Street
Rules

by
Baxter Clare

D1008914

Bella
BOOKS

Ferndale, Michigan
2003

Copyright © 2003 by Baxter Clare

Bella Books, Inc.
P.O. Box 201007
Ferndale, MI 48220

All rights reserved. No part of this book may be reproduced or transmitted in any form or by any means, electronic or mechanical, including photocopying, without permission in writing from the publisher.

Printed in the United States of America on acid-free paper
First Edition

Editor: J.M. Redmann
Cover designer: Bonnie Liss (Phoenix Graphics)

ISBN 1-931513-14-7

For

*Jules, Susan, Jender Bender, and the Big Pwincess —
all the people I should have thanked the first time!! —
and of course, always, Mrs. Binewski.*

Chapter One

"Hey, Frank. It's ugly in there."

Lieutenant L.A. Franco didn't like hearing that from a man who'd worked homicide twice as long as she had.

"How ugly?"

"Looks like six so far. Not counting the pit bull. All shotgunned. Me and Bobby saw what it was and backed out—figured we'd better wait for you."

Wiggling into a pair of latex gloves, Frank cast a cold eye over the excess of responding radio units. There were only three Figueroa cars. The rest were Sheriff's office, Compton PD, and Southeast Division. A Highway Patrol had responded, probably due to the proximity of the overpass. They were all

1

out of their jurisdiction, lookie-loos just hanging out and catching up on gossip.

"Ambo?" she asked her detective. A loose Windsor knot hung below Dan Nukisona's open collar and his suit was wrinkled. No doubt the one he'd changed out of when he'd gotten home.

"Don't need one."

Frank almost told Nook to straighten his tie, thought better of it. Looked like it was going to be a long night.

"We know who they are?"

"Looks like Julio Estrella, his family, and some guy."

"And the dog," Frank sighed.

"And the dog."

She turned her attention to the unfamiliar house, one of the Craftsman bungalows typical of south-central Los Angeles. The police strobes were lighting it like a Christmas tree.

"I thought Julio lived on Gramercy."

"He did. Used to anyway. Looks like they moved here not too long ago. There's boxes and stuff."

She motioned for her detective to lead the way and they retraced his steps. A large uniformed woman stood at the door holding an entry log.

"You the RO?"

"Yes, ma'am."

"Heard you passed the detective's exam."

"Yeah," Lewis grinned.

Frank nodded, "We'll get you into homicide yet."

Lewis was a good cop and Frank was pleased she'd been the responding officer. She took in the pile of torn and empty cartons in the corner, stacking plastic chairs, some toys and a two-wheeled trike, garbage bags, a couple empties. It was cluttered but not disrupted. Nook opened the screen door with a "here we go" glance and Frank followed.

The heavy, metallic tang of fresh blood weighted the enclosed air. Frank's first thought was how much she hated

2

shotguns; they made such a fucking mess. She stood in the living room, noting the woman puddled up in the hallway, then the two children sprawled over each other on the couch. Frank knew Estrella's older son, but probably wouldn't have recognized the younger ones. One of the kids on the couch was missing the left side of his head and had fallen backward over the other kid. From the sticky long hair hanging over the edge of the couch, Frank assumed the second kid was a girl. The major organs plastered onto the couch and the blood soaked cushions assured Frank they were both dead. Accompanied by tinny laughter from the TV, she gauged their positions. It looked like they'd been shot from the hallway.

Frank moved in that direction, careful not to step on the bloodied floor or brush against the spatter on the wall. She bent to look at the woman. It was Marta Estrella all right. Beyond her, just inside the kitchen, Julio's eldest lay on the floor. Leo Estrella was only about twelve years old and he looked very surprised. From the blood behind him, it looked like the shotgun load had knocked him into the wall.

Red footprints from a rubber-soled shoe decorated the linoleum. Frank zig-zagged around them, toward an older Hispanic man crumpled on his side by the kitchen table. He looked familiar but Frank couldn't place him.

"Do we know who he is?"

Nook shook his head. "Bobby thought maybe he'd seen him around Gramercy, where they used to live."

"Speaking of your partner, where is he?"

"Out puttin' some of those useless flatfoots to work. That transfer from Shootin' Newton — Hunt's his name — he's a lazy mother. He'd put a third generation welfare mom to shame. We get here — Muñoz and Lewis are working it — and I ask him to talk to some people, you know, at least names and addresses, and he looks at his watch and says he's almost 10-7. Just came by to see what was going on."

The man's wallet was just out of his rear pocket. Frank slipped on a glove and spread it open with her thumb and forefinger. James Barracas. Hollywood address. She flipped through the plastic card holder, grunting, "Check it out."

Nook squinted over her shoulder at the ID card she pointed to.

"Well, I'll be dipped in shit. Retired LAPD."

Frank replaced the wallet, noting the pit bull that had bled out near the back door. There was another beautiful footprint in the blood, a rubber-soled print, and she quickly glanced at the victim's feet. The men were in loafers and cowboy boots. The boy was barefoot. One break, Frank thought, fixing her attention on Julio Estrella. He was slumped in front of the open refrigerator, parts of him clinging to the milk and lard. It looked like he'd turned and caught his blast in the upper chest and throat. His head was tucked toward the floor as if he were embarrassed he'd been caught slipping. Frank squatted, peering up into his face.

She and Julio Estrella went back a long way. Dealing with strangers wasn't so bad, but knowing the people who'd been slaughtered suddenly made Frank feel too old and too tired for this kind of work. She glanced around. Bobby Taylor had stepped gingerly into the kitchen. She was amazed, as always, that a man so big could move so lightly. She'd have loved to have seen him play football. In the voice as incongruous as his agility, he offered softly, "Kind of a drag, huh?"

"Kind of," Frank agreed. She stood abruptly, focusing on work. "You call SID?"

With a mess like this she couldn't imagine Bobby hadn't called in the Scientific Investigation Division, but Frank didn't like making assumptions.

"Yeah. Coroner, too."

Frank instructed, "Let's not mess with the techs. Get Lawless here, case this thing explodes into a shitstorm. Any muck trucks out there yet?"

News vans didn't cover south-central homicides with the zeal they did in more affluent neighborhoods. Frank was hoping the radio call to dispatch had been subtle enough to dull their curiosity.

"No, the vultures haven't got wind of the carrion yet."

"Check the rest of the house?"

"Yeah, we walked through. Lewis and Muñoz checked it out, too."

Frank wanted to see for herself anyway. She found the phone in her pocket and called her supervisor, studying the kitchen table: a vase with plastic flowers, three cans of Tecate, an open bag of Doritos, an ashtray with butts, an envelope with an address scrawled on the back. While the phone rang in her ear, Frank said, "Nook, you get the address? Cigarette brands?"

"Kool and Marlboro," he grumbled, waving his notebook. "Someplace on Lester. I didn't fall off the turnip truck yesterday."

"What was I thinking?" Frank muttered. All her detectives were top-notch. Supervising them at a scene basically meant handling the brass and admin details so her men were free to do what they did best. Buying them beers, scolding them when they needed it and praising them when they didn't was how she best managed her crew.

Picking her way to the bedrooms, Frank said, "Hey, John. Frank. Thought you might want to know we caught a multiple."

She gave her captain the body count, but withheld James Barracas' ID. Anything other than a straight-forward domestic or drive-by made Foubarelle's Jockey's bunch and she didn't want him flying through her crime scene in a high panic. Frank ducked into the bathroom. The shower curtain was open, nothing in there, and though there wasn't even room for a gnat's ass, Frank checked behind the door. She'd learned that one the hard way.

Her captain asked for a motive. Surveying what appeared to be the master bedroom, Frank answered, "Not sure yet."

The ROs had left the closet open and the bedspread flipped up, but other than that the room was tidy. Marta Estrella kept a nice house. Resigned to the fact that her captain would never get a handle on the timing of a homicide investigation, Frank placated him with guesstimates as she glanced through the closet. Clothes hung neatly. Men's and women's shoes were arranged in rows, except two pairs in the corner. Crooked and overturned, they were jarringly out of character with the general orderliness. She looked at the clothes hanging above them. They were tightly bunched. Fubar was asking about the media. Frank silently folded the phone shut, trading it for the 9mm under her arm. Adrenaline crackled into her bloodstream, narrowing her vision and sharpening her smell. She noticed the carpet was slightly darker under the gathered clothes just as the tang of urine hit her. She stepped to the side of the closet, reaching in slowly. With a deep, steadying breath, she used her gun barrel to part the clothing.

A little boy — he couldn't have been more than six — gaped up at her, terror-stricken. Frank's adrenaline fled as quickly as it had come and she holstered her weapon before the shakes hit her. She stood in front of the kid, calmly getting her breath back. Poor little bastard was shaking in his underwear. Frank knelt, extending her hand, and the kid pressed himself even flatter into the corner. He was all huge brown eyes and open-mouthed horror.

"Sssssh," Frank whispered, not knowing if the kid spoke English or Spanish. "It's okay. *Esta bien. Todo esta bien.*" She didn't know how to say she wasn't going to hurt him, so she repeated everything was okay. The kid just stood quaking in his own pee. Frank got up slowly and stripped the blanket off the bed. She knelt again, holding the blanket open, urging him to come into it. He sobbed, hyperventilating, but he allowed Frank to gently wrap the blanket around him. She pulled him carefully from his hiding place, securing him even tighter, making sure to cover his head so he wouldn't see what was in the living room.

Nook and Bobby stared when Frank said, "Call Child Protective Services," walking past them with the little feet dangling under the blanket.

"Who the fuck is *that*?" Nook hollered behind her, but Frank just whispered, *"Todo esta bien,"* and kept stroking the boy's head. Outside, Frank searched for the nearest Figueroa car. Muñoz was walking the chief coroner toward the house but Lawless paused, watching Frank head toward her with the blanket.

"Hey, doc," she greeted quietly in passing, "Nice outfit."

Gail Lawless was obviously dressed for something more glamorous than a coroner's investigation, and she grinned. Hefting a bulging briefcase, she replied, "Have scrubs will travel."

"Sorry to interrupt your evening, but I need you here."

Hunt was resting against his hood and Frank nodded at the rear door.

"Open up."

"Yes ma'am," he said, taking his time moving off the car. "Who's the prisoner?"

Frank ignored him, looking around for his partner as she settled the boy in. She leaned out and called, "Waddell!" feeling the kid jerk under her hand.

"Sssh," she whispered, smoothing his hair. *"Esta bien."* She wished she could think of something more reassuring to say but her limited Spanish was eluding her. Hunt's partner jogged over and Frank told him CPS was on the way. Waddell was to accompany the kid and not leave him alone for a second. Nor be alone with him for a second. Frank wanted it to be impossible for a defense attorney to claim the LAPD had fed the kid ideas.

Frank studied the boy for a moment. His head protruded from the blanket and he stared back at her. Frank moved away from the car, guiding Waddell next to her.

"You got kids, right?"

"Three," he nodded.

7

"If he falls asleep, stay next to him. He's going to have some nasty nightmares."

Frank turned toward Lawless, as Hunt sniggered, "Aww. I never knew you were so maternal, *Lieutenant*."

Frank faced him. He was a big son of a bitch, mean and stupid too. Bad combinations in a cop and she wondered what he'd done to get busted from Newton to Figueroa.

"That's not maternal, Hunt, that's business. We need that kid. He's a material witness. You might want to learn how to do that."

Giving him her back, she said, "Come on, doc. I've got six bodies for you. Not counting the dog."

Chapter Two

After Gail released the bodies and when SID was all done, Frank met the rest of the 93rd Squad back at the Figueroa station. She gathered them at M&M's for breakfast, and while they ordered and drank coffee, Nook and Bobby filled their colleagues in. Neighbors said Julio's brother, Luis, lived in the garage behind the house. No one had seen him since yesterday, but one of the neighbors ID'd his car at the house after she heard the shots fired. The car was gone by the time Lewis and Muñoz arrived.

"Yeah," Bobby added, "and we found an empty gun bag in the garage, just lying on his bed."

Smoothing his silk tie Ike Zabbo said, "Sweet."

Next to Nook, he was Frank's oldest, most seasoned

detective. Before he'd transferred to Homicide, Ike had worked Narcotics at Hollywood. He told his colleagues he knew Barracas fairly well, but couldn't figure what had gotten him into this mess. While the waitress delivered platters of eggs and pancakes, the detectives speculated on what SID would find. They'd lifted prints from the garage and the detectives were curious to see if they'd match any found on the beer cans or Dorito bag. Frank pulled her crew off their current cases to focus on this one and she delegated assignments.

"Taquito," she said to Lou Diego, "You and Ike canvass the neighborhood. I'll try and shake a couple uniforms loose for you, take a look around for the shotgun. Noah, you and Johnnie go back to the office-"

"Aw, come on, Frank," Johnnie Briggs protested, as Frank knew he would. She checked his condition this morning, pleased to see his eyes clear and hands steady. She turned her attention to Noah Jantzen, who finished her sentence around a mouthful of hash browns.

"And find out whatever we can about Julio and Barracas."

Frank nodded, "Run a trace on Luis' car. Nook and Bobby, go over to Claudia Estrella's, see what she knows about her brother's whereabouts."

"I don't think it's him," Johnnie announced, chewing on a piece of toast.

Noah mocked his partner, begging, "Enlighten us, oh please, Wise One."

"Simple," Johnnie obliged. "The dog. Why would somebody who lives there risk the extra hassle of killing the family pet? Julio and Barracas posed the most threat. And maybe the oldest kid. Once they were eliminated, the rest of the family was cake. If Luis lived there, the dog knew him. He wouldn't have had to take him out. But what if the suspect's someone the dog didn't know? Man, if *I* walked into a house and there was a pit bull staring at me — blam — I'd take him out right away. A stranger'd *have* to waste the dog. He'd take that extra little risk. Where was the dog laying?"

Hm, Bobby murmured. "That's interesting. It was right by the back door and it must have been shot right away because I don't remember seeing any dog prints. Do you?" he asked Frank and Nook. They both shook their heads and Johnnie smirked, "See? Whoever did it took the dog out when he walked into the house. You live there, you're not worried about the dog. You're a stranger — booyah — out he goes, ASAP."

Noah marveled, "Don't we all sleep better at night knowing Johnnie's out there?"

"You're just jealous you didn't think of it first," Johnnie gloated. Frank admitted he had a point, but Luis Estrella still looked like their best lead.

As the 93rd filed out chomping on toothpicks, Noah stayed at the register with Frank. He asked, "Doc Law say when she'd get around to the posts?"

It wasn't unusual to wait two or three days for an autopsy, so when Frank replied, "Sometime this afternoon," Noah whistled in admiration.

"Sure pays to have the inside track," he teased.

"Hey, I didn't ask her," Frank shrugged. "She volunteered."

Lowering his voice, Noah said, "That's 'cause she *likes* you."

"Don't start with that old auntie crap," Frank warned her ex-partner.

Lifting his eyes to the ceiling, Noah sighed, "And this is the thanks I get."

Frank pushed him toward the door.

"I'll thank you when you get our Dog Killer. Let's go."

~ ~ ~ ~ ~

11

Normally Frank didn't tell the next of kin about the victim's death until after she'd questioned them, but she didn't have the stomach for that with Jimmy Barracas' widow. And maybe because Lorrie Barracas had been expecting the news ever since she'd been married, she reacted stoically when Frank told her, graciously offering to answer a few questions. She didn't know of any specific threats against her husband, but as she pointed out, "When you're a cop, threats are made against you every day."

Jimmy Barracas was Julio Estrella's nephew. When Frank asked what sort of relationship they had, Mrs. Barracas proudly said that Jimmy had assumed the role of surrogate father after his sister's husband died. Jimmy was close to his niece, Claudia, and his nephews.

"Even Luis?"

"Of course," his widow answered. "Jimmy's as —"

She caught her mistake.

"Oh, my. I guess I'll have to get used to saying was. Jimmy was . . . as good as gold to that boy."

The correction was painful and Frank gave Mrs. Barracas a moment to pull herself together. When she had, she continued, "He was too good, if you ask me. We had a lot of fights about Louie. Every dime Jimmy ever gave that boy went straight into his arm."

Frank didn't care for ambiguity, asking exactly what Mrs. Barracas meant.

"He's been fixing since he was fourteen. He'll shoot anything he can get into a needle, but heroin's his drug of choice."

Frank wasn't surprised. Claudia Estrella had chipped for years and Frank asked how her husband had felt about that, being a narcotics officer.

Lorrie Barracas shrugged.

"He was resigned to it. What could he do? The kids were older and they lived with their mother. Such as she was," Mrs. Barracas sniffed.

12

Frank had dim memories of a large, unwashed woman who sat in a dark room, staring out the window and drinking sweet wine.

Frank asked if she had any idea where Luis was and she said no, she hadn't had heard from him in three or four days.

"What happened then?"

"He called for Jimmy."

"Do you know what they talked about?"

"Business, I'm sure."

"What sort of business?"

An impatient gesture told Frank that the widow's brave front was fading.

"Jimmy set the boys up with a courier service. Cops always need things delivered here and there so Jimmy supplied the customers and the boys did the work."

"Mrs. Barracas, you've been extremely helpful. I know this is terribly difficult for you, but if you could just bear with me for a few more questions . . ."

"Of course," she answered, gamely masking the strain. She told Frank what she knew about the business, which wasn't much, and provided names and phone numbers of her husband's two closest friends. As is common with cops, they were his ex-partners.

Frank thanked Lorrie Barracas for her time and patience, leaving her with the standard appeal to call if she thought of anything else, anything at all, no matter how silly it might seem.

On her way over she'd passed a Peet's and now she went back to it. Sitting in the parking lot, she considered the phone numbers Lorrie Barracas had given her. She poked one into the cell phone, but didn't hit "send". Telling Barracas' wife had been bad enough. Telling his partners would definitely have to wait until she was well fortified with designer coffee.

~ ~ ~ ~ ~

The day dragged on but by late afternoon Frank managed to get to the coroners office. Cause, manner, and mode of death were blatantly obvious in the Estrella case, so she didn't really need to be there, and at least one of the boys would attend, most likely Bobby as Nook always managed to weasel out of being the attending detective. But because bodies sometimes gave up unexpected clues, and because ME's often rendered opinions that couldn't be printed in a protocol, Frank attended autopsies whenever she could. Gowning up, she tried to figure who was being cut. Gail had just started on Barracas and it looked like the Mangler was finishing with Marta Estrella. Bobby was watching a new baby-faced ME peel someone's scalp over his face. From the brands it looked like Julio.

"How we doing?" she asked him.

"Well, we still don't know where Luis is. Seems like he's got a pretty bad jones, so maybe he's on the nod somewhere. I asked Claudia who his main suppliers were, but she wouldn't say. If he's as bad as she says he is, I wouldn't imagine he'd go too far away for too long."

"Talk to anybody at Narco?"

"Not yet. We talked to some sources, a couple baseheads. Nook's checking on some of the names they gave us."

"When was the last time Claudia saw him?"

"Friday. He stopped by to borrow some money. She fed him and he hung around for a couple hours, playing with Gloria's kids. She didn't say much, neither did Gloria, but they know something."

"Too quiet?" Frank guessed and Bobby nodded, "Too evasive, too vague."

"I'll stop by later, see if I can't squeeze some blood out. You know Barracas set the boys up in some sort of courier service?"

Bobby shook his head and Frank told him to check every service in the phone book.

"Wife said Barracas set it up because cops always need deliveries and that he supplied the nephews with customers. Talked to the partners. They didn't know much about it. Went by Hollywood and no one had heard of this alleged service. Depending on what you find, we might want to subpoena some IRS records."

Bobby recorded their conversation into his notebook, mentioning that he'd managed to get a good picture from Claudia.

"It shows him from the waist up, showing off his tats. The guy's got stars inked all over him. You know Estrella means star in Spanish?"

Bobby never asked rhetorical questions so Frank shook her head that she didn't know that.

"I dropped the picture off and Donna's making a bulletin. She thought she'd have it by shift change."

"Good."

Gail and a massive black tech were turning Barracas onto his back, and Frank asked, "How's it going so far, Doc?"

"I just got started. I had to do a missing kid that finally turned up. Well, at least parts of him turned up. It looks like a mountain lion got him, mauled him pretty badly. That's my second mountain lion attack already this year."

"Where'd they find him?"

"Out around Malibu somewhere. I guess somebody's dog dragged one of his arms home. Can you imagine?"

"Yech," the tech said, "That's why I have cats."

"Me, too," Gail replied. To Frank she said, "We did Marta Estrella already. She was about six weeks pregnant."

"Make that seven and a dog," Frank noted.

Gail looked up sharply, then said to her tech, "Charlie, see if you can find me some vinyl gloves."

"We're out. We've been out for weeks."

"Check for me anyway."

"Okay."

The doc finished a dictation, then clicked her recorder off.

"What's going to happen to Estrella's little boy? Is there any family any he can stay with?"

"I don't know. CPS'll handle that. Maybe he'll stay with his aunt, Julio's sister. Might become a 300 kid."

Frank referred to the legal code wherein a child was mandated to the care and custody of the state. Gail flicked a curious glance her way, asking, "Did you mean what you said to Hunt last night?"

"What did I say?"

"When he accused you of being maternal, you said it wasn't maternal, just business. Was that true?"

Frank thought about the question.

"The kid had just seen his whole family butchered. He was petrified. Hunt's got about as much compassion as a bullet. He wouldn't have understood if I'd told him anything else."

Gail returned her attention to a fading cut on Barracas' forearm.

"Why?" Frank quizzed.

"Because what you said was so cold. I didn't want to believe you could be so heartless."

Charlie came back.

"No gloves," he said. Without looking up from her work, the doc thanked him, her eyes crinkling in a smile. Frank almost smiled too, realizing that Gail knew damn good and well there weren't any gloves around.

Chapter Three

Frank was summoned to the Estrella's at 9:47 PM on Sunday night. By 7:00 PM Tuesday she and her detectives had worked around the clock, through the most critical hours following a homicide. They were beat, and Frank sent everyone home. That's where she should have headed to, but she was working her way to the Alibi on surface streets. The freeway might have been faster but Frank wanted the comfort of the old roads. It pleased her to pass a Rexall that used to be a jazz club where Duke Ellington played. A little farther down the block she'd made her first collar. Two streets down, she and Noah had responded to a domestic and almost been knocked out by a charging 400-pound woman. At the corner of Avalon and 51st she slowed to admire a brand new strike. It was so fresh the paint still glinted.

Old English letters, four feet high in blue and orange, cryptically announced "**W52K-R213**." As dusk lowered around the swirling letters, their highly-stylized tips seemed to twitch and flicker like flames. Frank didn't need to stare long to know who'd done the strike.

Passing the next side street, she caught the artist's familiar, bad-ass shuffle half way down the block. Placa Estrella, revered OG of the 52nd Street Kings, was deep into Playboy territory. Taking out an old gangster like Placa would be a hell of a coup for an up and coming rival. Frank pulled up alongside her, watching Placa's hand move to her waist. The girl braced, waiting for the gun barrel to come poking out the window. Frank rolled ahead so Placa could see who she was. Only then did she roll the window down.

"Aren't you in the wrong neighborhood?" she called, driving beside her.

"I got a right to be here."

"Playboy's might not agree with you," Frank countered. Placa shrugged, kept walking.

"Want a ride?"

Placa shook her head, her long braid like an anchor to the sidewalk.

"Okay. I asked you nice, now I'm *telling* you to get in."

Placa planted her feet and glared.

"What I gotta get in for? I ain't done nothin'."

"Bet you're strapped. Want me to pat you?"

"So? I still ain't done nothin'."

Frank pushed the door open, moving slowly, and told Placa to get in. Placa protested feebly but got in. She slunk down in the seat so no one would see her.

"What I done?"

"Nothin'. But there's been enough blood spilled in your family lately. I don't want to be the one to have to tell Claudia I left you here and some Playboys capped you."

"Yeah," Placa snorted, "you'd be all tore up."

"I would," Frank insisted, "and your sister'd kick the shit outta me then put a hex on me."

She was pleased to see the corner of Placa's mouth twitch. As they waited for the light to change, they both watched a Baby Playboy cross the street on a bike.

Frank teased, "Bet he stole that off a King," and Placa immediately shot back, "That bitch wouldn't be walkin' if he stole that off a King."

Moving through the intersection, Frank asked "How's your mom doin'?"

" 'Kay," Placa shrugged.

"How about Toñio and your sister?"

" 'Kay."

"And your Uncle Luis?"

"I don't know."

"When was the last time you saw him?"

"I don't know."

"See him Sunday?"

Placa shook her head.

"Since then?"

Again her head shook.

"You always were talkative," Frank said. "You do that tag down the block?"

"Tagging's illegal," Placa responded ambiguously.

"Since when's the law ever stopped you?"

Placa didn't answer and Frank asked, "Still in school?"

"Sometimes."

Frank nodded. They'd come into 52nd Street territory, and Placa put her hand on the door handle.

"How about Rolo? How's he doing?"

That earned Frank a sideways glance.

"Why you wanna know for?"

"Just wondering," Frank shrugged. "He's your dog, ain't he? Heard he took a knife a while ago."

That wasn't all Frank had heard. Rolo had lost a lung in

that fight and word was he couldn't fight anymore. Placa still used him for drive-bys and for peeping when they hit a liquor store or Quik Mart, but she was getting a lot of shit from the other Kings. They said he was too slow, that he couldn't take care of himself and that somebody'd get hurt having to rescue him someday.

Placa said proudly, "He's okay. He just needs to get his strength back."

Pulling onto Placa's street, Frank slowed in front of her house, studying the dark windows.

"Where is everybody?"

Placa just offered another shrug. Frank pulled a card out of her pocket and pressed it into Placa's hand.

"You need anything, you call me. *Claro*?"

No one ever looked a cop in south-central squarely in the eye so when Placa gave Frank her full attention she was taken aback by the intense scrutiny.

"Is that all?" Placa asked.

"You want me to tuck you into bed?"

"Naw, I just . . ."

Placa suddenly found the seats ripped upholstery fascinating. It was the opening Frank needed.

"What's going on?"

Placa plucked a piece of foam then glanced at the street. There was a naked flash of pain, then it was gone.

"Nothin'."

She jumped out of the car before anyone could recognize her in the strange company of the law. Frank waited until Placa was inside before accelerating through the quickening night. Fatigue and memories wrapped her in a thick fog. She'd watched Placa come up from toddler to feared gangster. It was a deep bloodline.

Her father and her uncle Julio had been OGs in the Westside Kings and her brother Chuey had claimed for 52nd Street after the Kings splintered into three fractious gangs. Claudia had been a revered Queen, but lost her standing when

Placa's father was shipped off to Chino for twenty-five years. Before she had her babies, Placa's sister Gloria had been a fierce 52nd Street Queen. Frank remembered a rookie who rode with her when she was a field training officer. He'd sliced his finger to the bone patting Gloria's hair down. While he was bleeding and wondering what the hell to do, Frank had suggested he check Gloria's mouth to see if she had razors in there too.

Like a lot of bangers, Placa started her rise to ghetto stardom by spraying her gang's name on anything that didn't move. Her artwork was bold and inspired. It pleased the Kings and they made her a Baby Queen, but that insulted Placa. She'd already seen how the Kings treated Queens and she didn't want any part of that abuse. She told the 52nd Street homeboys that she wanted to be jumped in like her brother Chuey. She would stand with them as a King or she would stand against them. The OGs had laughed, but they'd given her missions. Frank picked her up on a break-and-enter the day after her tenth birthday and that was only one of many infractions.

Placa's reputation grew in proportion to her juvenile arrest records and on her twelfth birthday she was jumped into the Kings. She'd since risen steadily and Frank knew that the 52nd Street *vatos* didn't make decisions without Placa's council. That had happened once and the next day two Kings ended up at King/Drew with concussions and multiple compound fractures.

Frank was glad when she got to the Alibi that there was an empty booth. She snagged it, noting Johnnie already at the bar, an empty shot glass and a beer in front of him. He was arguing with Hunt, and Frank swore if he got into a fight she wouldn't help him. Even as she thought it, she knew her promise was empty. Johnnie could be a pain in the ass but at least his intentions were good. Frank had no such faith concerning Hunt. She was glad to see Nancy approach her booth. She and Frank had been flirting since Frank was in

Homicide. Nothing ever came of it, Frank made sure of that, but it was an amiable routine.

"How you doin', hon?"

"I'm good, Nance. You?"

"I'm better now that you're here. Coffee, scotch or stout?"

"Scotch. Double. Cobb salad and fries. Busy tonight?"

"Enough."

Frank allowed herself the simple pleasure of Nancy's ample ass in motion before turning her attention to a legal pad stuffed with notes. She had to squint at the letters to make them stop jumping. She skimmed Noah's report with the kid in the closet, Julio Estrella's youngest.

He'd been sleeping in his room before the shooting went down. When he'd gotten up to go to the bathroom he heard booming and yelling and ran into the kitchen. He saw his father and brother bleeding and a man in black clothes walking down the hallway. The kid had run into his mom's closet. He thought it was a good place to hide because his sister couldn't find him there when they played hide and go seek. When asked if he knew the man, the kid had said no. And when they asked if the man looked like his uncle Luis, the kid had been vague, but thought his uncle was smaller.

She flipped through more pages, scanning copies of her detective's notes from dealers and crackheads, neighbors and friends. No one had seen Luis Estrella more recently than Sunday afternoon. That bothered Frank. Everyone described Luis as a friendly guy, always ready with a joke and a smile. His nickname was Payaso, clown, and he was always looking for a party. He was a small man with a limp from a broken ankle that had never mended well. Where other men tattooed gang insignia and weapons, Luis had branded himself with stars and was known to coo poetry at pretty girls. The squad was sniffing out gang affiliations but that was looking like a dead end. They still claimed, as all *veteranos* did, but it had

22

been years since either Julio or Luis was actively involved with the Kings.

In a 'hood where guns were as common as roaches, no one could recall Luis strapped and why should he be? Everyone liked him. It sounded like he'd made a good niche for himself — joker to the lords of the street, a threat to no one, loved by all. That he had suddenly disappeared meant two things to Frank, he was guilty or he was a witness. From all she'd heard about Luis in the last twenty-four hours, the latter seemed the most probable. He didn't sound like a killer. In fact, the pit bull had been his. He'd rescued it as a puppy from a guy who fought dogs. The man was going to cut its throat because one of its paws was deformed. When Diego had told her that, she'd said, "Chalk one up for Johnnie."

Luis didn't fit the profile of a man who'd shoot his own dog, nonetheless his own family; the killing spree didn't square with anything she'd heard about him. That his car had been at the scene meant he might have fled after the shooting started. Or maybe he'd come in on the middle of it, then grabbed his own gun for defense. He might have run then or he might have looked into the house, seen the carnage and taken off. Luis was a clown, not a fighter. He had to have known the shooter grossly outmatched him. It made sense that he'd get in his car and fly.

And that was another gnat buzzing in Frank's ear. They'd talked to Claudia's neighbors and two of them remembered seeing her brother's junked Bonneville outside her house on Sunday night. Both wits pinned the time around nine PM, about fifteen minutes after the Estella's had been gunned down. One saw a figure get out from the driver's side but wouldn't say more than that. It looked like a man in dark clothes, but at night, with the street lights shot out, the wit couldn't even swear with certainty that the driver had been male. But they were both pretty sure about the Bonneville because of its size and coughing muffler.

Frank glanced around when Nancy brought her drink. She recognized lawyers, ADAs and detectives. Johnnie had peaceably wandered over to a table crowded with secretarial types and Hunt was hunched over the bar with a couple off-duty sticks. He was dressed in tight jeans that pegged over expensive boots and his muscles squeezed out from under a tight LAPD T-shirt. A black Stetson clung magically to the back of his head and his belt sported a silver buckle the size of a salad plate, the type cowboys won in rodeos. Frank thought he'd look more at home in a juke-joint than a bar full of suits. Usually the Figueroa uniforms favored a rougher bar called Red's, and she wondered idly why Hunt spent so much time in the company of the suits he seemed to despise. Then it occurred to her he'd probably gotten eighty-sixed from Red's.

When Nancy brought her salad, Frank ordered another double. The first drink had untied the knots in her shoulders and the second would undo the knots in her mind. She attacked her dinner, careful not to spill on the papers clamoring for attention.

Chapter Four

While Frank and her crew had been catching up on sleep, a heads-up sheriff was comparing Luis Estrella's old Bonneville to the one on his APB sheet. Through a not uncommon assortment of red tape and miscommunications, Frank didn't hear about the car until Thursday afternoon. Given the antagonistic relationship between the LAPD and L.A. County Sheriff's Department, Frank was glad she'd heard at all. Swearing more out of excitement than frustration, she and Noah grabbed jackets and headed out to Old Topanga Canyon Road.

The car was parked in an isolated turnout in a grove of eucalyptus trees. Thick chaparral rose steeply from the north shoulder of the road, and fell away to the south. It was hot and still in the scrub-covered hills and the air smelled of dust and heated plant oils. The car was dusty inside and out, loaded with all kinds of crap, like Luis had been living in it. They quickly poked through the litter, finding nothing more interesting than Luis' works on the passenger seat and a clean Bowie knife. The trunk was locked and the keys were missing but it didn't smell like they had pudding in a cup, or in civilian terms, a body in a trunk.

Noah tried to videotape the scene, but the camera battery was dead, as always. He settled on Polaroids while Frank sifted through eucalyptus leaves and old trash. As they waited for SID's arrival, Frank scanned the random homes perched on the steep hills, noting the sparse traffic pattern. She wanted SID to process the trunk before they jimmied the lock. Depending on what they found inside, SID could either continue at the scene or have the car hauled back to the print shed to finish their evidence collection in a more optimal setting.

The SID van pulled up and Noah groaned when Dave Grummond's gangly form emerged. He was a tall man, balding, thin, and vaguely reminiscent of a cadaver. He was born without a sense of humor and had never thought to cultivate one, but he was a meticulous forensic technician. Frank greeted him quietly, outlining the situation for him. Her idea was to dust the trunk area so they could pop it open. If there was a body inside, they'd process it *in situ* to preserve the evidentiary value. If not, they'd tow the vehicle to the LAPD print shed. Grummond nodded gravely. When he spoke, he sounded like a butler in Masterpiece Theatre.

"I should like to start by wanding with cyanoacrylate and RAM. I should think that would show up well against the dark paint while yielding as many prints as possible."

"Whatever you think's best," Frank agreed, backing away so Grummond and his tech could get started.

Noah asked, "Aren't you going to do the Rappenwhiph test first?"

Grummond frowned, "I don't think I'm familiar with that test."

Noah bent near the trunk and sniffed. He tapped the metal hood, listening to the hollow sound it made.

"No dead body," he said. "It passed the rap an' whiff."

The older man studied Noah quizzically, then gave up, returning his attention to the laborious process of getting into his gloves. Noah grinned at Frank, delighted with himself. Frank shook her head and watched Grummond load cartridges into his Super Glue gun. When he was finished he walked all around the car, completing his circuit near the right rear bumper. Aiming his wand like a magician he released a mist of fumes and dye over the trunk's surface area. Prints popped up like acne on a teenager.

While the tech held the light, Grummond started shooting them with his 1-to-1, methodically setting up each photograph.

"Jesus Christ," Noah griped in Frank's ear. "This isn't Yosemite and he isn't Ansel fucking Adams."

Frank lifted her shoulders but made no move to rush the tech. Noah sighed and went back to toeing the leaves around the car. His impatience amused Frank. They'd always been a good team. Still were. Frank's conservatism tempered Noah's enthusiastic tendency to trample details while he rushed headlong into a case. In turn, Noah gave Frank the push she needed when she mired in too much caution and deliberation. The traits they carried into their professional roles applied to the personal as well. Noah was a good mirror for Frank. Because he had earned her elusive and implicit trust, he was able to tell her things that would have landed anyone else flat on their ass.

Frank rolled up her sleeves, enjoying the dry heat. The sun on her skin brought an unbidden image of Kennedy and the sensation of their bodies touching. Frank blinked the memory back to its hiding place, glad for the distraction of her pager. Glancing at the number, she returned the call in the privacy of the unmarked. A secretary put her on hold, then Frank said, "Hey. What's up, doc?"

She winced, realizing she sounded like a cartoon character. Either Gail was used to it or didn't notice, because she answered matter-of-factly, "I think I've got someone here you might be interested in."

While searching for the mountain lion that had mauled the young girl in Topanga, a park ranger had literally stumbled over a body about a quarter mile from where Luis Estrella's car had been found. The Sheriff's office was called and after the coroner investigated, the decomposing body was hauled out of the canyon amid curses and insults to the dead man's mother. Gail had been checking the daily roster when the stinker had been brought in, and she thought Frank might want to check out his tattoos.

After Grummond popped the trunk, confirming there wasn't a body inside, Frank had the Bonneville towed to the print shed, then she and Noah fought through traffic to the USC medical complex. After badging their way into the coroner's office, they were met by Homicide Deputies from the Sheriff's office. They had jurisdiction over the body and Frank recognized them with dismay. They were old-school deputies, with fully evolved contempt for women, non-Anglos, the LAPD, and all outside investigative authorities — not necessarily in that order. Cooperation was going to be a bitch.

Frank patiently explained the LAPD's involvement. One of the LASD dicks told her to cry him a river. The upshot was she'd have to subpoena the case file from them. Frank hadn't expected any less. She and Noah stood apart from the deputies as they waited for Gail. She'd been paged, but it was another twenty minutes before she arrived, flushed and breathless. A handful of pathology students trailed behind her like ducklings.

"Sorry," she gasped, "I'm going to get into some scrubs and be right back."

Frank followed, speaking to her for a short minute. When she rejoined Noah, he breathed, "Ahhhh," as he watched the docs skirted legs disappear.

"Did you ask her for a date?"

"Don't start," Frank warned, gowning up.

When Gail returned she ushered everyone into Room C, the small, air-tight room within the main autopsy suite. Frank hated C autopsies because it meant the corpse either carried an infectious diseases or, more frequently, was decomposing nastily. This time it was the latter, and as Frank filed in she clenched her teeth against the stench. The men bitched and swore, and the students struggled vainly for nonchalance.

"We already x-rayed his teeth so maybe we can get a dental ID, but these should do for now, " Gail said, referring to a number of tattoos on the deceased. They squeezed against each other in the fetid room and as the deputies feigned disinterest, Noah produced a color copy of a photograph. The picture tattoos corresponded perfectly to the tats on the body. It looked like they'd found Luis Estrella.

The eye sockets were vacant, and jays and small mammals had stripped much of the facial tissue down to the bone. A print ID was impossible because they'd also gnawed away at his fingers. Estrella was as fat and swollen as a steamed bratwurst. The bacteria digesting him from the inside out gave off the malodorous gasses that caused his limbs and abdomen to swell. The swelling, plus a green discoloration spreading from his belly around a network of darkly rotting veins suggested he'd been dead at least a couple of days. That and the occasional maggot that continued to fall out of his head onto the steel table.

Gail innocently asked the deputies if they had the case file with them and they grudgingly handed it over. Noah tried to look over her shoulder but Frank gave him a quick, surreptitious shake of her head. He looked puzzled until Gail asked, "Mind if I make a copy?"

She passed the folder to her tech and the smaller of the two men protested, "What for?"

"New protocol," she sighed. "You should've gotten the memo already. Admin wants us to have copies of the initial investigation in all questionable deaths, in case the techs have missed something."

"Shit," the other dick breathed. "I'm already buried in fucking paperwork and they keep piling more on."

"Tell me about it," Gail commiserated. She and a new tech cataloged Estrella's bloody shoes, sweatshirt, and the rest of his personal effects, including three baggies of heroin. After weighing and measuring the body, Gail started the exterior exam.

"Autolysis is well advanced," Gail noted into her microphone. "What would you say the average daytime high's been the last few days?"

"Hot," one of the deputies offered uselessly, but a student said, "It was 88 yesterday and its felt like that most of the week."

Gail nodded, "And it looked like he was found in a pretty sunny area, so I'm guessing he probably hasn't been dead more than three or four days."

Frank quickly counted backward. That would have put his time of death at Monday or Tuesday. Plenty of time to ace his family, score some dope, wander up to Malibu and fix on a remote turnout . . . then what? Get out of his car to take a leak and fall down the hillside?

Gail was studying various lacerations, scabs and contusions, and as if reading Frank's mind, Noah asked, "Any of those consistent with a tumble down a canyon?"

"Not really," Gail said, pointing. "The coloring on these

bruises indicates he probably incurred them before death. The lacerations are scabbed, except for this one." She indicated a fresh two-inch tear on his upper forearm that corresponded to a tear in his sweatshirt.

"That doesn't look like it bled much," one of the deputies said.

"So he was dead when he was cut?" Noah added.

"Possible," Gail murmured, "but given where he was found there could be any number of postmortem explanations."

Continuing into the mike, she spoke about bilateral needle marks on the arms and a fresh hemorrhage in the antecubital fossa of the left arm. She catalogued old scars and tattoos, noting lividity and lack of rigor. He'd already gone in and out of the latter and the former was consistent with the position his body was found in.

Having finished the external portion, Gail sharpened a knife and gave her students time to ask questions and form opinions. As she made the "Y" cut she apologized for not having any half-face masks available, and Frank breathed through her mouth. One of the students fled the room, followed by a second. The men swore some more, as if that would help lessen the smell issuing from Estrella's rotting body, but the fact was they'd all carry the thick, gagging smell with them for the rest of the day.

"Welcome to the romantic world of pathology," Gail grinned. Slicing connective tissue, she flipped Estrella's chest plate over his chewed face. After cutting through the ribs she pulled them out, exposing lungs and the pericardial sac. A few more slashes with the knife and the green sides of Estrella's abdomen fell away, exposing the discolored abdominal organs.

The younger of the two deputies pawed his foot, muttering, "I hate this fucking job," and for once, Frank had to agree. Gail let the path residents make conclusions before she lifted out the organ block and laid it on the dissecting table. Then she sawed through Estrella's skull and lifted the

31

calvarium, giving them a look at his brain. Frank thought she saw a slight edema but no obvious trauma, and Gail confirmed that into the dictaphone.

After years of self neglect, Luis Estrella was in pretty bad shape. Clusters of bacteria around his heart indicated mild endocarditis from using dirty needles. As the autopsy progressed, he turned out to be a compendium of the "-itis's" associated with long-term drug abuse — esophagitis, pyelonephritis, pancreatitis, cholecystitis, and his liver looked more like paté than beef, indicating advanced alcoholism. All his organs were congested and his bladder contained almost 700cc of urine. A conscious person would have been in considerable pain with such a full bladder, so Gail assumed Estrella was unconscious at the time of death, explaining why he hadn't voided. Coupled with the respiratory edema and no obvious signs of trauma, Gail's preliminary ruling was that Estrella had overdosed into coma and eventual respiratory arrest.

Leaving the mess for the tech to clean up, Gail led her troupe out of Room C into relatively fresh air.

"Depending on the lab results, what I'm calling it right now is accidental death due to overdose. Questions?"

The sheriff's men shook their heads, happy with Gail's verdict. They left before she could change her mind and the students went to wash up.

"Their paper," Frank reminded.

"Oh, yeah," Gail said slipping away.

Noah asked, "What do you think, boss?"

Frank shrugged, "Looks like we're in the dark until we get some lab results back."

"Okay, here's what I'm thinking."

"We've got blood spatter on the sweatshirt. We've got what looks like the same pattern on this guy's shoes. With blood on them. For whatever reason — and maybe this is what his sister's holding back from us — he's pissed at his family and he whacks them. He takes off in his car. Maybe he's stoned out of his fucking mind. He stops at his sisters, tells her what he's done — which would also explain her lack of cooperation — and he takes off. Just driving anywhere. The guy's a junkie, probably all he wanted to do was get a stick in his arm. So he shoots a hot load — he's not being too careful 'cause he's shook — he gets out of his car at the overlook, maybe to take a leak or something, wanders down the road. He's disoriented, he slips, down he goes. It's dark. He can't find his way out 'cause he's too stoned. Goes into coma. End of story."

"Very tidy," Frank said, watching Gail return with a manila folder.

"Here you go," the ME said, "Those two are positively antediluvian."

"Think we could get a bug guy to look at those maggots? Make sure they're not from a housefly?"

"I can do that," Gail nodded.

"And you'll let me know tox results as soon as you can?"

"Of course."

Noah asked, "So we gonna see you at the Alibi tomorrow?"

"I don't know," Gail said doubtfully. "Last time I was there Johnnie set some poor woman's hair on fire."

"Ah, that was an accident," Noah insisted.

The woman was a redhead that Johnnie had been lusting over. She and her friends had been snubbing him all night, so in an inebriated moment of vengeance Johnnie'd "accidentally" lit her hair while he was lighting his cigarette. This enabled Ike and Johnnie to douse her with their fresh drinks and put the fire out.

That little antic had cost Johnnie another conduct unbecoming write-up and Frank suppressed a frown. Sober, Johnnie was a great cop; drunk, he lost all impulse control. That was his third CUBO in just over a year, not good stats to have in his file.

"Come on, doc. You're due."

"I assume you'll be there," she said to Frank.

"Most likely."

"We'll see then," she replied, fanning her nose. "You stink. Go change."

Chapter Five

On Friday night the Alibi was thick with suits, civilians, and a handful of uniforms. The ninety-third squad ringed a table in the middle of the crowded bar with a shapely rookie in the center. Ike and Johnnie were barely giving the pretty boot room to breathe and Frank wondered what might happen before the night was over.

She surveyed her crew, happily awaiting the lab work that would convince them Luis Estrella was responsible for his family's homicide. Not only that, the nine-three had had two closures during the week, one a double homicide. Frank wished she could celebrate with her boys but she was catching this weekend. Besides, she wasn't as convinced about Estrella's guilt.

Drinking old coffee, she circled her finger over the table when she caught Nancy's eye. A few minutes later the harried waitress set down two slopping pitchers of Budweiser, confiding into Frank's ear, "You'd think I'd lose all this weight on Friday nights."

Nancy glanced around, making sure everyone was taken care of, and Frank encouraged, "Don't lose an ounce. Looks perfect just where it is."

She batted Frank's shoulder and disappeared into the throng. Noah poured more beer and smiled. Over the din, Frank said, "Guess who I saw the other day."

Noah played their old game, answering, "Elvis?"

"Not so many sequins."

"Pat Boone?"

"Not so white."

"Tupac."

"Not so dead."

"Hey, he's not dead. He's headlinin' at Caesar Palace with Elvis."

Frank shook her head. The rules required the right answer to be given up after the third wrong answer, so Frank said, "Placa. Gave her a ride home the other night. She was walking through Playboy 60 turf like she owned it."

"Oh yeah? How's she doing?"

"Good. Too skinny. Big circles under her eyes."

"Think she's using ?"

"Didn't seem like it. You know how intense she is. But then guess who calls me at work today."

"The governor?"

Frank shook the blonde hair against her neck.

"That was yesterday."

"Hmm. The president?"

Frank shook again.

"Much more interesting."

Swirling a finger in his beer foam then licking it off, Noah settled back, enjoying the game.

"Let's see . . . Julia Roberts?"

"Not *that* interesting."

"I lose," Noah sighed, hands up.

"Placa. Said she wanted to meet me Sunday. Six o'clock. Behind Saint Michael's."

"S'up with that?"

"Don't know. Kinda odd though, don't you think?"

Ike bent an ear to the conversation and interrupted, "You said Placa wants to see you?"

"Yeah."

"What for?"

"No clue. Said she had to show me something and would I be there or not? I said sure and asked her what it was about but she said I had to promise not to tell anyone. Then she whispered something — I couldn't hear what she said — and hung up, like she didn't want to get caught talking to me."

Noah's face clouded.

"Think she's in trouble with this Estrella thing?"

"Maybe. Seemed like something was buggin' her the other day, but you know Placa. Stoic."

Ike asked, "What else did she say?"

"That was it. Like she was rushed."

"Maybe it's a set-up," Ike said.

"Why me? For what?"

"Want me to go with you?" he offered.

"No. It's at the church. That's a pretty neutral zone. Probably wants to drop a dime on somebody."

"Placa?" Noah said dubiously. "Since when's she calling us to do her dirty work?"

"We'll see," Frank shrugged. Ike started to say something but Noah called out, "Hey-hey! Look who's here."

Heads at the Nine-three table swiveled to watch Gail Lawless snake her way toward them.

"Who's dead?" Nook grumbled and Johnnie cried, "Well, hell! If it ain't Doc Law."

"Don't pay any attention to 'em," Noah ordered, waving

her into the seat he'd wedged between himself and Frank. He shouted, "Gin 'n tonic for you, Doc?"

She nodded and Frank watched the coroner taking in the faces around the table. Frank studied Gail's almond-shaped eyes. They had an almost Asian cast but were set in a distinctly western, raw-boned face. When they settled on Frank, they sparkled.

"Hi," Gail smiled.

"Hey. Thought we'd scared you off."

"I figured my hair wasn't long enough to set on fire," she smirked. "Besides, how could I resist the tall tales?"

Diego was telling a story about an interview he and Ike had done. Their wit was an old lady and her dead husband, who she assured the detectives, was right next to her on the couch. Diego would ask a question, and she'd say she wasn't sure. The old lady would turn to her husband and ask what he thought. Then she'd look at the detectives and smile as if they'd heard the answer too. Diego finally got the hang of it, and asked the lady to repeat the husband's answers, "on account of my partner and me being so deaf from all the gun battles we've been in."

She was a great witness, even they couldn't put her on the stand because she was loony-toons. Diego made small talk as they left and she complained about making dinner for her husband. He insisted on supper at six o'clock, but he never ate a thing anymore. She always ended up scraping his plate into the garbage can.

"After that," Diego rapped on the table, "Every night, six sharp, Ike was at her door."

"That's like the old lady I had when I was still in uniform," Johnnie said launching into his own story.

Nancy plunked a tall glass in front of Gail and swept up an empty pitcher. Noah kept interrupting Johnnie's story, showing off for the ladies at the table, and Nook grumbled interjections. Taking in conversations from other tables, monitoring the mood of the bar and her own detectives, Frank

38

tested the atmosphere like a wild animal, too sober to let her guard down. She didn't anticipate trouble, but was ready for it. Part of that was her natural character; part of it was too many years as a cop.

For a moment, Frank gave the coroner her full attention. She seemed to be having a good time and when the boot at the other end of the table asked Gail the trickiest case she'd ever had, the ME launched into an animated story of an anesthesiologist who'd poisoned his wife with succinylcholine. Frank watched as she explained the wife's exhumation, charmed by Gail's flying hands and lively accounting.

Nook took center stage after Gail, recounting a body he'd found under a swimming pool. The ice was melting in Gail's glass and Frank leaned over to ask if she'd like a fresh drink.

"I'll get it," she insisted, but Frank waded to the bar, caught Mac's eye and yelled, "Gin and tonic." He nodded and Frank continued to the bathroom, grateful for the momentary quiet. Drying her hands she glanced at the face in the mirror. Nestled within shadows and a wreath of fine wrinkles, cobalt blue eyes stared back. She'd turned forty in January and looked every minute of it.

When she returned with Gail's drink, the ME protested, "You didn't have to do that."

"You know the rules," Frank said. "Tradition is, you drink at the Nine-three table, the LT picks up the tab."

"Who started that anyway?"

"That would have been Joe Girardi, my old boss."

Gail sipped, eyeing Frank from under a fringe of dark lash.

"You must have plenty of stories," she observed.

Frank did, but the boys were usually so busy trying to get their own tall tales in, they seldom asked. Frank mostly settled bets, paid the bill, arbitrated discussions, and nodded in the right places. Even after work, she was still the boss.

"Yeah," she nodded, tilting her head at the detectives, "But this is good for them. Lets them blow steam."

"And how do you blow steam?"

"Listening to them," she smiled.

She wobbled her coffee mug, watching the film on top shimmy. Johnnie was questioning Nook's story and he asked the doc a technical question. She jumped into the fray, and deftly defended Nook's story without deflating Johnnie's ego. No small task, Frank thought. Gail went on to top Nook's story and Frank admired how she fit in with the Nine-three.

Bobby took a turn and Frank's thoughts drifted idly to Kennedy. She wondered what the manic detective was up to this Friday night. If she wasn't working, and if conditions were right, she was probably surfing. If not that, then cruising on her in-lines or 10-speed, or defeating imaginary foes at kick boxing. Whatever she was doing, Frank was certain she'd be moving; the girl couldn't sit for long. She reflected on the fling they'd had, an affair comprised mainly of passionate and aggressive love-making.

Frank indulged in the memory of that last time with Kennedy. They'd stumbled around the apartment, groping each other like school kids, finally landing on the floor and filling themselves with each other. Then Kennedy'd given her that damn cocky smile and said, "I'm starving. Want pizza?"

Still somnambulate, Frank had dumbly replied, "Sure."

They'd eaten dinner, talking about their week. Kennedy had pried (as always) into how it was going with Clay at the BSU. Frank had hedged (as always). It was going well but she hadn't wanted to get into the details. Instead she'd told a story about a case Ike had caught. Kennedy had laughed around a bite of pizza, accusing Frank of changing the subject. Frank argued there was no changing subjects with Kennedy, only delaying them.

"You know what?" Kennedy had asked. Expecting the inevitable confrontation, Frank had answered, "I'm afraid I don't."

"I think we need to make love again. Slow this time. What do you think?"

"Second best thing you've said all night."

"What was the first?"

"Let's get pizza."

Three days later Frank surprised Kennedy at her apartment. Not only was Kennedy surprised, so was Frank and a very disheveled Nancy.

"Isn't that right, Frank?"

"What?"

"162 stab wounds?"

"Where?"

"That Salvadoran woman who shredded her boyfriend, remember? Cut him 162 times. Crochetti had to count each one. Man, he was pissed."

Frank nodded, verifying Bobby's story, and Gail laughed from the back of her throat.

"God, I can hear him now. *'Worse than a damned .22',*" she rasped in imitation of the old ME.

Noah caught Frank's eye and he cocked his head at her, wondering. She winked and he tapped his mug to her cup.

"To Fridays."

"Here, here," Gail joined in, raising her glass to Noah, then Frank. This precipitated a whole series of toasts around the table, in Spanish, Polish, Chinese, Japanese, and Czechoslovakian. Then the conversation turned to the NBA playoffs and Gail edged toward Frank.

"You follow basketball?"

"Nope. I'm pretty much a football fan. How about you?"

"I like to watch the Niners and Giants. Those are my dad's teams and I kind of grew up with them."

"You're from Berkeley, right?"

"Good memory," Gail nodded. "How about you?"

"Back east."

"Where back east?"

"New York City."

"Really?" Gail said, surprised, pushing her dark bob away from her face. "I'd have never guessed."

"Good," Frank said, watching Noah's face crack into a big

grin. She looked over her shoulder just as she heard Kennedy's wicked drawl.

"Yes sirree, I reckoned this was where I'd find you bar rats along a Friday night."

Johnnie and Noah greeted the young detective, imitating her accent, and telling her, "Make yerself to home."

There weren't many seats available and noting her predicament, Bobby gallantly offered his. She protested but he said, "Hey, I got to be getting home. It's late as it is. Leslie's gonna bust a move on me."

Kennedy took his seat and Nancy came over with bright interest.

"Darlin'," Kennedy drawled, eyeing the waitress up and down, making her blush.

"Hi," she answered shyly, avoiding Kennedy's eye by wiping rings off the table. "Coke?"

"*Por favor*," the detective said in horrible Spanish.

When the waitress left, Kennedy turned her full attention to the ME.

"How ya doin', doc?"

"Fine," Gail replied, with a slight edge. The young narc held the doc's cool gaze a beat longer than necessary, then turned to Frank.

"How you been?" she asked.

Conversation drifted back to the DA's office and below the rest of the table talk Frank answered, "Good. S'up with you?"

"Nothin'," Kennedy shrugged, "Just thought I'd drop by and see what ya'll were up to."

Frank shrugged, "Working hard, hardly working."

"You taking care of yourself?" the younger woman asked, with no trace of an accent.

"You bet. And you?"

"Stayin' fit as a fiddle."

"You look it."

Kennedy leaned closer, dropping her voice even more.

"Ain't too late to change your mind, you know."

42

A thin smile reflected off Frank's coffee.

"Thanks, but no thanks."

"Suit yourself," Kennedy dismissed, scanning the crowded room. Spotting Nancy, she said, " 'Scuse me."

Frank watched the two women talking, joking, Kennedy's hand on Nancy's arm. Frank would have shaken her head if she were alone; the girl had moxie, and then some. Frank had ended their affair when she saw the situation with Nancy, but Kennedy had been unrepentant. She'd insisted her relationship with Frank wasn't monogamous, so what was the big deal? She still didn't understand why Frank had ended it.

Kennedy made her way back to the Nine-three table, winked at Frank, and said goodbye to the detectives. Knowing Noah was watching her, Frank refused to look at him. She finished her coffee and stayed for another round of one-upping, then dropping some bills on the table, she said, "Make sure Johnnie doesn't take this for alimony."

"Johnnie, hell," Diego answered. "Make sure Ike doesn't take it for the ponies."

"Hey, where you goin'?" Noah asked

"Going home. Been a long week baby-sitting you guys. Doc, good to see you again," Frank said amiably. "Always nice to have fresh blood at this table."

When Gail asked, "Pun intended?" Frank answered with a rare and genuine smile.

Chapter Six

"Hey. What are you doing here?"

Noah slapped into the squad room in rubber thongs. Wearing faded red shorts and a cut-off, paint-stained sweatshirt, limbs dangling, he looked like a Southern California scarecrow.

Frank's squad worked 6:00AM to 2:00 PM, Monday through Friday, rotating on call outs after hours. Unless they'd caught a new case, Frank usually had the squad room to herself on weekends.

"Aw, Trace and Markie got the flu. I got 'em some videos and the girls are at the mall with some friends. I figured I may as well come in and get that Torres report wrapped up."

"Yeah. You're late on that. I want it by Monday."

"I know, I know. So how was your night?" Noah asked innocently, sniffing the coffee pot.

"Fine," Frank replied, equally innocent.

"Get any sleep?"

"Plenty."

Noah chuckled at her and said, "You're drivin' Johnnie batty. All these women lining up for you and he can't even get *one*. He was gettin' *bitter* last night."

"What'd he say?" Frank asked, unsettled by the vision of Johnnie rambling drunkenly about her love-life.

"Aw, nothin'. He was just thinkin' he'd do better with tits and a ponytail."

"All I got's the ponytail," Frank corrected.

"You got somethin'," Noah pressed, "I'm tellin' you — Nance, Kennedy, the doc . . ."

"You'd probably make more money on Love Line than you do here, No."

"Damn right," Noah agreed. "I should be charging you a finders fee. The doc was asking questions after you left. I like this, she called you — and I quote directly — intriguingly impenetrable."

"What did she want to know?"

"If you and Kennedy were an item."

Frank raked Noah's face for signs of a joke.

"What'd you say?"

"I told her she'd have to ask you."

"Nice. Very subtle."

"What was I supposed to say?"

"Could've tried no."

"Then I'd be lying . . . wouldn't I?"

Now Noah looked for answers in Frank's stony face.

"Are you two not . . . you know . . . ?"

"No. We're not."

Frank tried to walk away, but Noah blocked her.

"Since when?"

"Since when's that any of your business?"

"It's my job to keep abreast of these things. So to speak. So since when?"

"Since a while ago," she relented. "Okay? Can I get some work done now?"

"That's *perfect*," Noah exclaimed. "Now you can make your move on the doc. *Trust* me, Frank; your efforts won't go unrewarded."

"So you keep telling me," she muttered, then to change the subject she demanded, "Listen. Guess what I did this morning."

"Let's see. You hired a hooker?"

Frank shook her ponytail. "Couldn't find one at six AM."

"You're lookin' in the wrong places," Noah suggested. "Okay. You registered for a cruise around the world."

"Cruise is partly correct."

Noah narrowed his eyes, carefully assessing Frank. The faded, neatly pressed jeans, the blue LAPD shirt, were standard weekend attire, but the battered running shoes weren't.

"Knowing you . . . at six AM on a Saturday morning, you'd probably worked out already and you were probably back at work, either at home or here. But cruise is part of the answer . . . let's see. I know you're not happy that we're pinning the Estrella case on Luis . . . I'm guessing you cruised out to Topanga and did a little bush-whacking. That would explain the scratches on your arms. Correct?"

Frank chuckled, surprised, pleased, and a little embarrassed that Noah knew her so well.

"Did I hit the jackpot?"

"Three cherries, my man. Not that it did any good. All I found were ticks and gnats."

"Lucky that man-eating cougar didn't find *you*."

"I'm too tough. She'd have spit me out after one bite."

"So what were you lookin' for?"

"I don't know. Anything."

46

Frank hadn't expected to find a smoking gun, but she'd needed to see for herself where Luis Estrella had been. She'd half walked, half slid down the angled hillside, and from the surprisingly accurate LASD notes, found the exact location of the body. Searching for the anomaly in the scenery, she'd spent a couple hours crawling through prickly-leaved shrubs and poison oak.

But for a small assortment of the usual litter, it was a surprisingly clean canyon. Frank had cleared some duff to bare soil and nestled herself against a large boulder. She'd let the mild sun play over her face. Closing her eyes against it, she'd shut out the scenery and gradually deafened herself to the birdsong and bustle in the underbrush.

She'd concentrated on Luis Estrella's face, the proud picture of his tats. She imagined him in his room, at the kitchen table with his family, driving in his beat-up car. Working hard at becoming him, she'd absorbed everything she knew about him — his heroin habit, his limp, his ill health, his easy-go-lucky clownishness. She put herself in his tennis shoes and sweatshirt, on the dirty bed in the garage, scratching himself, picking at his sores.

Frank didn't have to shoot up to know the effects of horse. She'd grown up around the drug and been surrounded by it throughout her career. When a junkie was happy, he shot up. When he was sad, he shot up. When he was breathing, he shot up. A gutter-hype like Luis lived for only one thing, and that was to dip steel. The only thing that mattered to him was scoring and using. A junkie on the nod couldn't be provoked into the rage necessary to waste an entire family. A crashing junkie could be angered, but his rage would be focused on finding his next hit. Nothing else mattered to him. The horse obviated any other needs; food, sex, shelter — it all paled compared to the craving for that next hit.

Sitting in her patch of sunshine, Frank had tried to feel how a hope-to-die junkie could muster the wherewithal to efficiently and cold-bloodedly kill six people. And his dog. The dog that slept in the garage with him, on his own bed. Johnnie was right. It didn't make sense.

She repeated that to Noah, who just shook his head. She couldn't blame him. With a case load like theirs, a detective had to take the most obvious leads and run with them. In a few days, sometimes a few hours, another call would come in and his already heavy load would have to be shifted to accommodate the new burden. The ninety-third didn't have the luxury of chasing wild hairs and shaky leads. If the evidence pointed north, a detective went north, even if his gut screamed south. The detective could only indulge his gravitational pull if and when the opposite course had been proved a misdirection.

Rather than arguing when they both had more pressing demands, Frank conceded, "We'll see what the lab comes up with."

Long after Noah had typed up his 60-day report and gone home, Frank could almost see the top of her desk again. She was satisfied with the progress she'd made on the reams of budget projections and overtime justifications, payroll forms and vacation requests, multi-jurisdictional faxes and memos, 60Ds and preliminary reports, plus dozens of warrants, weapons registrations, rap sheets, DMV printouts . . . and still there was a pile. Determined to return to an empty desktop Monday morning, Frank crammed the remaining papers and photos into her briefcase. She palmed the light switch, leaving the squad room dark behind her.

On her way out she asked Officer Heisdaeck about his upcoming back surgery and swapped quips with a B&E artist in the holding tank. He'd been on the streets since Frank had been a boot. A few weeks back his 13 month-old grandson had been grazed by a .22 meant for the boy's Crip father and she asked how he was doing.

"He be awright. Ain't nuttin' but a scratch. Got his first

taste a Blood, dat's wha' da was. He gone be a big time slob killuh."

The man in the holding cell was Frank's peer, but bad food, worse liquor, and a lifetime of combining drugs made him look twenty years older. No doubt he'd been brought in on a D 'n D but he was subdued now, remorseful.

"Yeah, he'll be alright," Frank agreed. "Got his Gramp-C reppin' him."

" 'Da's right. Somebody gots to hep the lil' ones comin' up."

"Don't reckon there's anyone knows as much about these streets as you do."

She slapped his cell bars and he clucked, " 'At ain't no lie, Franco. 'At ain't no lie."

Slipping out the back, she was on the Harbor Freeway in two minutes, headed north to Pasadena. The drive usually only took fifteen, twenty minutes but the crush of Saturday evening traffic slowed her down.

Squeaky brakes and idling engines competed with talk radio shows and the powerful *boom-boom-boom* of car stereos. Frank sat with her arm out the window, aware of each sound, but knowing they didn't demand her attention. The same went for the pastel dusk folding softly around the downtown skyline. Seventeen years with one of the largest police forces in the world had exquisitely honed Frank's senses. She hadn't been in uniform for over a decade but she still needed to hear the heartbeat of the streets. That was why she listened to the hip-hop stations and could recite N.W.A. and Da Brat lyrics.

Frank had spent her entire career in the corner of the western world infamous for the Watts riots, and then thirty years later, the Rodney King riots. She'd missed Watts, but the second series of riots had been a succession of nights straight out of Dante. Frank had been "riot-baptised" with bricks and bottles, bullets and fire.

Clay had asked during one of her earlier sessions what it

was like to work in such hostile environs, especially as a female, and a white one at that. Frank hadn't thought much of it. Born and raised in New York City's lower east side, there was nothing she hadn't seen by the time she entered the LAPD Academy; landing at the Figueroa Station had merely rounded out her education. The hard streets afforded Frank an excellent outlet for her natural wariness and aggression and as a younger cop she'd looked forward to the physical confrontations of the job. The demands of her rough exterior world commanded Frank's constant attention, offering diversion from her own complicated interior. Like the kids growing up in Compton and Inglewood, Frank had survived by refusing to show fear or pain. Softness was equated with weakness, and weakness meant death. She'd lived by that street credo for forty years. Ironically, it had almost killed her.

Frank absently tracked a jet gleaming silver in the dying sun. Despite the terror of suicides and homicides witnessed, of bullets and knives passing through her flesh and that of loved ones, none of it had scared Frank more than one desolate night with Kennedy, the night she was sure her brain had cracked and that whatever she touched was dripping in blood; her blood, Kennedy's blood, her father's blood, Maggie's blood, all the blood she'd seen puddled and sprayed on sidewalks and cars, walls and carpets, cribs and school chairs. Everywhere she looked, blood.

Exiting slowly onto Colorado Boulevard, Frank was guardedly optimistic that she could handle the memory of that night so easily. She figured the Wednesday afternoons with Clay must be paying off. Turning down her street, she noted the dusky gloom of the big oaks over the road, the neighbors windows glowing yellow. Frank realized that she was finally enjoying coming home again. Just as she pulled into her driveway, her pager thrummed against her hip. She left the car running on the vague superstition that if she stopped it, she'd have to start it again. She called the front desk on her cell phone.

Sergeant Romanowski ceremoniously informed her, "Lieutenant, your presence is requested by Detectives Nukisona and Taylor at the corner of Hyde Park and South Wilton."

Frank backed out swearing. So much for superstition.

Chapter Seven

Back in the warren of traffic on the One-Ten, Frank shook
her head at Nook and Bobby's run of bad luck. Not only did
they get the Estrella homicides, but they'd caught two
mysteries in the last two weeks — each case a bad boy shot
with no witnesses, no motives, and no suspects. She considered how the two didn't make an ideal homicide team.
They were both more tenacious than aggressive and tended to
plod through cases, bogging down in detail. Especially Bobby.
Though they both earned high marks for sheer determination,
she wished there was more fire in their partnership. As it was,
she'd have to settle for stubbornness and resolve. Because of

their tendency to err on the side of caution, Frank figured they were calling her out on a grounder.

She poked the radio's preset button to KLOS, hoping electric guitars and pounding backbeats could pump her up for what was looking like another long night. Creeping off at the Downtown exit, she worked her way south using a maze of side roads. The cool spring evening belied the deadly summer heat just around the corner.

Bummer of a nice night to die, she thought, arriving at her destination. A Sheriff's unit and two LAPD radio cars worked their lights where the road made a dogleg. The coroner's van split the night with glaring halogens. Handley was stepping into a pair of coveralls so Frank figured the investigator had only beaten her here by minutes

"What have you got?" Frank asked Bobby. He twitched his head at a body on the sidewalk. Its legs were off the curb, hidden by a line of parked cars.

"It's Placa, Frank. She took a couple rounds."

Frank swallowed hard, holding Bobby's gaze a beat, before lowering it to his tie. She took in the LAPD tie clip and starched creases in his shirt. She appreciated the time he took to get dressed for a call-out. In the matter of seconds it took for Frank to formulate those thoughts, she had morphed into stone and ice. Now she swung her head toward the body which was suddenly not just a body. The ice in Frank's veins warned her that this was personal. It also warned her to be especially objective. She walked over to Placa, squatting on her heels in front of the dead girl.

Give it up, she silently willed. *Show me how it went down.*

Placa's left cheek was pressed against the broken concrete. From the shattered look of it she'd been dead or disabled as she went down and hadn't been able to break her fall. Her braid went through the back of a Dodger's cap, tilted almost off her head. Frank could make out a tiny blue tattoo just under the eye socket and the "52K" jarringly tattooed under her bangs. A sexy female devil with flowing hair and pointed tail peeked from under Placa's right sleeve. Her left hand was arched awkwardly in a blood puddle. The name "ITSY" stood out in blue on the webbing of her thumb and forefinger.

Frank unconsciously held her own ring finger, stroking it lightly as she studied the dead girl in front of her.

Handley knelt too, but Frank said, "Hold up."

"I don't have all night," he pointed out. The look Frank cut him was enough to send the tech a respectful distance away.

"Anybody see anything?"

"Not yet," Bobby answered quietly.

Frank looked around. Nook was talking to two of the uniforms. The Sheriff's deputy was making conversation with Handley. Waddell was working paper in a radio car and Hunt was in his usual position against the bumper of another. Frank gave Handley the nod and walked over to Waddell. Twitching her head toward Hunt, she asked, "You short tonight?"

"Yeah. Couple guys called in sick. Guess its just coincidence that it's Saturday night, huh?"

"Who's got the log?"

"Hunt."

"Who was Responding Officer?"

"They were," he said at the cops Nook was talking to. Frank moved toward Hunt, telling him she wanted the scene log. He sneered and moved slowly off the bumper, retrieving the list from inside the unit. Frank scanned it and as she did, she murmured, "Are you 10-7?"

"No, ma'am," he drawled, his answer sounding lazy and snide.

"Then I suggest you get your ass off this car and find some witnesses."

Hunt grunted, "There ain't a fuckin' monkey in this jungle that's seen shit."

"You're probably right," she answered, "but you better start knockin' to prove it."

Swearing under his breath, Hunt hitched up his heavy belt and sauntered off. Frank assessed the area. The east side of South Wilton was residential. It was a nice neighborhood lined with old, graceful palms. Each small, neatly kept bungalow had a trim patch of lawn sloping gently to the street. It was a solid working-class street where pride was still evident. Despite the hype, much of the south-central neighborhoods were like this one, quiet and modest, occupied by decent people trying to earn a decent living. Then there were the kids like Placa, who lived hard and died fast.

The rule of the streets, Frank thought, resuming her sweep of the area. The west side of Wilton was industrial, with privacy and security fencing running the length of the sidewalk. Where Frank stood, Wilton took a deep curve to become Hyde Park. Tall fences continued along the north sidewalk, but a building supply company took up the entire south corner.

Most of the adults on Wilton had gone back inside, bored with yet another gang-related shooting, but the kids still hung around, gawking. A radio played on a porch. A couple of young girls sang and mock danced with each other. Frank recognized the tune, the one all the pop and hip-hop stations played every twenty minutes. The irony that the band was Destiny's Child didn't escape her.

Frank caught the heavy odor of frying food in the air as she watched Hunt and Nook knocking on doors. Few of the houses had air conditioning. They would have easily trapped the heat of the day. Little kids would have begged to play outside before they had to go to bed. Grandmothers or grandfathers would have watched them, collecting the evening breeze on stoops and porches. Aunts or uncles might have joined them, sharing 40's or iced teas. Siblings would have been kicking by someone's car, bumpin' and swapping tales.

Still Hunt was probably right; nobody would have seen anything.

Frank returned to Bobby, who was searching the wallet Handley gave him.

"She strapped?"

"Nope, nothing."

"What do you think about that?"

Bobby nodded, "Kind of weird for that G to be running around without a gat. Is that what you're thinking?"

"Yeah. Especially Placa. She favored those little deuce-fives. I could wallpaper my bathroom with her concealeds alone. Find out what time this was called in, and when the first unit showed up."

Nook sauntered up, and asked, "Why's the LAPD better than the AMA?"

Both Frank and Bobby stared at him, and he grinned, "We still make house calls."

Neither of his colleagues responded, and he said, "What?"

"Do a weapons sweep. Look for a .25."

Bobby asked, "You want to knock with us on this one?"

Frank nodded, watching Handley shove Placa's shirt up. She knelt next to him, noting the entry wounds.

"How many you see?"

"Well . . . looks like five. So far," he said, pointing. Placa had taken a round dead center in her back and another through her left shoulder blade. A third grazed the left side of her neck, and Handley exposed another a few inches abover her beltline. The fifth made a tiny hole at the base of her head. Whoever smoked her had made sure she wouldn't get up again.

"Trajectory?"

Handley gingerly examined the most lethal wounds. He boasted, "Hard to say for sure until we get her on the table, but entry appears to relatively level, maybe angling slightly left."

Nook had recovered a fresh case from a .25, roughly 150 feet south of the body. It had been on the road and was flattened.

"Show me where the jacket was," she said to Bobby.

He walked Frank in front of a battered pick-up parked at the crook of the curve. Frank stepped on the spot. Raising her arm, she sighted along the sidewalk at Placa's height. The trajectory of Placa's wounds would have been consistent with a shooter in a tall vehicle or standing where Frank was. She wondered if it was coincidence that she'd been shot with a .25. Maybe it was her gun. She tried to imagine Placa fleeing, Placa who'd rather suffer a beating death than run. Placa with her outrageous and dangerous pride.

Was she outnumbered and outgunned on foreign turf? Frank thought this was Rollin' 60's turf. Frank didn't think the Kings had a quarrel with them. Maybe she'd rounded a corner and a rival happened to be coming around the other way. But she was running north. So the danger would have to have been from the south. From where the casing was, the shooter had been just at the bend, not enough time for a shooter to accidentally round the corner, recognize her, and open fire. Unless they knew she was there, as if they'd been following or chasing her.

Frank was doing her best to be objective, but events were becoming too coincidental; within one week Julio Estrella's family was massacred. A few days later his brother winds up OD'd in the bottom of a canyon. After that, Placa mysteriously calls to tell Frank to meet with her, then ends up fatal. Another convenient drive-by statistic.

Frank needed a good witness. There had to be one. It was pretty hard to ignore a girl running down the street and shots being fired; even as jaded as south-central residents were, they would have instinctively glanced up to see which way the bullets were coming from. Was there shouting, screaming, anybody claiming? When the first shots sounded, they'd have all ducked for cover. Before that though, someone must have seen or heard something. But this was south-central; ratting in the 'hood was often deadly and rarely done.

Adjusting the bite of the harness under her left arm, Frank drew a long breath and joined her men in their search for a witness.

Chapter Eight

A couple hours later, the best the detectives had were two people who thought maybe the car that had driven up on Placa was some sort of sedan. They couldn't even give them a color or guess at a make. Too dark. No street lights. The usual frustrating responses. But the first witness was pretty sure she'd seen a sedan pulling away from the curb around the pickup, as if the sedan were leaving a parking space. When they asked the second witness where the car was in relation to the street, he'd said, come to think of it, the car looked to be parked.

"Right in front of that pickup," he'd said pointing. And the car had a rounded back, not a square one. "Like a T-bird," he'd added.

Frank stood on the dark street listening to a helicopter whock-whock overhead, it's Night Sun cutting a path through the sky. Frank watched it fly out of her jurisdiction. Bobby stretched, cracking his back, and Nookey complained, "I didn't even get a chance to have dinner."

He gallantly volunteered to go back to the office and start the odious paper work. Frank knew his ulterior motives were to get a little nap and avoid doing the next of kin. She told him to go get some dinner, and then he and Bobby could round up the homies. Frank said she'd do the notification and Nook looked at her curiously.

"Why are you gonna do it?"

"My turn," Frank said simply, not wanting to explain her long ties to Placa's mother. She'd wanted to tell Claudia Estrella about her brother Luis' death but Foubarelle and the Deputy Chief had claimed her time that afternoon.

Frank drove slowly north-east, finally parking in front of a house that wasn't quite as tidy as the rest on the block. She couldn't think how many times she'd rolled to a stop here in a black-and-white. A Spanish TV show blared through the open windows and a yellow mosquito bulb dangled from a socket over the front door. She knocked loudly, and when the door opened, the face in the crack betrayed recognition and a weary animosity.

"Hey, Claudia. I need to talk to you."

Claudia Estrella stepped back into the disheveled living room and the lieutenant followed. Frank took in a dark-eyed girl on the plastic-covered couch, distracted between the stranger and the television. A toddler crawled on the floor with a sagging diaper, and Placa's older sister stared at Frank from the kitchen. Drying her hands on a towel, she asked disgustedly, "What you want now?"

Frank didn't answer, facing Claudia instead. She noted the gray roots under the black dye, the hard set of her face and deep lines.

"When was the last time you saw Carmen?" she asked, calling Placa by her proper name.

"Two, three o'clock."

"Where'd you see her?"

"Here."

"What was she doing?"

"I don't know."

"Was she eating, or watching TV, hangin' out? What was she doing?"

"I don't know. I just saw her going out."

"Where was she going?"

"I don't know."

"Was Gloria here too?"

Claudia bit some skin around the edge of her thumb and stared at Frank with a sharp, wary expression.

"Yeah."

"Gloria," Frank called. "Come out here. I need to talk to you."

They heard swearing in the kitchen and a drawer banging.

"I ain't got nothin' to say to you," Claudia's eldest daughter said from the doorway.

"When was the last time you saw your sister?"

She shrugged, just like her mother.

"Earlier, like she tol' you."

"Not since?"

The young woman shook her long hair. When she'd been a banger she'd worn it in a teased pile, now it just hung limply. Permanent bags under the big eyes replaced the black circles from makeup, and like her mother, her hips had spread with each child. Babies had ended their days of hanging with their girlfriends and fighting over boyfriends. They had handed their legacy down to Placa and this was were it ended, in a stuffy house smelling of old diapers and grease, with the TV on too loud and Del Taco bags covering a chipped coffee table.

"What was she doing?"

"Nothin'. She wasn't even here most of the day. Probably being a lazy-ass and kickin' it in the park, I don't know."

"Did you talk to her before she left?"

"No."

"She didn't say anything to you?"

Gloria shook her head.

"She talk to the kids, anybody else?"

"I don' know," she answered, her irritation growing. "What, you think I had some tape recorder goin' on or somethin'?"

"Did she look like she was upset when she left? Happy? Anything?"

"*Normal*," she said in Spanish, flipping a shoulder.

Frank asked Claudia, "She get any phone calls before she left?"

Gloria aborted a glance at her mother, but not fast enough to escape Frank's notice. Claudia's son, Toñio, emerged sleepily from a bedroom. Skinny and gangly, only fourteen, he scratched his hairless chest and asked in Spanish what was going on.

"*Estan preguntando de Carmen. No les diga nada.*"

Frank wouldn't say she was fluent in Spanish, but after years of listening to it everyday, she could understand a fair bit.

"Don't say anything to me about what?" she asked Gloria, who stamped her foot and said, "Nothin'. Why you police comin' aroun' askin' all these questions when we tell you we don' know nothin', eh?"

Ignoring her, Frank faced Claudia instead. She'd struck this pose so many times. It was never pleasant, but at least it was easier with a stranger. Nonetheless Frank did her job perfectly, speaking levelly and gauging Claudia's reaction, as she said, "Somebody shot Placa."

Claudia's mask slipped for a second and Frank was aware of Gloria careening into the room, screaming, "That fucker! I'll kill him! That fucking p*endejo,* I'll *kill* him!"

The old adversaries stared at each other, even as the little girl on the couch and the toddler picked up their mother's wailing, even as Gloria fell to the floor and her brother rushed to Frank demanding to know where Placa was and how she was. Both women had done this too many times. Stoically they shared the silence of bad news delivered and bad news received.

As if in confirmation, Claudia said, "She's dead."

Frank nodded. Seemingly without effort, Claudia rearranged her face into a quiescent tableau, a still brown desert that revealed nothing across its landscape but the inevitable play of time and gravity.

Taking a knee next to Gloria, Frank asked, "What *pendejo* are you talking about, Gloria? Who did this?"

Rocking and sobbing, she moaned her sister's name. Frank repeated her question, with no effect. Finally she asked, "Is it the same *pendejo* that shot Julio and his family? Is that who you're talking about?"

Gloria halted her hysteria, staring at Frank through her tears. Then she laughed, crying, "You don't know nothin'! You fuckin' *jura* don't know *nothin'* 'bout what's goin' on. Get out of here! Get out of my house! Leave my family alone!"

She resumed her moaning and Frank stood. Claudia opened the door, staring implacably at Frank. Frank hovered over her.

"She called me. She wanted to meet me tomorrow morning at Saint Michael's. Said she had something to tell me. What was it, Claudia? What was she going to tell me?"

Claudia's only response was to close her eyes.

Quietly, tenderly, Frank said, "Claudia. You and me, we go back a long way. And Placa, too. What do you know about all this?"

Claudia said nothing, just gnawed on her thumbnail. She looked old. Older than she should have.

"Look at me," Frank said, so low only Claudia could hear. "Look at me."

The woman's dusty eyes flickered across Frank's but she couldn't maintain the gaze.

"What's going on?" Frank whispered. "Tell me."

Like a lover denied, Frank implored, "Give it up, Claudia. Talk to me."

She waited, but she may as well have been talking to the table. Frank nodded, her hand on the doorknob.

"Okay," she said gently. "I'm leaving now, but I'll be back. You know something. And until I find out what that is, I'm gonna be here every day. *Claro?*"

Placa's mother stared tightly and Frank opened the door. On her way out, she paused.

"Take your time. I'm in no hurry on this. I got eight more years before I retire, *entonces,*" she shrugged, "if I have to be here everyday that'll just be another part of the job."

Chapter Nine

The night had cooled and felt good on Frank's tired face. She lifted her head to search for a sign of stars or the moon, but the LA sky reflected only a dull red pall. It was as if heaven had turned its back on the City of Angels, leaving it in a fiery, Stygian gloom. It was reminiscent of the night Kennedy had dragged her to the beach and they'd lain on their backs, trying to catch sight of the elusive gems in the sky. For a moment she missed Kennedy. *No, that's not true* she told herself, *you miss being in bed with her*. That was true. It would have been nice to find Kennedy and hold her tightly enough to forget everything for a while.

Frank pulled in a lungful of the tainted sky. She was beat. She should go home and grab some sleep, but she knew that history would overtake her the minute she stopped moving. She wasn't ready to face all its ghosts. She would, she promised herself, just not yet.

Firing up the Honda, Frank caught the freeway, merging smoothly with the cars and trucks that flowed at all hours. She drove and listened to the talk on KFI, Tammy Bruce sparring with a homophobe. Frank tried to listen to the banter, but kept seeing Placa on the sidewalk, and Claudia's calm, prescient acceptance of her youngest daughter's fate. She drove faster, making the Honda shimmy, relieved to finally see the warm glow of the Alibi's front window, iron grate and all.

Inside, Frank returned a nod from a couple Vice detectives out of Parker. It was almost closing time and she took a seat at the empty bar, surprised to see Nancy.

"What are you doing here?" she asked.

The waitress slipped onto a stool next to Frank and purred, "Filling in for Dee. Now, what are you doing here?"

"Working."

Nancy wagged her head, "It's Saturday."

"I'll make sure to tell the bad guys that."

"Have you had dinner?"

"Nope. Kitchen still open?"

"He's closing down, but I can get you something. What do you want?"

"How about a ham and Swiss on rye? That shouldn't be much trouble."

"You got it." Slipping off the stool, Nancy asked, "Stout?"

"No. Scotch. Double."

Frank watched Nancy squeeze back behind the bar and pour her drink. Frank kept her eyes on the waitress as she talked to the cook. Nance had put on some pounds but she still filled a skirt nicely. Nancy reclaimed her stool and while she tallied receipts, Frank asked how her son was doing. Nancy and the liquor loosened the evening's death grip on

Frank. She kept drinking, paying attention to Nancy as she scarfed the sandwich the cook brought out.

"When are you gonna get someone to take care of you?" Nancy clucked.

Frank was grateful for the familiar banter, answering, "You mean a secretary?"

"You know what I mean," Nancy chided, then in a lower voice she added, "I mean a real live woman."

Been there, done that, Frank thought.

She said around a mouthful, "You applying for the job?"

"Shit," Nancy retorted, "I've had my application in for years. I'm still waiting to hear about it."

"Takes a long time to get to these things," Frank assured her.

"Well, I guess some things are just worth waiting for."

"Things okay with you and Kennedy?"

Nancy sighed and said, "Yeah. You were right, though. She's not real long-term, is she?"

Kennedy had alluded to Nancy that there was nothing serious between her and Frank, and Nancy had believed it, had needed to. She'd even checked with Frank, who by then agreed that, no, there was nothing between her and Kennedy. But Frank had warned Nancy to be careful. She glanced at Nancy, who said, "I know, I know, you told me. But still, even if it doesn't work out . . ."

"It won't."

"How can you be so sure?" Nancy pouted.

"She's a player, Nance. It's in her blood. She's not going to change just 'cause you get hooked on her."

"I'm not hooked," the waitress defended.

"Good. Don't get that way. She's fun, and that's all."

"I know," she groaned.

Nancy changed the subject, chatting while Frank savaged her dinner and worked on another double. The cook said goodnight, and Frank thought she should go home and let Nance close up. Thing was, she didn't want to go yet. Frank appraised the handsome woman beside her, wondering as she often had, what it would be like to take her up on her offer. The welcome mat had been out for a long time, but as tempting as it was, Frank liked Nancy too much to use her like that.

Frank drained her scotch and left a hefty tip. It had been a while since she'd spent the night on the couch in her office, but that was where she reluctantly headed. Crashing on the chrome and vinyl relic, she hoped that sleep would take her instantly. No such luck. The old faces came, as she'd feared they would, swirling around her like a windy fog. She bent an arm across her eyes as if that would fend them off

She and Claudia and Placa had traveled a far stretch of time together, their histories sometimes subtly, sometimes overtly linked. They'd grown up and grown older together. Made right choices and wrong ones. Lost people they'd loved. One was an ex-junkie, one a notorious banger, and another a commanding peace officer. Still they had more in common than not. And they'd all been young once, with more promise than not. But that had been before the junk got Claudia, before the streets got Placa, before Frank . . .

She flipped uneasily on to her side, quite aware of the familiar dread trying to get a claw into her. *I should just let it take me wherever it wants to go,* she thought, *have its little ride, then be done.* She threw off the thin blanket she kept in her locker for nights like this and stabbed at the light switch. Her desk was irritatingly clean. She picked through a cold case, hoping to ease her discomfort. But she knew by now that work just postponed it. Nothing eased it.

She closed the binder and sank into her old wooden chair. Rubbing one of the scarred, skin-polished arms, Frank thought, *been a long way with you too.* They kept trying to give her a new chair, one with wheels and springs and a dozen different positions, but she refused to give this one up. She wondered if maybe she should cave; how could she bring her head into the present if her ass was still firmly planted in the past? So much of her was in the past and she was bone weary of that.

She tried to convince herself to think of everyone, even Maggie, then let them all go. She could do that. She was stronger now, thanks to Clay. And Kennedy had helped, too. Propping bare feet on the desk, Frank tilted the chair back, hovering on the narrow cusp between forward and backward motion. Picturing Claudia young and not yet beaten, and Placa, giggling in diapers, Frank was grateful for all of Clay's instruction. Not only was he teaching her how to salvage the good memories, the best ones, but he was also showing her how to move on from the bad ones. She sat a while doing just that.

Chapter Ten

Noah put down a box of doughnuts and gave Frank the once over. Spraying powdered sugar on his too short suit, he mumbled, "What were you doin' here all night?"

Her hair had given her away. It was still slick, dripping onto her shirt collar from the shower she'd taken in the locker room. Frank didn't look up from the paper in her hand.

"Pretty much camped here all weekend. Somebody capped Placa Saturday night."

The doughnut fell away from Noah's mouth.

"Oh, *man*. Who?"

"Don't know."

Noah shook his head and said, "Goddamnit."

"Hardly a surprise," Frank responded curtly.

Noah's mouth dropped open. No one else was in the squad room yet and he said, "Jesus Christ, Frank! I swear I just wanna *hurl* this doughnut at you! I been workin' with you nearly twelve years and I swear to Christ sometimes it's like bein' with a stranger."

Frank glanced up from the warrant in her hand, seemingly unmoved by Noah's outburst.

"Something bugging you?"

"Yeah," Noah said angrily, "You! How can you be so fucking blasé about a girl half this squad raised?"

Facing him squarely, Frank made Noah wait for his answer. The overheads accentuated the purple shadows under her eyes and she absently rubbed the back of her neck. Frank rarely verbalized a feeling, but for someone who'd had as much practice reading her as Noah had, words weren't necessary. A sudden frosting and narrowing of the dark blue eyes indicated she was plenty pissed. If this was accompanied by bouncing jaw muscles it was likely someone or something was about to get broken. When she was engrossed in thought she often stroked the spot on her ring finger where a band used to be and squeezing the back of her neck was a dead giveaway that something was eating her. She tried to control her mannerisms but sometimes, like now, she simply forgot.

Dropping his doughnut back into the box, Noah's temper sputtered as quickly as it had flared.

"Never mind," he said, as Bobby and Ike came in together. Frank asked, "You want to talk in my office?"

"No. Sorry. Just lost it for a sec."

Frank's phone rang and she went to get it. Johnnie was calling in, said he had a migraine and he'd be in around ten.

"You know you're out of sick time," Frank responded.

"Yeah, yeah, I know," he wheezed on the other end. "What am I supposed to do, huh?"

"That's a good question. Might want to think about it while you're nursing that hangover."

He started to protest and Frank hung up, making a mental

note to talk to Noah. When all her detectives arrived, they had their morning meeting. Even-keeled and calm, Frank sat with her feet crossed on Gough's old desk. Ike was sporting a bruise on his cheekbone. From rough trade, he claimed. While the boys razzed him, Frank's hand strayed to the back of her neck. This time she caught herself and stopped kneading the tense muscles, but Noah had already seen her. She thought about how long they'd been friends, how there was a time when he would have died to rub Frank's neck for her. Popping the rest of a doughnut in his mouth, he stared at her, as if reading her thoughts. She swore he could sometimes, and she looked back down at her notes.

"All right," Frank said, starting business. She brought Ike, Diego, and Noah up to date on Placa's case then asked Nook and Bobby what they had. The smaller man flipped through his notebook.

"Well, we've been chasing homies all over town. Nobody knows nothing, and if they do they're not tellin'. The one thing we got is that Placa was really making a move on Playboy territory, specifically 51st Street. The corner held by Ocho Ruiz. You remember him?" Nook asked Frank.

"Refresh me."

"Got the octopus tattooed on his back? The tentacles wrapped around his chest?"

"Oh yeah," Frank nodded. "Lot's of time in stir. The tentacles connect to a big M."

"That's the one. And he's out again, but word is he's slippin'. Sampling too much of his own product."

Ocho Ruiz had started as an entrepreneurial hustler, keeping an eye out for ballers doing business on the corner, hollering when the heat came near. He'd fought and killed for his turf, stabbing and clubbing his way to a profitable corner of the drug trade in his barrio. He'd managed to stay on top even in lockup. Reputedly this had been done with the aid of the Mexican Mafia, hence the large M tat.

"Best part though, turns out he drives a yellow '91 T-Bird.

We've been tryin' to find him, but he ain't around. I figure maybe we'd go over to his crib after we're done here, see if we can catch him nappin'. But my bet is his ass is in the wind for a while."

"And nobody's claiming this?"

"Not a whisper," Bobby said. "I persuaded his mom to consent to a search. We found two .38s and a .45, but no quarter."

"Confiscate?"

Bobby nodded and Frank said, "Good. Get ballistics on them."

If they couldn't get Ocho for Placa, they might be able to nail him on another case.

"How about Itsy?"

Bobby said, "She's pretty torn up. We couldn't get anything out of her. The other girls, Negra and Payasa, they saw her around ten that morning, then she disappeared for a couple hours. Evidently she did that a lot, but nobody knows where she went."

"Keep at them. And both of you drop by and have a chat with Claudia and the kids. I know they know something, but they're not letting on. And hit Itsy again, and who's that little dark gal that's been putting in work for the set?"

"La Limpia," Noah piped in. "She's Rolo Hernandez' sister."

"What's he got to say?"

"Nothing. He was home in bed. Has the flu or something."

"All right. Keep hitting the homes. Let's hit the Playboys too. Find Ocho's dogs, bring them in if you have to. How about that CI of yours, Nook? Think she could help?"

"I'll see."

All the detectives had snitches or, confidential informers who'd trade a piece of news for a twenty. After everyone updated their cases, Frank moved on to other business, then the small group dispersed. Checking her watch, Frank told Noah to step into her office. When she closed the door, he said "Uh-oh."

"Tell me about your partner."

"What about him?"

"How's he doing?"

Noah looked uncomfortable and Frank knew she was putting him in an awkward spot, but cops usually knew more about their partners than they did about their own spouses.

"He's all right. Same old Johnnie, pissin' and moanin' about the IRS, and the government, and his exes all suckin' him dry. But he's okay."

"He's drinking a lot."

Noah pulled his aw-shucks face and opened his hands wide.

"Which one of you doesn't?"

"Look, I don't care what he does on his own time, but when it starts interfering with my time, we've got a problem. I'm not asking you to cheese him out. I just want a handle on what's going on. If he's got a problem, I owe it to him to help before it gets worse. Protecting him isn't helping him."

"I know, I know. But he's not drinkin' on the job, I can tell you that. But yeah, he's hung over almost every morning. I had to pull over last week so he could puke in the street."

Frank stared grimly.

"Don't come down on him too hard," Noah pleaded.

Frank nodded, knowing what a softie he was. Noah and Tracey joked that in their house, it was "wait 'til your mother gets home," because Noah just couldn't discipline the kids. He looked for the best in everyone and when he found it, he'd cling to it, refusing to look at the bad. It was one of the ways he kept his sanity in an insane job.

"This doesn't go out of here," she said, opening the door. No sooner had she returned to her desk than Diego poked his head in.

"*Quivo*, Taquito?"

"Got a minute?"

"Sure."

He tilted his head and Frank followed. He and Ike had a

74

suspect in one of their cases but couldn't get him into the box. Zabbo wanted to pull him in on a technicality, but Diego wanted to wait, let it ride until the suspect did something stupid. If they pulled him in now and he didn't tell them what they wanted, they'd have to let him go. Then he'd know he was wanted and could take a powder.

"This guy's rap sheet covers the floor, man. He'll fuck up any day now and then we've got him," Diego reasoned. He sat relaxed in his chair, the faint outline of a tattoo still visible under his left eye. He was an old *cholo*, a White Fence homeboy who'd turned his life around to play on the other side of the law. Nothing perturbed Diego, but his partner was a hothead. At 53, Ike was the second oldest member of the nine-three. The boys called him "Pinkie" because of his rings, and there was much speculation but no proof as to how Ike managed to live like a shot-caller on a detective's salary.

Waving a sticky maple donut in the air, he argued that their suspect knew he was hot and that they already ran the risk of losing him. Ike was confident if they brought him in on a minor that they could break him down in the box. Just as Frank was about to side with Diego her phone rang and she sprinted into her office. She was waiting for the coroner's office to call about Placa's cut.

"Homicide. Franco."

"No, no, no," the voice at the other line argued. "You worked *hard* to get where you are, Frank. You've got to answer the phone, *Lieutenant* Franco."

Frank recognized Joe Girardi's high-pitched voice.

"So they know exactly which office to send the bomb to, right?"

Joe chuckled and asked how it was going.

Frank's hand found her neck when she answered, "Not so bad. I've got one detective out on maternity, another that's retired, and one that should be in AA meetings. Other than that, things are good."

"Let's see. That redhead you hired would be the ML.

Gough's wearing out his lawn mower, and the drunk would be Ike or Johnnie. Or you."

Frank smiled into the phone.

"That'd be Johnnie."

"What are you doing about it?"

"I gotta talk to him. Tell him I'm worried about him, worried about his job performance."

"And he'll spit in your face. That's what I did when Dougherty called me on my shit. Let me know if there's anything I can help with. How's Fubar treating you?"

"He's getting kind of antsy. Stats were down last two months, closures were sixty-nine and fifty-two respectively."

Her old boss whistled, "That's low for you, my girl."

"Tell me. And the little man ain't happy."

"Tell him he better get you some more bodies — live ones, that is."

"Yeah, he keeps saying he's going to, but they never materialize."

'Things heating up yet?"

The body count at Figueroa always increased with the summer temperatures. People were outside more and their tempers started fraying in the unrelenting city heat. Trivialities quickly escalated into traumas, and by August it wasn't unusual to have daily homicides. Joe had escaped it all when he retired to the fishing in Minnesota. For a second Frank felt a pang of envy.

"Nah, still pretty quiet." She paused. "Remember Placa? Claudia Estrella's daughter?"

"Sure, sure. What did she do now?"

"Somebody smoked her the other night."

"Aw, geez. That's a goddamned shame."

The disappointment in Joe's voice made Frank uneasy and she worked the tightness just under her hairline.

"Yeah. Not only that, week before, her uncle and aunt and cousins got capped."

"You got a turf war going on?"

She told Joe how the Kings were muscling into Playboy territory, but that so far all the killing was strictly related to the Estrella clan. There was no broader indication of an all-out gang conflict. She mentioned the lead on Ruiz and how they'd spent the weekend trying to find him. When that topic ran out Joe casually asked, "Are you still going over to BSU?"

Frank squeezed harder.

"Yeah, once a week or so. It's going well. I'm glad I did it."

"Good. Good girl. It's a hard thing to do, believe me. I know. Christ, after that Palmisanto case? I thought I was going to swallow the magic bullet, I tell you."

Frank hadn't been working with Joe when he'd pulled his first serial killer case, but she'd heard about it dozens of times over dozens of beers. Joe was telling it again now, and Frank's mind wandered to the Delamore case last year. It had taken a huge emotional and physical toll on her and was part of the ugly spiral that had landed her in Clay's office.

Frank asked about the fishing and the cabin that Joe was building. He laughed, saying if the fishing kept up the way it was he'd never get the damn thing finished. He launched into a story about a pike and a mosquito and Frank had to smile. It was good to hear his voice. He had a knack for buzzing her out of the blue, usually when she was chewing on a particularly vexing problem. Joe had 'good bones'; his instincts were strong and he listened to them. He'd taught Frank how to trust hers and molded her into a first-rate homicide detective. With his retirement looming, he'd started grooming Frank to succeed him. He'd had to fight like hell for it, but his legacy was creating Figueroa's first female homicide lieutenant.

"Well, you know, we old retired folks get on the phone and forget that you kids still got work to do. I should let you get back to it."

"Good talking to you, Joe."

"Hell, I'd be more likely to finish that cabin tomorrow than get a phone call from you."

"Yeah, I know. Just get busy."

"Tell me about it. Well, listen. You know where I am."

"Yeah, I do, Joe. Appreciate it."

Frank replaced the phone and sat back, hands clasped behind her head. She allowed herself the brief luxury of missing Joe, then cut it off to avoid being buried in the emotional avalanche of people she missed.

There was nothing in the office urgently requiring her attention, so she grabbed her coat and decided to wake up Claudia. Fifteen minutes later, Alicia, Claudia's oldest granddaughter, opened at Frank's knock.

"*Buela*!" Alicia yelled for her grandmother. Looking Frank up and down she called, "It's the *policia*."

Frank waited until Claudia came to the door in a long T-shirt and sweater.

"Morning, Claudia," she chirped, holding up a bag of donuts. "Let's talk."

"I already tolt you ever'thin' I know," the woman argued sleepily.

"Aw, you know that's not true. Am I coming in or are you coming out?"

Claudia unlatched the steel screen. Frank followed her into the kitchen, watching her make coffee. Alicia asked for cereal and Frank asked, "Do you want a donut?"

Suddenly the girl was shy and hid behind Claudia. She stared curiously and Frank held the bag out to her, "Go on. Take one."

Alicia looked up at her grandmother.

"*Vaya*," she grunted and the girl grabbed one from the bag, then another, and scampered into the living room where the TV was already blaring.

"She's cute," Frank grinned. Claudia leaned back against the counter, eyeing Frank blankly.

"So tell me, how many funerals you been to lately?"

Claudia looked away.

"Let's see," Frank said. Starting with Claudia's oldest son, Chuey, Frank named the dead in order. She finished with,

"And that leaves Carmen on Saturday. Then who? Toñio? Is he next in line? How old is he? Thirteen? Then does the little one get it? Is Alicia next?"

Frank let that work while the old coffee machine burbled and wheezed.

"Claudia. You've spent the last week burying most of your family, including your *daughter*. I know you're a good mother. You've done all you can do, given your circumstances. Maybe you didn't make all the best choices, but you did pretty good. And you never had any help, did you? You've done it all alone. I know that's hard. My mother raised me alone. I know it's not easy. And I know you don't want to lose any more of your babies."

Frank paused. It didn't surprise her that a mother living in south-central wouldn't turn in the person who'd gunned down her daughter. She knew the high price of retaliation. And there was nothing Frank could do to prevent it. It was what made homicide at Figueroa so frustrating. Even when they knew damn well who'd done a hit on someone, and knew they had witnesses, they couldn't make the wits talk. Hard-core bangers were hope-to-die killers who thought nothing of wasting a witness if it would keep them out of Chino or San Quentin.

Frank pleaded, "I want to help you, Claudia. I don't want you to lose any more of your family. Christ, I've known you since you were Placa's age. In all that time, have I ever lied to you? Haven't I been *carnal*?"

Claudia nodded. Frank was encouraged she was at least listening.

"I've always been straight up with you, haven't I?"

Again Claudia nodded.

"Then be straight up with me now. Talk to me. Tell me what's going on here. All I need's a name. That's all you got to do. Drop me a name."

Frank could see the strain on Claudia. It was subtle, but it was there — the eyes narrowing by a fraction, the lips becoming a little more bloodless against each other, shoulders squaring just a tad. Frank gently stretched the breaking point.

"You want to tell me, but you don't. I understand. It's okay. It's okay to be afraid too. I know what you're up against."

Claudia's brown eyes flickered, becoming even more wary. Stepping into the woman's personal space, Frank stared down at her, but Claudia wouldn't raise her head.

"Who's the *pendejo* Gloria was talking about? Tell me, Claudia. Tell me," she begged gently.

"I don't know who it is," she mumbled, taking a nibble around her thumbnail.

Focusing on a black scuff mark on the linoleum floor, Frank said, *"No te creo."* They stood that way for minutes. Frank relinquished. The coffee was ready and she nodded at the pot.

"Can I have a cup of that?"

Claudia shrugged but made no move to pour. Frank got up and found the cups, pouring one for Claudia.

"You're standing here, putting up with my shit, and in a couple days you're gonna bury your baby daughter. You're a brave woman, Claudia. You're strong. I seen you raise five kids alone. I seen you give up the *carga,* and that's hard, specially when it's still movin' in and outta this house."

Claudia stiffened. It was a slight motion, but something about dealing smack had touched a nerve.

"Digame," Frank said softly. "What about the dope, Claudia?"

"I told you," she answered tersely. "I don't know *nothin'.*"

"And I told you I don't believe you."

They stalemated again, then Frank told a story about breaking up a fight Placa was in and how Placa'd been so full of fury and pride that she was ready to take Frank on after the *cholos* had been shooed along. Frank smiled at Claudia.

"She was your daughter, but a lot of us helped raise her.

She was a good girl. I'm not quittin' 'til I find out who did this."

Putting her cup down in the sink, Frank said, "I'll see you later."

Chapter Eleven

The sergeant took roll. He made a few jokes, took a couple, and then let Frank have the floor.

"Thanks, Sarge. Some of you've been here awhile and you knew Carmen Estrella. Street name was Placa. She was a King, big OG in the Fifty-second Street clique. She took five rounds from a .25 on Saturday, at South Wilton and Hyde Park, around 1715 hours. Wits tell us the shooter may have been parked in a sedan at the corner."

Frank held up a handful of flyers.

"This is our primary suspect. A lot of you probably know him. Name's Octavio Ruiz. Goes by Ocho. Drives a yellow '91 Thunderbird, lives at 50th and Broadway but he hasn't been home for a few days. If you see him, bring him in. Don't mention anything about this case. He's got outstanding GTA and weapons felonies you can use."

Frank walked around the cops as she spoke, handing each of them a flyer. One of them, Dimmler a young, muscle-bound blonde with a crew cut, fanned himself with the sheet asking, "Hey, Lieutenant. What's the big deal with this chick? I mean she's just another banger, right?"

Frank nodded, his words clattering around in her head. Just another banger. She understood the mentality. Cops had to establish and maintain distance from the public they served. It was ironic they pinned their shields over their hearts. To do what they had to do, cops had to develop emotional armor against the insanity and violence they encountered on an hourly, daily, weekly basis, month in, month out. They lived in a grim world where only the cops capable of emotional detachment survived. Frank did the same thing. Usually. This time it was personal and Dimmler's words stung.

He hadn't meant them to, just like the cop who'd stepped over her father's body hadn't meant to wound Frank when he'd complained, "Dumb fuck. My shift was almost up." For that cop, her father had been an obstacle to dinner and a hot shower. For Frank, her ten-year old world had just imploded. She never forgot that cop. Thirty years later, no matter what low-life scum bag was leaking into the street at her feet, she remembered that he might be the center of one person's universe. And though the vic was nothing to Frank, there was probably someone beyond the yellow tape Jonesing for an explanation about what happened to their boyfriend, husband, son, daddy. Frank had never gotten an answer. She didn't think about it, but that lack of resolution had impelled her into homicide, and kept her there, still gamely looking for answers. Even if they weren't hers.

"Just another banger," she agreed bloodlessly. "And Ruiz is just another felon that I'm trying to get off the street, Dimmler. Just doing my job. And the more felons we put away the sooner you can get back into the gym to work on those pretty pecs of yours."

Lewis wolf-whistled and someone threw a wadded paper. Dimmler blushed. Frank raised her voice above the catcalls, deliberately keeping it in a low register.

"Ruiz runs with the 51st Street Playboys. He has a tattoo of an octopus on his back that extends around to his chest. Got a big M tattooed under his collarbone. On his right shoulder he's got BPBOYS, under that, 51, and under that, an upside down exclamation point, R, and another exclamation point."

Hunt mumbled, "Gee. How will we know if it's him?"

"He's got a scar running up the right side of his neck, stands 5'11", weighs a buck eighty-five. If you spot him, approach with caution. Call me at my pager number, it's on the flyer or have desk notify me immediately. Questions?"

Sitting in back, Heisdaeck asked when was the last time anyone had seen Ruiz.

"Day of the shooting."

The old cop just shook his head and said, "Ain't gonna see him for a spell."

"Not if he's smart," Hunt added.

"He's a banger," Dimmler quipped. "How bright can he be?"

From the back of the room Muñoz threw another piece of paper at Dimmler and laughed, "You got a lot to learn, Pretty-Boy."

The beefy blonde waved irritatedly at the missiles, growling, "Cut it out."

Frank thanked the sergeant and returned upstairs. She ran into Foubarelle on the way.

"Frank! I was looking for you."

"What's up?"

The captain sighed, deeply wounded. Holding up a two-page memo, he said, "You want me to pull a unit when we're already understaffed to do survey on a banger's house? For a drive-by? What am I not seeing here?"

Fubar was a station queen; he worked inside, not on the street. She wanted to say that by the time she told Fubar all he wasn't seeing she'd be a week shy of retirement. He'd never been on the street in Figueroa and the little time he had spent on patrol had been at the Venice Division handing out public nuisance tickets.

"This guy's got a rap sheet longer than your arm, he's got three separate felony warrants on him, and he's the prime suspect in a murder case. He's an old timer with the 51st Street Playboys and he's been a bad boy for a long time. He's past three strikes now and if we can find him we have a good chance to keep him out of action until he's walking with a cane."

Frank shrugged.

"You don't want to catch him, it's no skin off my nose."

"Oh, don't give me that, Frank. Of course I want to catch him. We just don't have the resources to pull a car out of action."

"Whatever. Just thought I'd ask. Look, I'm on my way to the coroner's office. Anything else?"

"What's going on there?"

"Autopsy on the drive-by of-the-week."

"And why do you need to be there?"

Frank's eyes narrowed and dilated. She clamped her teeth together. Any of her men would have known to back off, but Foubarelle kept at her.

"It seems to me that your stats have taken a tumble and that you're spending almost as much time out there as a foot cop. Except for the one you closed last week —"

"— Two."

"What?"

"We closed two last week."

"Well, until those I hadn't seen a close-out or 60-day on my desk in weeks. What's going on, Frank?"

"You want to know?" she asked, nailing Fubar to the wall with twin steel-blue lasers. "I'll tell you. I'm working over one hundred cases a year. We get so many homicides here we're thinking of making it a misdemeanor. That's what's going on. A new case almost every third day. And when those new cases come in we're supposed to drop everything and give them highest priority. Even you know our best chance of closure's within 48 hours. I'm supposed to have a squad of ten and I've got six. That's almost half-staff, John. My supervisor keeps telling me I'll get replacements. I haven't seen a new body in this room in four years.

"And in case you haven't been out there in a while, this isn't a beach strip. I've got witnesses who won't talk because they'll get killed if they do. I've got kids out there who've done so many drive-bys they could teach John Gotti new tricks. I've got CIs that are hope-to-die users and as soon as we turn them into good sources they OD on us. I've got projects we can't get into to question a suspect without half a SWAT team backing us.

"If I'm spending time on the street it's so I can help my men do the work they're supposed to be doing. You want me in my office every day? Fine. You get me some extra legs out there. The stats don't just walk up to the front door and wait to get picked up like a morning paper. Somebody's got to go out there and dig them up."

Slightly shorter than his lieutenant, Foubarelle just stared silently up at her. Frank held the little man's gaze then shook her head disgustedly and started walking away. But she stopped and said, "Why don't you do a ride along for a couple days, John. See where your man-hours are being spent. Come with me to the autopsy. You can start there."

"I don't think that'll be necessary," the captain demurred.

"No, really," Frank insisted. "I think it'll clear up a lot of misunderstandings. Why don't you come along?"

There are thousands of written rules and regulations within a police organization, but the most critical ones, the ones that make or break a cop, will never be found in any book or memorandum. The rules that cops create themselves are brutal and rigorous and can only be tested through trial by fire. During that trial, a cop has to display two criteria. The first is courage. Will he go into a burning building or make excuses? Will she back her partner or run for cover? Will he go down the alley with the mythic 250-lb man or look the other way and keep walking down the sidewalk? The second criterion is loyalty. Will she turn her partner in for knocking off a piece on the clock? Will he snitch about the free booze and cigarettes from the Handi-Mart? Will he or she balance on that thin line and cover for more serious things?

If she passes, she earns an invisible badge of respect. She'll have to work every day to keep it, but with it, she is allowed entry into the inner sanctum of police work. If she fails, every cop will know it. They might tolerate her, but they will never trust her or treat her as an equal. Respect cannot be legislated or mandated. It can only be earned. Frank made the offer to Foubarelle knowing full well that he'd refuse. He was afraid of the street and his loyalty was to the department, not his men. Frank waited for his answer, giving him plenty of time to make his rope long. Then he hung himself.

"I appreciate the offer, and it's a good idea, I just don't have the time now. Maybe later."

Frank nodded gently, finding him not even worthy of scorn.

Frank had specifically asked Gail to perform Placa's autopsy but she'd been held up by the unexpected suicide of a sitcom star. The mood in Autopsy Room A was quiet as the new tech photographed Placa's clothed body. Frank and Bobby watched silently while Gail sharpened her knives. Frank doubted there was much the autopsy could tell them, still she wanted to see it all, no matter how routine or seemingly irrelevant it might be. They started the external exam by removing and bagging Placa's blood-encrusted clothing — baggy shorts, T-shirt, sports bra, men's boxers, the Dodger's cap. After photographing and x-raying the body, Gail noted all identifying features, including a homemade tat high inside her left thigh.

It had been crudely dabbed, probably with a sewing needle and pen ink, in the Old English style favored by Latino gangs. Frank and Bobby peered at it, and the big cop slowly read, "La Re-i-na," then whistled.

"What?" Frank asked.

"La Reina, man. I don't know if it's a coincidence or what, but that's what they call Ocho's girlfriend."

Flicking a curious eyebrow, Frank crossed her paper-gowned arms across her chest. That certainly lent a new complexion to the homicide. Poking at an old scab, Gail asked what Placa meant.

"It's a tagger's graffiti," Bobby answered. "Which is usually the name of his gang and set, and something like 'we rule' or 'Number 1'. She started tagging when she was what, eight or nine?"

He looked to Frank.

"Somewhere around there."

"Yeah, right around the time she stopped wearing the badge."

"What badge?" Gail asked.

"That's another reason they called her Placa. It means badge or shield in Spanish. She had this thing for cop's badges, " Bobby chuckled. "When she was just a toddler we'd find her in the middle of the street and we'd stop and pick her up, put her back in the house with someone. And she always wanted your badge. When you picked her up she'd finger your shield and stare at it, try to pull it off your shirt. That was back when Frank was my FTO. Remember when you gave her that plastic badge?"

Frank offered the outline of a smile and Gail glanced at the two cops.

"So what happened?"

"You tell her," Bobby said.

Frank shrugged. "She must have been about five then. She was walking down the sidewalk one evening, it was getting dark, she was all alone. Me and Bobby stopped and she came running over. She loved riding in the squad car."

"Yeah," Bobby interrupted. "We should've known then she was going to be an OG. Remember how she was always wanting to play with the shotgun?"

Frank continued, "We pulled up to her house, but before I took her in, I told her I had something for her. I grabbed a bag out of the backseat and gave it to her. She reached in, pulled out a plastic police badge, you know, a toy like you get at the five and dime. She looked at it, turned it over, had this really serious expression. Then she shoved it in my hand and shook her head. Told me it was *plastica* and jumped out of the car. She turned around and stood up on her toes, jabbed at my badge. 'I want that one,' she said and marched up the driveway."

Gail smiled, and Bobby took up the rest of the story.

"Frank, being the softie that she is —"

"— hey. That's an ugly rumor."

"Frank has us looking all over town for *metal* badges. I know Noah brought some in and Haystack found one, but no, they weren't good enough. It had to look like an LAPD badge. So we're looking all over town for a realistic badge and one of the PI's from — where was it? Newton?"

Frank nodded.

"His brother runs a machine shop, so he makes one up. It's perfect. It's got the gold and blue and the insignia, probably illegal as hell —"

"— he spelled LAPO instead of LAPD," Frank corrected.

"Okay. Other than that, it was perfect. And she wore that badge every day, didn't she?"

"Yep."

"She was a wild child," Bobby mused. "There aren't too many girls allowed into gangs. I mean they've got their own, but usually females aren't allowed to run with male gangs."

Addressing a puckered old bullet wound, Gail asked why Placa was allowed.

"Oh, she *earned* it," Bobby answered. "And it helped that she had an older brother in the gang. In fact he jumped her in, whipped her for fifty-two seconds. When her time was up she was still swinging. The other guys backed off quick but Chuey kept at her, laughing the whole time. He finally knocked her out."

"His own sister?"

"Yep. No room for softies in the 'hood. If you're going to make it you've got to be hard. Chuey wanted to make sure his sister was down, that she'd be there for her clique."

Bobby grinned at Frank, who couldn't help noticing the similarities between street gangs and cops.

"Remember that time she took the .22 in her head and everyone thought she was dead?"

"What happened to her?"

"We took her to the hospital and an hour later she's asking us to buy her a soda. That bullet went in behind her ear and just curved around her skull. It came out the other side. You'll see where when you open her up. She was getting quite the rep then and don't you know that only added to it. Then she started doing that hex thing, like Claudia and Gloria used to do. Started leaving dead chickens and rats everywhere. You know that freaked some of the *hermanos*. Dead homies are one thing but start messin' with that Santeria stuff . . ."

"What is it?" Frank asked. Gail was squinting at the girl's wrists, and answered, "Bruising. It's real faint, but it's there on both forearms. See? Like someone was pinning her down."

Both detectives leaned over and saw the faint purpling. Gail carefully continued searching the body. There were older cuts and bruises, but the only other thing noteworthy was what looked like dried sperm on Placa's right thigh.

"Let's see what the PERK comes up with," she said straightening up, arching the muscles in her back.

"Rape?" Bobby asked his boss.

"Be my first thought."

Gail frowned, "How did you jump to that?"

Bobby glanced at Frank but she just kept her mouth shut behind her fist.

"Placa didn't go for boys," he explained awkwardly.

"She was a lesbian?"

"Yeah."

Gail offered no reaction and Frank asked Bobby, "You talked to this Reina?"

"Yeah."

"Did she look beat up at all?"

"No. She's missing a tooth but that's old."

"She seem afraid?"

"No."

"She say anything about her and Placa?"

"This is the first I've heard of it," Bobby said. "But Nook found out Placa had dumped Itsy a couple weeks ago. Guess she's hitting the pipes pretty hard and Placa didn't want her around. She ordered the Queens to jump her out."

Frank studied the placement of the shots in Placa's torso. Three in the ten ring, as they taught in the academy, an accurate pattern for stopping someone. Forever. Was the shooter that accurate on a moving target or just lucky? Frank cautioned herself on the pronoun, considering Itsy and La Reina potential suspects.

Halfway through the internal exam, Noah and Johnnie came in. Johnnie hung back by the door but Noah gowned up.

"How's it going?" he asked, pulling on the cap.

"Interesting," Frank answered as he joined them at the table. "What are you doing here?"

He shrugged, "We're off the clock and were over at the Heights anyway. I just wanted to come by and see what was going on."

"Yeah, we're off the clock," Johnnie grumbled, "and we gotta stop and look at a fuckin' post that's not even ours."

"What's interesting?" Noah asked, ignoring his partner sulking against the wall.

"Looks like maybe she was raped."

"Wow. I'd like to see if that guy's still walkin'."

Johnnie whined from the back of the room, "Jesus, No, how long you gonna stay here, huh?"

Frank continued, "That's not the interesting part."

She explained the tattoo and Noah answered, "Son of a bitch."

Maybe he was thirsty and long past due for his first drink of the day, but for whatever reason, Johnnie lost it. He stomped to the autopsy table, demanding, "Give me the goddamn keys. Get a ride back to the station with Frank. I'm not standin' around off the clock to watch an autopsy on some fuckin' beaner that's not e-"

That was as far he got. Calling Johnnie an ignorant fuck, Noah whirled and slammed a fist into the big man's cheek. The shock of his own partner hitting him rendered Johnnie momentarily defenseless and Noah swung again. He was still swinging and cursing when Frank and Bobby stepped between them. Frank grabbed Noah's lapels, shaking him, yelling in a deep voice, "Hey! Look at me!"

Bobby stood next to Johnnie who, Frank was grateful to see, was still stunned or he could have made pulp out of Noah. The skinny detective was still mad-dogging his partner but she marched him back a few feet, holding on to him until he looked away.

"Give me the car keys, No."

He fished around in his pocket and slapped them in her hand.

"Johnnie," she called over her shoulder, tossing the keys at him, "Go on home."

Bending over to swipe up the keys, he told Noah, "You're fuckin' psycho."

"Fuck you, you drunken asshole," Noah spit back.

Frank patted his face roughly, "Hey. Knock it off. Johnnie, go home. Bobby, get back to the table."

Johnnie left, rubbing his jaw, swearing. Frank pulled Noah toward the door.

"What the fuck was that all about?"

"You don't have to drive around with him all day, Frank. He's a goddamn moron."

"He's been a moron for years. Why'd you decide to punch him now?"

Noah glanced at Placa, splay-chested on the table.

"He had no right to call her that. I mean look at her. She's defenseless. If she'd been here she'd have wailed on his ass."

"She'd a put a curse on him to make his dick fall off," Frank said softly.

"Yeah," Noah smiled, but he ducked his head against the tears welling up. Frank hurt for her friend. She rested a hand on his shoulder and he looked back at Placa.

"It's just, you know, some of these kids. You watch 'em comin' up and they're bright and they got so much potential and you just wanna see 'em make it out of this fuckin' cesspool. And she just had so much goin' for her. I mean if anybody coulda made it out, it'd been her, but no, she had to die cause she was wearing her barrio on her arm. I mean where's the fuckin' sense in it?"

He'd asked the question earnestly and Frank had to admit she didn't know. He hung his head again and she said, "Look. Go home. Play with the kids. Pat Trace on the ass. Have a couple drinks. Okay?" she asked, catching his eye.

He nodded and she squeezed his neck.

"There you go. You all right?"

He nodded again and she said, "Call me if you want. I'll be up late."

"Yeah."

"Bobby. Take No back to the station. I'll finish this."

"Want me to come back and get you?"

"No. I'll grab a cab."

The men left and Frank resumed her stand at the steel table.

"Sorry about that."

"Not at all," Gail spoke wryly. "That was exciting. We don't get many fistfights in here."

After the sudden outbreak the room seemed overly calm. The big air conditioner hummed efficiently and MEs dictated into their recorders and talked quietly to their techs. The whispering of paper gowns and click of metal on metal was almost soothing. Gail was slicing the diaphragm from the body wall and said without looking up, "She must have been pretty special to you guys."

Frank sighed like she'd trained herself to, slowly, so that no one could see.

"She was a good kid," she said, dispassionately.

Gail glanced at Frank and they continued the autopsy without conversation. When the ME finished, she had a tech replace the organs and stitch the Y. She peeled her gloves off and bunched her fists into her kidneys.

"I don't know about you," she said to Frank, "but I'm calling it a day. If you could wait around a bit, I'll give you a ride back to your car. Maybe we could stop for a drink somewhere. You can hang out in my office while I finish up these notes and grab a shower. What do you think?"

It had been a long couple of days. Frank was beat and not much in the mood for company, but a drink sounded good and a ride was better than popping for a taxi, especially in commuter traffic.

"Okay. I've got some notes I can work on too."

Pulling off her mask, Gail beamed, "Great! Give me half an hour."

Chapter Twelve

The man who'd created the building that housed the Los Angeles County Coroner's Office had been a flamboyant character and the Chief's office reflected his style much more than Gail's. Frank took in the big furniture, piled high with papers and folders and jars of she didn't want to know what. Clean bones, misshapen bullets, and excisions in plastic were scattered around like the toys of a very disturbed child.

Frank settled into a plush sofa, pushing the coroner's clutter to one end. She quickly jotted the highlights from the autopsy into her notebook. The most tantalizing clues were the evidence of recent intercourse and the name tattooed on Placa's thigh. Pulling the latest leads together gave Frank an interesting story with a beginning, middle, and end. Placa was doing it with Ocho's girl, which both Placa and La Reina kept on the QT. Dating rivals demanded an instantaneous beat-on-sight at the very least, not to mention the fall from grace that would ensue. But suppose Itsy figured it out. She snitched to Ocho for revenge. Ocho found Placa alone, got her in the back of his T-Bird and took her .25 away, then showed Placa what La Reina *really* liked. Knowing Placa she probably hurt him pretty bad and jumped out of the car. To save face, Ocho grabs the .25 and caps her as she's trying to run for cover. End of story.

That explained Placa, but did nothing to clear the rest of the deaths in her family. Frank allowed that maybe Placa had a boyfriend. With a bad-girl rep to protect, she'd probably kept that a secret too. Or if the dude was an off-brand, she wouldn't want that getting out. Placa was pretty hard-core King and Frank couldn't see her balling a rival *vato*. But Ocho's girlfriend, *that* would be the ultimate insult.

She made a note to ask Placa's home girls, some of the Kings, and the Playboys closest to Ocho, about a boyfriend. The Toluidine had stained Placa, indicating ripping and abrasion during the intercourse. Frank had asked if she was a virgin but Gail said no. The sex had been rough, consistent with a rape, which also offered a convenient explanation for why she wasn't strapped. That led back to the bullets.

They'd recovered three slugs at the scene and had found the other two lodged in Placa's thoracic cavity. Her chest was so smashed up it was impossible for Gail to follow their complete trajectory. Three of the five shots were immediately fatal and Frank thought again that the shooter knew what he was doing. Not only that, the trajectory of the bullet to her head indicated the shooter had fired from directly behind Placa once she was down. It was clear the shooter wanted Placa dead — not scared, or frightened, but stone dead. *Just like whoever shot Julio Estrella's family.* As with them, the shooter had done the job thoroughly and accurately. And just like whoever shot her uncle's family, the person who shot Placa had taken the time to pick up the spent .25 casings. The trajectory of four of the five bullets was consistent with the shooter standing in the spot where Nook had found the lone casing. But the other four casings were missing. Frank had seen a lot of drive-bys but never one where they'd stopped to clean up ejected shells.

Apart from the wound traumas, Placa's internal exam had revealed nothing unusual. Her organs were pale from hemorrhaging but unremarkable. The stomach was empty except for what looked like antacid residue. Frank didn't think it was common for kids to chew Rolaids, and wondered about the cause of Placa's upset stomach.

Because no one was around, Frank blew out a huge horse breath. She laid her head back against the comfortable couch, wishing they'd seen Placa's bruises in the dark. The chances were slim they'd have pulled anything useful, but still she would have liked to dust them for latents. Frank hated working scenes at night just for that reason. There was so much to miss and by the time they returned in the morning scenes had changed and were contaminated, sometimes even cleaned up.

"Sorry to keep you waiting," Gail breathed, bursting through the door. "A couple of the residents cornered me. They lie in wait for me outside the locker room."

"No problem. I was just going over what we found."

"Or didn't," Gail said apologetically.

Frank stood by the door, waiting for the doc to finish up. A fruity shampoo scented the office and Gail's dark bob concealed her face as she stood over the desk. She'd changed into jeans and a faded UA sweatshirt. The scrubs fleshed her out a little and Frank noticed when she was in regular clothes that she was very angular. Watching her leave the Alibi one Friday night, Noah had called her rawboned. Bobby had added that she looked like one of Modigliani's blue women, then Johnnie had chimed in that the doc gave him blue balls.

"Okay," she said straightening, swinging the damp hair from her face. "Ready?"

"Whenever you are."

Gail covered the room in long strides and was just about to turn the light off when she said, "Hey, turn your face this way."

Frank did as told. Gail put a fingertip below her temple and said, "Looks like you've got a bruise there."

Frank felt it gingerly.

"Must've intercepted a round meant for Johnnie."

"Ouch."

They walked to the elevator and Gail said, "That surprised the hell out of me. Noah seems so easy-going."

"He is. That's not like him to blow up."

"Was he close to Placa?"

"Kinda."

"You seem to have a pretty good rapport with those guys."

"We get along."

Gail took a sidelong glance at Frank and grinned, "Why do I get the feeling that if they had awards for understatement you'd bring home the trophy every year?"

"Don't know. Tell you what. Instead of driving me all the way back into town, why don't you just give me a lift home. You're in San Marino, right?"

Gail nodded and Frank said, "I'm on the way. I'll just catch a cab into work in the morning."

"You sure? I don't mind."

"I'm sure."

Once they were buckled into Gail's Pathfinder, the doc confessed, "I'm glad your boys had that spat. This way I get to spend some time with you."

Frank studied the ME's profile, glowing deep pink in the dying sun.

"What'd I do now?"

"Nothing. I just meant I only see you during autopsies or on Friday nights. Neither place is very conducive for conversation."

Curiosity edged Frank's fatigue out of the way and she decided to spar a little with the doc.

"No says you were asking questions about me the other night."

Gail immediately bristled.

"Did he say that?"

"Yep. He's my main dog. Tells me everything."

Enjoying Gail's embarrassment, Frank continued, "Now that we're in such a *conversationally conducive* spot, what did you want to know?"

"I was just . . . wondering about you," Gail stammered. "You're so reticent."

"If I'm not mistaken, your exact description was intriguingly impenetrable."

"My God, what'd he do? Recite our entire conversation verbatim?"

Frank was like a cat with a mouse.

"Said you asked about me and Kennedy."

"Oh, God," Gail cringed. "I will *never* ask him anything again."

"Not if you want to keep it a secret," Frank grinned. "No's the department gossip."

"So I see. Oh God, how embarrassing. It's none of my business, I know. I was just curious about you."

Frank didn't know the doc that well and calculated just how much she wanted to reveal. She and Mag had called themselves roommates, rarely acknowledging the carpet cleaner and muff diver comments. During the long drought between Mag and Kennedy it hadn't been much of an issue; people made presumptions and she'd let them. Besides, she was sure her relationship with Maggie was carefully documented in an IAD file somewhere. Being in the LAPD and having secrets was a contradiction. She'd believed in "don't ask, don't tell" long before Clinton had thought of it. Conversely, Frank didn't like lying to the people closest to her. Her partners knew, and Joe had known. Frank decided to let Gail off the hook, offering, "Kennedy and I are just friends."

She summarized their bad bust on Johnston, and how they had become close as a result. Then Frank appended, "There was something between us, but it's been over for a while."

"Thanks for leveling with me," Gail said, catching her eye. "You didn't have to."

"No big deal."

The light was red and Frank looked away first. Checking out the street scene, she said to Gail, "Your turn."

The doc hesitated. She seemed strained and Frank said, "You don't have to if you don't want to."

"No," Gail breathed. "That's not it. There's just nothing, and no one to tell about. I'm just starting to hate the way that sounds. I've been so busy building a career that in all honesty I haven't ever made the room for a relationship. There were affairs here and there, people I really should have tried harder with, but I was too selfish. And I'm wondering if it's too late now. If I'm too set in my ways."

The doc trailed off, staring straight ahead. She didn't continue and Frank didn't push.

"Where are we going for that drink?" Gail asked.

"Tell you what. I know a place that serves the meanest roast beef sandwich in L.A. with the coldest imported ale. You up for it?"

"Sure. Tell me where to go."

"My place," Frank said. Gail chuckled. The sound was low in her throat and Frank liked it, thought it was kind of sexy. She wondered if Gail did it for effect or if it was just natural. Taking in the doc's simple clothes and the lack of make-up or jewelry, she decided Gail wasn't into artifice.

"What's so funny?"

"Do you always play everything so close to your vest?"

"Always," Frank admitted.

"Does anybody at work know you're gay?"

Frank squinted out the window, "Except for Noah, it's something most of my squad just assumes. I don't talk about it and they don't bring it up."

"I would imagine the LAPD's not the most tolerant institution."

"Now *that's* understatement. What about you? Rumor mill's outted you."

"I'm not surprised," Gail smirked. "All you have to do is reject a couple Neanderthal's and that automatically makes you a dyke. I feel sorry for straight women."

Gail turned where Frank told her, continuing, "I'm not out at work and don't intend to be. I'm not real comfortable mixing boudoir with business." Making an apologetic face, she said, "I know it's not PC, but frankly I've worked too hard to get where I am and don't want to blow it because of who I sleep with or don't."

"You don't think the good citizens of Los Angeles could handle a lesbian in the Chief Coroner's office?"

"I don't know and I don't want to find out."

The doc swiftly rerouted the subject, asking Frank how long she'd been a cop.

"Closing in on seventeen years."

"You're almost ready for retirement."

"Not quite."

Gail flashed a bright smile, "You like what you do?"

Frank nodded, "A lot. Miss being on the streets, though. It's easy to lose touch."

"I know what you mean. I miss being in the trenches too. I try and do a post every day. Where were you before Figueroa?"

"That's it. Never been anywhere else."

"You're kidding? That's pretty unusual."

"Yeah. Everybody want's to get out of Figueroa, not into

it. That's where they put us — me — straight out of the Academy. Probably thought it would be a good way to weed the female boots out. But it was like home to me. Besides, it's a great station for homicide. I'd go crazy in one of the white-collar divisions."

Gail narrowed her green eyes. "You're not one of those adrenaline junkies, are you?"

Frank thought of Kennedy and said, "Definitely not."

They rolled into Frank's driveway. She switched lights on while Gail ooed and ahhed over the split level living room.

"Do I get the grand tour?" she asked.

"Soon as I get rid of this," Frank replied, emptying her bulging pockets. Gun, badge, and cuffs took their place next to case folders and manila envelopes on the crowded dining room.

"The place belonged to an architect," Frank explained, showing Gail the guest room and master bedroom to one side of the living room. She paused at the kitchen, open to the living and dining area, and pulled two Bass Ales out of the fridge.

Indicating the other side of the living room she said, "There's a den over there, and that second door used to lead into the garage. Now it's my gym."

She poured Gail's beer into a mug from the freezer. Hers she left in the bottle.

"Cheers," Gail said.

Frank nodded, draining a quarter of the bottle. She made the sandwiches as they talked easily about staffing nightmares and supervising men in a man's world. The conversation shifted to movies, then food, and Frank found Gail both articulate and amusing. Well after they'd finished the sand-wiches, they each nursed a pony of Ruby Pinto, and it hit Frank that she hadn't thought of Placa in hours. She felt a stab of conscience and decided that was pretty unreasonable. Clay was right, maybe she rode herself too hard sometimes.

Gail must have sensed that Frank had drifted from the conversation, because she said, "I think I'd better go. It looks like I'm putting you to sleep."

"No. Not at all. I was just thinking . . ." Frank hesitated, wondering if she should admit it. "What a nice night it's been."

"Yeah," Gail agreed, rising. "Maybe we can do it again sometime."

"Yeah."

Frank walked Gail out to her car, telling her how to get back onto Huntington. When she went back inside the house was too still. She put a handful of CDs into the player and tapped the random button. She paced through the dining room, the kitchen, back into the dining room, her hand lingering over reports. She glanced at her wrist, wondering if it was too late to call Noah. Probably not, she thought.

The phone buzzed in her ear and she was about to hang up when Tracey answered.

"Hey. Is this the most beautiful woman in L.A.?"

"Oh, hang on a sec. You want my twin sister who's forty pounds lighter."

"No, I think I've got the right sister. Hi, gorgeous. How's No?"

"He's okay. He's planted in front of a *Gilligan's Island* marathon. I'll get him, hold on."

Frank tried to protest but Tracey had already slammed the phone down. When he picked it up, Frank said, "Mr. De La Hoya, my man. Didn't mean to interrupt the cultural hour. Just checking up on you."

"Dudess. I'm sorry about this afternoon. I shouldn't have lost it like that, in the morgue and everything."

"Don't worry about it. I'll ream you out tomorrow. 'Sides, gave the doc a chance to give me a ride home."

"Oh, yeah? Did you ask her out?"

"Yeah, sure. You know what a play-uh I am. I made her

one of my killer roast beef sandwiches and we had a couple beers."

"Oh, yeah? Then what?"

Frank smiled into the receiver, glad No was okay and back to matchmaking.

"That's it, dummy, else I wouldn't be calling you."

"Aw, man."

"Look. Get back to Ginger and MaryAnn. I'll see you tomorrow."

"That's a big 10-4. Hey, dudess?"

"Yeah?"

"Which one you like better? Ginger or MaryAnn?"

"That's easy. You sleep with Ginger. You marry MaryAnn."

"Right on. Hey. Thanks for callin'."

"No sweat."

Frank tipped herself back on the barstool at her kitchen counter. She felt surprisingly good. She was warm and well fed, and had a nice buzz going, but she had to admit she'd had a really good time tonight. In a town like L.A., where people were obsessed with cash and flash, Gail's simple good looks and honest conversation were refreshing. Attractive, Frank decided, then dropped the stool back onto all fours. That was neither here nor there.

Stretching and sighing, she planned out tomorrow. She needed to talk to Johnnie and sit him down with Noah, have them make peace. Christ, she thought, I'm running a Romper Room, not a homicide squad. Miles glided into *Seven Steps* as she flipped open the *L.A. Times* on the table. It would have been a fine thing to see Miles live, she thought, wondering if Gail liked jazz.

Chapter Thirteen

Before Johnnie and Noah went out, Frank called them into her office. Noah sat on the thin couch and Johnnie straddled a plastic chair. Cocking a hip on her desk, Frank glared down at both of them, a rare vantage.

"What happened in the morgue yesterday was inexcusable. Johnnie, your comment about Placa was inappropriate, unprofessional, and offensive to everyone in the room. You apologize to Doc Lawless and her staff, today."

Johnnie started his usual bluster, but glaring at Noah she continued, "Your behavior wasn't any better. You apologize along with your partner."

Noah rolled his eyes and crabbed, "Whatever. But that crack —"

"I don't want to hear it," she said. "I want that apology today, in person, both of you. Got it?"

"Fuck," Johnnie said, "I got court all day."

"I thought that wasn't until ten."

"I gotta get a wit before that," he complained.

"Then you better get going. Morgue opens at eight."

"Come on, Frank," Noah tried intervening, "can't this wait until tomorrow?"

"Nope. I want this taken care of before you," she said to Johnnie, "open your fat mouth again, and before you," to Noah, "pretend to be Sugar Ray again."

Noah hung his head, but Frank could see the grin under his bangs.

"You can go," she told him.

Johnnie squirmed in his seat, whining like a schoolboy, "How come he gets to go?"

Frank ignored him, telling Noah to close the door. When he did, she answered, " 'Cause he's not using all his sick time on hangovers."

"Did he tell you that?" he said jerking his thumb at the door.

"Didn't have to. It doesn't take a genius to figure it out when you come in shaking and sweating, bloodshot as hell. Want to tell me about it?"

"There's nothin' to tell about! Shit, Frank, I don't have enough fingers to count the number times you've come in lookin' like something the cat threw up."

"You're right. Everybody ties one on sometimes, me included, but we don't skip work because of our hangovers, and when I'm getting complaints about one of my cops leaning out of his car and puking in the street, then I've got a problem."

"I had the flu or something. That fucking chicken at Popeye's."

"Johnnie. You can bullshit this all you want. That's your decision. I can't make you talk to me. But I'm telling you, you're walkin' a fine line. You got a problem? That's okay.

Everybody's got 'em. Hell, I got 'em, and I'll do whatever I can to help you. If you can handle it on your own, great. Show me. If you can't, and it starts interfering with your work, then it becomes my problem and I'll do what I have to to fix it. Do you understand what I'm saying?"

"There isn't a problem," he told the floor.

She studied him a moment, remembering how he'd come onto the squad, still lean and muscled, an old linesman like Bobby. He was all swagger and bragger back then, the Happy Clapper, cheerfully waving off his bouts with various STDs, convinced if they had a poster boy for LAPD cocksman, he'd have been it. But the long hours at a desk, and all the booze and fast food had softened him. He looked tired now, his charm as tarnished as an old uniform button.

"You know where BSU is. And you know my number."

"Is that all?"

"Yeah."

Frank watched him lumber out, feeling for him. She put the pity away and got ready for the eight o'clock ADA meeting.

"Hey, Frank," Johnnie called from his desk. "We gonna see you on the news tonight? LAPD Lieutenant pulls postal, slays supervisors. Coalitions and committees to blame."

Frank had finally broken away from back to back meetings and had gotten to the homicide room a half hour before quitting time.

"Just about," she answered, surprised he was in such good spirits. She wondered if he was making an effort to show everything was okay.

"Where's your partner?"

"Down in Property."

Frank headed to her office, but when Nook and Bobby trailed in with an armload of binders, she said, "Hey. What's the word?"

"We can't find Ruiz anywhere," Nookey puffed. "The fucker's in the wind. According to the aunt he's got relatives in Fresno, Calexico, Madera . . . not to mention Mexico. He could be anywhere."

"Did you put an APB on him?"

"You want us to?"

Frank stifled a sigh. As much as a pain in the ass as Gough was, at least he'd been a good partner for Nook. Between he and Bobby, she didn't think they'd wipe their asses without asking her first.

"Yeah. What else did the aunt say?"

Nook made a disgusted sound.

"The usual. Her nephew's a good boy. He'd never dust anyone. Specially not a girl. You know, just a real gentleman."

"But we had a nice talk with Lydia Alvarez," Bobby said.

"La Reina?"

"Yeah. She and Placa had been seeing each other for about six weeks. In fact, Placa was at her place Saturday from about 11:30 to 2:30. We're getting her day accounted for, but she didn't tell Lydia where she was going when she left. Just said she had to take care of some business."

"And according to her, nobody knew that she and Placa were doing it. She swears Ruiz doesn't know, and she doesn't know where he is. We asked her where she was when Placa got hit and she says she was at a party up in Eagle Rock and that Ruiz was with her."

"Where was the party?"

"She's not sure. It was dark and she didn't know where they were going. She'd never been there before."

"Better get more than that." Stroking her chin, Frank asked, "If Ocho didn't do anything why's he gone?"

Nook said, "Words all over the street that we're puttin' this on him, and he didn't want to stick around to defend himself."

"You talk to Itsy again?"

"Not yet. She's at a cousin's in El Monte. But we talked to La Limpia. She and Placa were hangin' at Hoover's from about 10:30 to a little after eleven. That's when Itsy showed up and Placa took off. She didn't say where she was going or anything, just left like she was pissed that Itsy was there."

Bobby was talking about a corner store were kids hung out and kicked it, sharing blunts and 40-ounce bottles of Olde English and Cobra malt liquor.

"She was only there for a couple minutes. Limpia said she was still in a bad mood and wouldn't talk much. They tried to get her to stay, said they'd go throw down some winos, but she was pissy and said she had to be somewhere. That was the last she saw her."

"Didn't say where she had to be?"

"Nope. Or where she'd been."

"Ask about any boyfriends?"

"Yeah, and everybody laughed at us. Don't know who it was that shagged her but I'm bettin' she ain't marrying him."

"How about a homie or an off-brand that tried to make her? Anybody she particularly dissed?"

"Shit," Nook laughed. "The girl was OG. Who *didn't* she dis?"

"Keep the heat on and let's talk to CRASH. See if they got any word for us. I called County OSS too, told them to keep their ears open. And if Itsy's not home by tomorrow find out where she is and get her. I stopped by the Estrella's this morning. They're upset but they're not saying anything. Claudia's got her lips sewed together, and Gloria's bouncing off the walls. She's pissed, but she's not talking. I don't know what they know, but it's something. Keep the heat on them too. I want one of you there at least once a day."

"Oh joy," Nook grumbled and Bobby asked, "Do you think Gloria'd do a payback?"

"I don't know. It's hard to say. Once they have the babies they kind of get out of that, but this is blood. And a lot of it lately."

"If they do, we'll never close this."

Heaving his shoulders in resignation, Nook pointed out, "It wouldn't be the first one."

He tried to move past Frank but she put a finger into his chest.

"I *want* this one, Nook."

"We'll do what we can, but I can't pull this guy outta thin air."

"Yes, you can."

She went into her office, leaving Nookey muttering under his breath, and Johnnie laughing. Almost out of earshot, he called Frank by her nickname, commiserating, "Damn, Nook! Is Le Freek on the rag or what?"

The comment was vintage Briggs and Frank marveled again at how well he was dealing with this morning's reprimand. Like mushrooms after a rain, forms and papers magically resurfaced her desk. Frank glanced through a few of them, then called Bobby into her office.

51st Playboy territory ranged outside of the Figueroa Division boundary and Frank had lost touch with the nuances of the set hierarchy. She vaguely remembered Ruiz coming up as a Baby Playboy who'd yet to earn his colors, but she had no recollection of Lydia Alvarez.

"What's up?" Bobby answered.

"You heading home?"

"Nah, I still haven't written anything up for today, and barely did anything yesterday. I was going to stick around and do that. Why?"

"Mind introducing me to La Reina?"

Chapter Fourteen

Driving down Broadway, Frank saw an old gangster and told Bobby to pullover.

"Colgate!" she shouted out the window. A thickset Hispanic man in his early thirties turned. Recognizing Frank he raised a hand in greeting and approached the unmarked, boldly marked by its inconspicuousness.

Frank stuck her hand out and they clasped in a casual street shake.

"*Qué vole?*" she asked. "Still packing a brush?"

The man flashed beautiful white teeth. Sometimes it was days, even weeks before a prisoner at the county jail could get any personal effects. Because Colgate was arrested so frequently and so suddenly, he'd taken to carrying a toothbrush like other men carried a wallet.

"I don't need that any more," he declared proudly. "You know I ain't bangin' no more."

Colgate had opened a church and was trying to attract young people to it before they got caught up in the cycle of gang life. Frank asked him what the word was about Placa and he was as dumbfounded as everyone else.

"But I'll keep my ear to the ground. I knew that *chica*," he said with a sad shake. "That's the shame of taking the devil's road."

"Yes it is," Frank agreed soberly, flipping him her card. "She was trying to get out of the life. She was a smart girl and she had some plans. But she didn't have enough time to get off that road. You hear anything, you call me. Okay?"

"I will do that," he said, tucking her card into his wallet.

"Take care," she said.

Her right hand stroked her left ring finger as they cut back into the traffic

"I don't know, Bobby. Doesn't make sense that nobody's claiming this."

The detective agreed, taking a side street.

"Check it out," he said, slowing by a large tag on a low concrete block wall. "That's fresh."

Highly stylized Old English letters, in blue and about two feet high, spelled "PLACA V2KING". Next to it was "187 LAPD", with a large X over the LAPD.

"What's that about?" Bobby asked.

"Beats me. Wonder if Toñio threw that."

"Yeah, he favors the V. His tats are all V2, instead of 52."

They rolled on, Bobby saying that he'd seen another strike like that at the 49th Street School, with the LAPD crossed out.

"Hey, there she is," he said swerving to the curb. Three girls were kicking it in the doorway of a bodega, and he said, "The one with the big hair."

The girls started to run off, but both cops jumped out as the car lurched into park, Bobby shouting La Reina's name. Even a four-year old knew that running from the LAPD could be deadly so Lydia Alvarez froze in her tracks. She turned slowly, hands behind her neck while her homegirls halted their flight.

"Go on girl, put your hands down," Bobby said in his gentle bass. "We ain't pronin' you. We just want to talk."

He waved her friends away as Lydia's petulant expression shifted from cop to cop. Her hair was dyed reddish brown, highlighted with purple streaks, and teased up high. Kohl-rimmed eyes, a pouty, mocha-colored-mouth and a shape like a figure eight, advertised Lydia Alvarez as some hot coochie.

"This here's Lieutenant Franco. She wants to ask you some things."

Frank's appraisal of the girl was cool and Lydia felt it.

"Like what?" Lydia glowered, stepping impatiently from foot to foot. Her tough bravado hid fear; it didn't look good for bangers to be talking to the law.

"Like where's Ocho?"

"I don't know. He come by Sunday mornin', woke me up early, and made me give him all my money I had. He said he was goin' away for a while, to hold it down for him while he was gone."

"Why'd he have to go away?"

Sullenly, she repeated what she'd already told Nook and Bobby.

"Where was he going?"

"He wouldn' tell me. Said if I didn't know, I couldn't tell."

When she talked, Frank could see her missing front tooth. She indicated the gap in Lydia's mouth, asking, "He knock that tooth out?"

"Oh no," she defended, "that was some White Fence bitch. I busted her ass. I can take care a myself."

"How old are you, Lydia?"

"Fifteen?"

"Any babies?"

"Not yet."

Her grin was quick and shy and she covered the gap in her teeth behind her hand, "But I'm trying to give Ocho a baby."

Opportunity was scarce in the ghetto, and as hard as it was for young men, it was even harder for young girls. Many tried to alleviate the endless poverty by hooking up with a ghetto star. The competition was fierce, but presenting a boy with his child gave a girl an advantage. Plus, being a mother took her out of the life. No self-respecting girl was allowed to bang if she had babies at home. Once into the life, babies and serious religion were the only safe ways out.

"Tell me about you and Placa."

Lydia's soft grin was instantly replaced by hyper-vigilance. She glanced all around her, even up at the roof of the bodega. You never knew where your enemies might be. She jammed her hands into her tight back pockets.

"What about her?"

"About why your name was branded onto her leg. Why you trippin' with a King?" Frank asked, getting into the lingo. Lydia rocked restlessly, eyeing every passing car, each pedestrian. She shrugged, glanced at the sidewalk. Lydia was reluctant with an answer so Frank pressed her on things she already knew, testing the girl's veracity. She passed.

"What did Ocho think about you and Placa being hooked up?"

"He don' know nothin' about that," Lydia spat. "If he did, I wouldn' be standin' here."

Frank believed that was true.

"Who else knew about you two?"

"*Nobody*," she avowed with deathly sincerity.

"How about Itsy?"

"Psh," Lydia snorted. "Ain't no way."

"Why you say that?"

" 'Cause she a skank," Lydia said in disdain. "She ain't down. She's a baby. She'd a cried it out to the world if she'd a known."

It was common to trash the enemy, but as Frank recalled, Itsy was almost as hard-core as Placa. She ostensibly ran the Queens, though she deferred in all gang matters to her former girlfriend. Itsy was devoted to Placa and their break-up must have devastated her. Not only did she lose her lover, she'd lost her status in the set. Word was that La Limpia and Payasa were running the Queens now.

"How about her brother, Toñio?"

She shifted uneasily. "I don' think so."

"Did he ever see you two together?"

She repeated her answer.

"How about drugs? You and Placa ever slang?"

"No. We din' do no business together. What we had goin' on . . . it was personal. You wouldn't understand."

"Did Placa ever use?"

The multi-colored hair shook like a beast about to loose it's chains.

"She only smoke weed. She tell me once she'd kill me herself if she ever caught me crackin' or shootin'. Like that bitch Itsy."

"Itsy was using?"

"Yeah," Lydia snorted meanly, "that girl's a rock monster. That's why Placa didn't want nothin' to do with that bitch and they was tight."

"I hear you were at a party in Eagle Rock the night Placa got smoked."

"Yeah." Lydia hung her head and Frank couldn't see her expression.

"Where was the party?"

"I don't know."

116

"I want you to take a ride with us, show us where that party was."

"I don't know," she protested. "Me and my homegirls was in the back gettin' high and messing around. I don't know *where* that party was at. Ocho was drivin'."

Frank lifted her jacket sleeve away from her watch.

"I'm gonna give you one hour to find out where that party was."

Lydia pouted at the cracked concrete.

"What if I can' find out?"

"Then word on the street's gonna be that Ocho's girl was ballin' an off-brand. I'll let Ocho figure out who."

Frank let that sink in, then added, "*Si estas firme,* your boyfriend can come home."

La Reina made a face suggesting that wasn't much of a reward for her troubles.

Chapter Fifteen

Frank was talking to Nook and Bobby, about to call Northeast CRASH to see if the gang division would give them a liaison to help ID bangers who might have been at the Eagle Rock party.

"We don't need any help," Nook protested. "I can —"

"— you know that area?"

"Not so well, but I can figure it out."

Frank put her hand on the phone.

"No offense, but this'll go a lot faster if we're working with someone who knows the place."

Frank saw that a lot, cops hating to give help or ask for it. They were greedy with their knowledge, hoarding it like provisions during famine. They were most disinclined to lend assistance to other agencies, but were even possessive within their own divisions and with their own colleagues. Frank guessed because most cops were men, it was a pride thing, like not asking for directions. She thought it ridiculous and had no trouble asking for or giving help to other jurisdictions. With the advent of computerized databases, sharing information was becoming increasingly easier, and some of the "I got mine, now you get yours" attitude was breaking down. Still it was common with old-timers like Nook, and Frank wasn't about to let him get away with it. Especially on this case.

But the CRASH cowboys were as reluctant to offer help as Nook was to accept it. A lieutenant told her they couldn't possibly break anyone loose until Monday. Frank had no alternative but to let her boys do what they could alone, and meanwhile, they could track Itsy down too. She sent them out and reached for her ringing phone.

"Howdy," came the long drawl at the other end. "How ya doin?"

"Hey, sport. What's up?"

"Not much. I'm at work. Luchowski's got me back on paper. Doesn't want me gettin' *over-exposed*," she complained dramatically. Frank almost smiled. Kennedy loved undercover work and resented when she had to stay behind the desk for any length of time. Frank didn't say he was probably right, only offered condolences.

"Well, I reckon as I'll live. Not happily, but I'll live. I been sittin' a spell, goin' through this joker's file, trying to find some aliases and I came up with a homey name a Custard Pie. I ran him in the computer but nothing came up. I remembered Diego was talking about him one night at the Alibi. I remembered on account a how that infected eye gave him the name. You know the dude I'm talking about?"

"I know the guy, he's an Eight-trey Crip. Deals mostly weed and Sherms."

"Yeah, that's him," Kennedy said languidly, "only now he's hanging around elementary schools trying his hand at crack."

She needed whatever Frank had on him and Frank promised to get it for her.

"Cool. I'd shore appreciate it."

Annette Funicello meets Dale Evans, Frank thought.

"No problem."

There was a slight pause, then Kennedy said, "Now be honest, you miss me, don't ya?"

The moment she heard her voice Frank figured something like that was coming, and she was steeled for it.

"Can't sleep at night."

"I know you'd never tell me anything like that if it was true," Kennedy countered, correctly. Then she pushed even further, saying, "Looks like you and Doc Law are gettin' along real good."

"No better than you and me."

"You sure about that? You two look awful snug together and don't I get some hairy eyeball whenever I come around."

"Don't read too much into drinks after work, sport. Not everybody has your appetite for bed-hopping."

"Oo-o," Kennedy drew out, "did I hit a nerve?"

"No," Frank lied, irritated by the conversation. "You've just spoiled me for other women. Look. I've got to get back to work. I'll get the Custard Pie data to you ASAP."

She hung up without waiting for Kennedy's goodbye.

Frank sniffed the gummy coffee at the bottom of the pot and put it back down. She'd much rather have a beer at the Alibi with her feet propped on a chair but she had an appointment with Clay at 4:00. Checking her watch, she calculated she could squeeze in a quick visit to the Estrella's. She did, and was pleased to find them all home.

"One big happy family," she noted affably, perching on the sofa arm. "But every family's got secrets, right?"

Gloria juggled the baby and didn't take her eyes from the

novela on the TV. Claudia leaned silently against the wall and Toñio looked like he'd been doing some herbal, sprawled in the worn easy chair, dull-eyed and slack-mouthed.

"Tell me something. I thought Itsy and Placa were hooked up, but now I hear they busted up a while back. Who was Placa's new tight?"

They all stared at anything but Frank. Zero reaction.

"What if I told you she was twistin' Ocho's girlfriend?"

"You'd be fuckin' crazy," Gloria laughed, but Toñio threw Frank a hasty glance. He licked his lips and wiggled deeper into the chair. Frank smiled inside, knowing he knew.

"*De verdad,*" she continued. "Placa had La Reina tattooed on her leg, right up here," Frank drew a line across her thigh. Toñio didn't look but the other two did. Gloria stopped bouncing the baby.

"*Mentirosa,*" she growled.

"*Te juro,*" Frank pledged, hand held in the air.

Gloria jumped up in a full and sudden fury, screaming, "*Jodida puta!* How could she be disrespecting her *clica* like that? That fuckin' *bitch!*"

Claudia merely watched her grandchild crawling on the floor and Frank asked, "You knew?"

She waved a hand, "I don't know about that kinda thing. Carmen, she aways have to be different. Always want to be somethin' she not. I don't want to know nothin' about that business of hers."

Claudia crossed herself and Frank looked at Toñio for an answer. He wouldn't meet her gaze. She wanted to talk to him, but she wanted him alone. She'd wait. She was running out of time for today. With a grin, she said, "I hope this was as much fun for you as it was for me. I'll see you tomorrow."

She let herself out, pondering how to approach Toñio as she crept through side street traffic to the freeway traffic. She was five minutes late for her meeting with Clay, but his secretary apologized that he was running late too. Frank nodded, quickly disregarding the mental health brochures scattered around as reading material. A bottled blonde, rail-thin and heavily made-up, rattled through a Good House-keeping. Must have brought it with her, Frank thought, wondering who she was waiting for. Husband? Boyfriend? Frank decided to wait in the hallway, not wanting to bump into whoever came out of Clay's office.

She paced, chumming her thoughts back to Placa. Maybe it was inevitable, but like Noah and Bobby, Frank had hoped Placa would turn out differently. She wasn't the only one who must have thought that; there probably wasn't a cop in Figueroa who at some point hadn't picked up that baby girl padding happily along the sidewalk in a loaded diaper. She'd laugh and wiggle when you held her and always tried to pry your badge off. As an older child she'd become wary, but quick to smile when she recognized you. When she started banging, she'd become hostile and insolent, but still able to summon a trace of civility for the cops she knew best. Despite the rough tagger exterior, there was still a tenuous respect for the past if nothing else. It was that faint memory, of a time before gangs, that cops like Frank and Noah had hoped would jettison Placa out of the life.

Claudia had chipped during Placa's earliest years. When she wasn't in the spoon she took good care of her kids, and with their overwhelming backlog, Child Protective Services never got around to taking them. There were occasional men around, the longest lasting being Gloria's father. He was a ratty punk and Claudia had his name tattooed over her left breast. Frank had broken up more than one bottle-flying, fist-smashing catfight over him and it wasn't unusual to get a Saturday night domestic violence call from Claudia's house. What money he didn't make hustling and fencing cars, Claudia made by selling junk, and doing minor B and E's. She'd been busted dozens of times, from misdemeanors to grand theft auto, and Frank had taken her in at least seven or eight of those times. But there were so many more "serious" offenders on the LA County court dockets. When she shyly appealed to the judge that she had three babies at home that needed taking care of she got off on probation or her cases got tossed or pleaded. At worst, she'd end up at Sybil Brand for a couple months and Julio's wife would take the kids in.

Frank had a softness for Claudia. They ran into each other frequently, and while Claudia was uncommunicative, she was never as openly hostile to Frank as she was to the other *jura*. The last time Frank had taken her in had been years ago, when she was a Sergeant, and Claudia'd been on the nod. Her hair was dirty and there was no make-up to cover her yellowing skin. Where she'd fallen onto the sidewalk her cheek was gouged and her upper lip was split. Frank had propped her in the back of the squad car and flies tried to cluster around a bloody scrape on her knee. Frank had waved them away, closing the door carefully. Behind the wheel she'd flipped the rearview mirror so Claudia could see herself.

"What happened to that pretty girl I met my first day on patrol?" Frank wondered aloud. Claudia had stared cloudily at her reflection, as if trying to find the answer. Maybe the question had done some good. When she went into Brand that time, she'd been forced into quitting the smack. She was also carrying her second son, and when she came out she'd stayed clean.

It was a couple years later that Frank presented Placa with the metal badge. She'd pinned it on the chubby girl's thin T-shirt and she'd beamed. She couldn't stop staring at her chest. Every time Frank saw Placa after that she had that damn badge drooping off her chest. Until one day Frank saw her playing on the sidewalk, in a bare shirt. When Frank asked her where the badge was, Placa's face darkened and she said some boys had ripped it off and jumped on it till it was flat and crumpled. So Frank had paid the cop with the machine shop to make her half a dozen and the cycle continued until one day Placa didn't want the badges anymore.

"How come?" Frank had asked.

"My *tio* and brother says they're stupid, only the police wear badges and I'm not a police."

"You could be a police," Frank said, "when you're a little bigger."

Placa considered that carefully.

"Then I could wear a badge all the time?"

"Everyday. And no one could ever take it away from you."

"No one ever takes your badge?"

"*Nunca.*"

"But how big do I have to be?"

"You have to be as old as your brother Chuey."

Then very seriously, Carmen said, "*Entonces*, I'll wait to be a police. Then I can have my own badge and no one can take it from it me."

She and Frank had exchanged a low-five. Thing was, Carmen never got to be as old as her brother Chuey.

The receptionist told Frank she could go in. Clay rose to meet her and they shook hands. After she settled uneasily into one of his chairs he asked how her week had been.

"Okay," she answered noncommittally, knowing she was buying time. Clay stared over the glasses at the tip of his nose. Frank knew what was expected and Clay always gave her the option to waste the hour or be productive.

"Had a girl get shot up this week. Knew her for a long time. She was a banger, but she was a good kid, good grades. She was a mean OG so nobody gave her trouble. She could get away with being smart. Could have gotten a scholarship to art schools."

Holding her thumb and forefinger together, Frank continued, "She always got this close to convictions. Managed to wiggle out of them like her mother. Would have been fun to see her come up."

124

When Frank didn't continue, Clay said, "How does her death make you feel?"

Frank tossed a shoulder, shying from the answers. They swirled on the edge of her consciousness, waltzing like women in gauzy ball gowns. It took her a moment to pick out individual feelings and give them names. She walked over to the window. The pane was cool and solid against her fingers, a comforting contrast to the turbulence within. Knowing what Clay wanted to hear, she quickly catalogued and labeled her feelings.

"Mad. Sad. Frustrated."

Then Mag's parting words rang in her ears.

"When are you going to grow up?"

Did Frank really want to drag her ass in here once a week to try and pull one over on Clay or did she want to get on with her life? She conceded the former was more appealing but the latter more necessary. She didn't ever again want to come close to the abyss she'd stepped into after the Delamore case.

She'd conveniently blamed her crash on the burden of that case, knowing full well that if Delamore hadn't tipped her over the edge, something or someone else inevitably would have. Kennedy had her flaws but Frank would always be grateful she'd been around that night. Next time, if there *was* a next time, there might not be someone there. She turned and faced Clay.

"She was only seventeen. She was actually going to graduate from high school in a few months. I don't think anyone else in her family had ever done that. She was born the year I joined the force. Fact, I met her mother first day on the job. She was hanging with some *cholos*, drunk off her ass. She was pregnant, just huge, about to deliver any day and she was swigging out of a bottle of Boone's Farm. It's funny. I smell that stuff and it's pow — total flashback to that day."

Frank paused. The memory was as clear as the window she looked through.

"My FTO and I were driving around, and he saw her in this alley. He pulls up. He's already pissed that he's being forced to work with a woman — and that would have been the nicest thing he ever called me — so by the time we get to these homes, he's on a royal tear. He swaggers down the alley, slapping his stick in his hand, and I'm still trying to get out of the car. I'm jamming my hat on, trying to get my stick in my belt, juggling my field book. I've got no idea what's going on, got no clue what's being said on the radio. I thought, maybe he heard something, but then I was wondering, why didn't he respond? So whatever, I'm following him like a lost dog, and he says something stupid to these kids, which doesn't surprise me after having driven with him for an hour.

"They're all just staring at the ground, kicking at it. You can tell they're not happy. And no one answers him, so he swings his stick at the kid closest to him and says 'Hey! I asked you a question.' I heard his stick connect and thought, man, that must have hurt. Well this kid says they're not doing anything and that Roper, that was his name, he didn't have to do that. Of course this just pisses Roper off even more. Then the girl says something really stupid in Spanish, about a fat pig or something. She is totally pasted, and I'm thinking, 'Oh Christ, the shit is going to fly.' But Roper's cool. He just goes and stands over her. He puts his shoe on her shoulder and she tips over. I want to help her but I'm thinking I better just stay out of this. But the guy who's already mouthed off, he tries helping her and Roper swats at him with his stick, like he's playing with him. He says, 'You want to fight me over this, Juan? Huh? You want to fight me over this *cunt*?' just totally baiting the guy. And this kid knows he's fucked.

"Roper tells them all to leave, but this guy, he wants a piece of Roper so bad he can taste it. He stands there, staring at Roper and I'm thinking, 'Just go home, buddy. For Christ's sake.' But he reaches down to help Claudia up, she's out of it, all sticky with wine, and Roper goes *whap!* with his stick. Right on the guy's wrist, just shattered it. If he'd been playing baseball he'd have had a homerun. The kids *got* to be in pain but he just makes this little yelp and jerks his hand away. It starts swelling up like a fucking basketball, but the kid doesn't say a thing, just holds his arm and gives Roper the evil eye. Roper gets into his face, saying all sorts of shit, and he's backing this guy out of the alley. The other homeboys are *gone*. They saw the shit going down and they flew. So Roper finally gets the poor sonofabitch out of there, and he comes back into the alley, all happy now. He's got this wicked grin on his face, and I don't know what's happening next but I know it's not going to be pretty.

"And he's a big guy. LAPD beautiful. Tall, dark, built — the kind of cop straight women just *pray* will show up to their calls. So he strolls over to Claudia, unzipping his fly. He grins at me, an evil fucking grin, and he says, 'You can watch this or go back to the car like a good little girl.' "

Frank stopped. She watched a man lean into a bronze sedan, talking to the driver. He wore a gray suit and carried a briefcase. His hair was sandy and thinning though he looked trim and fairly young.

"I knew that was a defining moment. Either I was in with Roper or I wasn't. I could just see my whole future. It was like a long highway with a fork in the middle. On the one side, I was down. I'd go along with him. I'd be part of the team. What was happening was ugly, but that's the way it was. I'd seen it in my own neighborhood growing up. That was just the way the world was. Nothing I could do about it.

"On the other road, I was alone. There was just me in the middle of this goddamn highway, no team, nobody. And I *wanted* to be part of the team. I remember thinking I'd always been alone and that it would be so nice to be part of something, just once. I'd busted my ass to get where I was and I didn't want to lose it. That other road was calling me and God, I wanted to be on it."

The man stuck his hand into the car, seeming to shake the driver's hand.

"I remember I just kind of looked at my feet. That alley was filthy. Busted bottles and beer caps, cigarette packs, tossed garbage. And it smelled like rotten vegetables and piss and wine. I thought I was going to throw up. Roper was saying something to Claudia and I saw her spit on him. Goddamn. He had her by the hair and he yanked her head back so hard I thought he was going to break her neck. And then I just snapped. It was so fucking weird — I literally saw red. I slammed him with my stick, I mean with everything I had and that fucker went *down*. And son-of a-bitch, I was *excited* by that. He looked up at me, surprised at first and with just this trace of fear, and I loved it. Then he got pissed and I got scared — well, not really scared, but just incredibly amped and wired and *wanting* to take him on. I was ready to kill the sonofabitch. I understand how that happens. I understand why people do what they do out there.

"He reached for his baton, but I'd fucked his arm up and he couldn't use it, so I let him grab it with his left. I figured Roper was crazy and I'd rather have him swinging his stick at me than pulling his gun. In fact, he told me I was going to die. Told him I'd take him out with me. I was ready for him. God, I was ready. It was almost like sex. But better, more intense. I was *flying*. It was like something got released in me, a trip-wire. We circled around that fucking alley for *hours* it seemed like. He connected once on me, hurt like a motherfucker, but I must've jumped quick enough that it didn't do any damage. I was trying to work him back to the street and I was getting tired. The edge was wearing off and I realized what a stupid thing I'd done. Taking on the field training officer, not even before our dinner break. Thought I'd make the record for shortest time served on job by a female. But I was committed. I'd chosen my road."

She took a resonant breath, studied Clay for a minute.

"Saw a guy today, used to be a banger. Now he's into God and saving kids. Asked him if he'd heard anything on the street about who offed Placa. He said no, that he knew her.

That it was a shame she'd taken the devil's road. I told him she was a good kid, that she just hadn't had enough time to get out of the road."

Puzzlement shadowed Frank's face.

"Thing is, that road's always there. Even if you get off it, it doesn't mean somewhere down the line you don't find yourself right back on it. And damned if you know how you got there."

She looked out the window. The sedan was gone. A woman in a grey skirt suit and black boots walked briskly along the sidewalk. Power haircut, full leather briefcase. A lawyer? Frank wondered, on her way home? Husband, two kids, and a nanny, Frank bet, watching her until she stepped out of view. Clay had a clock that ticked quietly. Frank listened to it over the moan of a city bus. Behind her, he asked, "Do you ever feel like you're on that road?"

"Sometimes."

"Are you on it now?"

Below, the bus farted thick black smoke. The city was switching to electric soon. That would be good.

"I feel like I'm on the curb."

Tic, tic, tic.

"What does the road look like from there?"

A delivery truck idled at the light. Frank thought of her father, how dark his hair had been. It was thick and curly on his arms and had tickled her face when he held her. Sometimes she'd give anything to feel that arm around her again. She closed her eyes against the window, grateful for its coolness against her forehead.

"Looks like where I've been."

Clay let her sit with that before asking what was the best thing that happened to her that week.

She tweaked her mouth into a deprecating line.

"Had dinner with a nice lady."

Clay's smile was warm and he urged, "Tell me about that."

Feeling silly, she briefly described dinner with Gail,

adding, "It was nice. She's easy to talk to. Smart. And funny. Pretty, too."

Remembering her conversation in the car with Gail, she added, "She keeps it real. I don't see much of that."

"Are you going to see her again?"

Frank almost said sure, but she'd learned there were no guarantees in life.

"Probably. We run into each other in a professional capacity."

"I meant in a personal capacity, like having dinner again."

"Hadn't thought about it," Frank admitted.

"Well, consider it," Clay advised, ending their session.

As always, he left Frank with something to chew on. And as always, she was glad to be out of his office and back on the street where she knew the rules.

Chapter Sixteen

Frank cheerfully presented Claudia with another box of donuts. Sleepy and rumple-haired, she pulled a cheap robe around herself and let Frank in. The baby began crying and Gloria screamed from her bedroom. Something about *jodida* cops and harassment. Claudia started to make coffee, but Frank took the pot from her hand.

"No, no," she said, exaggeratedly solicitous. "Let me. You sit down. Have a donut."

Half asleep, Alicia stepped into the kitchen, coming to when she saw the pink box on the table. She was the only one who liked Frank's early morning visits. She sat at the table, mooning over the unopened box. Alicia's eyes gleamed when Frank lifted the lid. The little girl examined the donuts, and maybe because she was getting more comfortable with Frank, she asked, "Why you don't bring syrup ones like the other *policia*?"

Claudia hissed at her grandchild to be quiet and jerked her from the chair. Swatting her bottom, she gave the girl a push into the living room. A moment later the television blared. Her grandmother yelled at her to turn it down.

"What other *policia*, Claudia?"

"*El negro*," she said quickly. "He brung donuts the other day."

Frank poured them both coffee, putting milk on the table for Claudia. Waiting until Claudia was adding the milk to her cup, she said, "Tell me about the heroin."

Claudia dripped milk on the table, glancing up into Frank's attentive blue eyes. She grabbed a sponge out of the sink and swiped angrily at the spill, then picked up her cup and stood with her back to the counter. Frank watched her like a snake tracking a mouse.

"Tell me about the heroin," she repeated.

"What heroin?"

Frank laughed, "Damn, Claudia, you think the police are so stupid they don't know you're serving out of here? What I want to know is if you're chippin' again."

Claudia looked disgusted. "I give that up a long time ago."

"What about the kids?"

"They don't mess with that stuff. That's the devil's candy. I kill 'em myself before I let them shoot up."

"But you let them sell it."

Claudia held Frank's gaze. "Sometimes," she admitted.

Frank considered a curious paradox of ghetto morality. You could do shit to strangers, other gangs, even your friends, but never to your gang or your family. They were blood. But it was perfectly okay to fuck up everybody else. Frank had seen the rationale time and time again, that if someone was stupid enough to use it, why shouldn't someone else be smart enough to hustle it? Claudia admitted none of them used smack and she didn't want it near her, yet she felt no compunction about dealing it and addicting other people. This blind eye to suffering was a common survival technique in communities with few resources and intense competition.

"Who do you sell to?"

"*Gente*. Whoever's looking," she said, flipping her tangled hair behind her shoulders.

"You sell to Fifty-first Street Playboy's?"

Claudia shook her head, "I don't know who that is."

"You have a steady clientele?"

Frank realized she didn't understand, and amended, "You have regular customers."

"Sometimes," she shrugged.

"I want their names. I want to know where they live."

"*Mierda*," Claudia snorted. "*No se eso*."

Frank went along with a cool smile.

"You're telling me you deal to strangers?"

"*No son stranjeros, pues, pero no sabemos sus nombres propios o dirreciones*."

"In English."

Claudia started chewing on the flesh around her nail. Claudia denied much involvement in dealing, saying it was infrequent. When Frank asked how she supported three children and two grandkids, Claudia cited child aid and welfare.

Alicia sidled back to the kitchen table and Frank pushed the donuts toward her. She grabbed one and ran off with it. The child looked healthy and well fed. The shelves behind Frank were well-stocked and she'd noticed when she took the milk out, that the refrigerator was full. You didn't see that too often in government aid homes.

Claudia's nails were ragged from chewing, but her hands were smooth. She thought about the junk food wrappers and pizza boxes scattered perpetually in the living room around toys and piles of CDs and Nintendo cartridges. Frank knew there was more then welfare coming into this house. She stared at Claudia, deliberately making her uncomfortable as she gauged her best angle of attack. At length, as Claudia ate away more skin around her nails, Frank asked, "How many more, eh? How many more have to die because you're afraid to tell me the truth?"

"I got nothin' to do with it," Claudia defended herself.

Disgusted, Frank shook her head.

"How can you say that? People are *dying*, Claudia. Your blood, your *family*. For Christ's sake, someone killed your daughter and you know who and you won't let me help, so don't tell me it's got nothing to do with you. *Christ*," Frank swore again. "If you know who's doin' this and you ain't done nothin' to stop it's like you've pulled the trigger on your own daughter! You killed your own flesh and blood Claudia, now you're just sittin' around drinkin' coffee while you're waitin' to see who gets it next."

Quivering, Claudia hissed, "So I should die, too? Eh? Who's gonna look after my babies? Who's gonna look after Alicia and the gran'babies if I'm not here, eh? You tell me that! You cops come in tryin' to run everybody's lives like you know what's goin' on, and you don't know *nothin'*," she spat. "All you fuckin' *jura*, all you want is it your own way — what's good for you. And you come in here tryin' to tell me what I need to do. How to protect my family. *Fuck* that. You don't know. Where are you at three-thirty in the morning when he comes knockin' on my door? Eh? How much do you care then? You don' know nuttin' about what I need to do. You don't know nuttin' about keepin' my chil'ren safe. Don't you be tellin' me what I need to do. I'm *doin'* what I need to do!"

"Who comes knockin' on your door at three-thirty, Claudia?"

"*Fuck* you. All you fuckin' cops."

Claudia's eyes were lit with rage, the old fire had finally been stoked back to life.

"Who's at your door at three-thirty?" Frank tried again,

knowing as Claudia coldly recomposed herself that she'd lost her. She'd had her for a sec then played her wrong. Frank slowly drained her cup, then stood, scraping her chair against the floor.

"Thanks for the coffee. I'll see you at the funeral tomorrow."

When it was Frank's weekend on call she usually didn't get to the Alibi until the drinking was well under way. She found a space on the street and pulled in just as Gail was getting out of her car. The ME hadn't seen her and Frank caught up, following quietly a few steps behind.

"Hey."

"Oh, Christ! Thanks, Frank. I hadn't had my daily coronary yet."

"Got to be more careful out here. I watched you get out of your car and then I followed you. You didn't even see me."

"I wasn't expecting to get mugged."

"Nobody ever is. That's what the bad guys count on."

"Yes, Officer Friendly."

"Just be more careful. Look at what's on the street before you get out of your car."

"My God, you sound like a public service announcement. Are you always this didactic?" Gail asked reaching for the bar door. The noise assaulted them and Frank raised her voice, "Be a shame to see you laid out on one of your own gurneys!"

"Ha, ha."

The Nine-three was holding down two tables and as Frank threaded toward them, nodding here and there, she recognized Hunt, Dimmler, and a couple other uniforms around the tables. Johnnie was arm-wrestling Muñoz, and actually winning for a change. Frank offered Gail the only empty seat and scavenged another one, putting it next to the doc. Bobby and Diego welcomed Gail, but Frank overheard Hunt mutter to Dimmler, "Somebody must've left the door open at the pound. All the bitches are loose."

Frank was surprised Hunt was smart enough to make up a joke and wondered if he'd stolen the line. She glanced at Gail who didn't seem to have heard.

"This place is mobbed," she semi-shouted to Frank. "What's the occasion?"

Frank replied quickly, "They all heard you were coming."

Picking Nance out among the harried waitresses and noting Ike cruising a knot of females from the DA's office, Frank asked Diego, "Noah come by?"

"He's in the can."

Frank leaned close to Gail and asked, "Gin and tonic?"

When Gail nodded, she said, "Be right back."

Frank went to the bar and yelled her order at Mac.

"Comin' up," he yelled back, slamming bottles and pouring with both hands. While Frank waited, Noah came out of the bathroom, saw her, grinned.

"What up, dudess?"

He flipped his palm up and she greased it. Mac slid the dripping drinks over and Frank carried them carefully, wondering how Nancy flew around with them on a tray.

"Move over," Noah said, wedging a chair between Diego's and Frank's. Gail clanked her glass against Frank's.

"To Fridays."

"Here, here."

As Dimmler vied for Gail's attention, Noah said close to Frank's ear, "I see Dim and Dimmer have joined us. Dimmler's all right," he conceded, "but Hunt's a freak. He'd rather be out knockin' heads than working."

Bobby and Diego cheered as Muñoz' arm went down, then Frank looked down the table, asking Bobby how his talk with Itsy had gone. She'd come back home last night and her detectives had paged Frank so she could be in on the interview, but she hadn't been able to break away. She'd told them to throw another girl in Itsy's face but not to mention who it was.

"She was pretty strung out, wasn't in much better shape than when Nook talked to her the last time. We rattled her cage about a girlfriend and she took it pretty hard. She was asking us who it was, begging us to tell her. She's a mess. She couldn't even tell us where she was when Placa got shot. Thinks she was hanging around with a guy named Droopy. They were both trying to score."

"You find him?"

"We're looking. I got a CI might know who he is. He used to be a King until he got jumped out for using."

"So you don't think she knew about Lydia?"

"I doubt it. About all she thinks of anymore is where to get her next hit."

"Does she have wheels?"

"No. She went to El Monte with her mother. She's got an old Riviera. We asked about Ocho, if anything was going down with him and Placa. She said she didn't know. She's been out of the set for a while and most of the Queens just diss her now."

Frank watched the bubbles pop in her club soda, mulling this over. Putting her head close to Frank's, Gail asked, "Are you narrowing in on anybody?"

"Well, at first we had a good possible suspect, then we had two more, but they seem to be slipping through our fingers. At this point, I have to say no."

Bobby and Nook had checked out the other Playboys Lydia said were at the party, but had gotten nothing of substance. When pressed, they all admitted being there with Ocho, but were vague about the party's timeline. Ruiz could have slipped away anytime.

Dimmler vied for Gail's attention as a cop in civvies bumped Frank's chair. Kneeling behind her he said hello to the ME.

"Hello," Gail replied, obviously annoyed.

"I was wondering if I could buy you a drink."

"I already have one."

"Well, when you finish that one."

"I'm only having one."

"Hey, pal. She's at *our* table," Dimmler growled.

"Whatever," the cop in civvies said, then snickered, "Arnold."

Coming out of his chair, Dimmler said, "You want to make something outta this?"

"No, man, just relax."

When the cop stood, he was taller than Dimmler but not nearly as buff.

"Maybe later, doc. See you around."

"I hope not," she said to Frank.

"Sorry about that," Dimmler said. Gail took him aback when she said, "What are *you* apologizing for?"

Hunt grinned nastily while Dimmler stammered, "Well, for his behavior."

"Like yours is so much better? Honestly, you guys are like wolves fighting over meat scraps."

Her tone got the attention of the rest of the table. Noah started to say something but Hunt interrupted.

"Hey, lady," he drawled, his cowboy boots propped on the rung of Gail's chair.

Hunt reached into his lap as Gail glared at him. Unzipping his fly, he cupped his dick in his hand, and said, "I bet you've never seen one of these before."

Everyone at the table froze. Frank quickly decided the best way to deal with the situation, but Gail calmly peered into Hunt's lap and replied, "You're right. It *looks* like a penis but I've never seen such a *small* one."

Hunt's sneer faded, and Johnnie groaned. Frank was about to usher the cop out when Gail added, "I'm a doctor, you know. You should really have that looked at. It might need to be removed."

Nervous chuckles went around the table, and Dimmler, not as dim as his friend, thought it best to leave.

"Come on," he said tugging on Hunt's arm. "Let's go."

Hunt stood but shook him off, righting the cowboy hat on his head.

"Yeah, let's leave the cunt-lickers and their faggoty friends," he jeered. Johnnie jumped to his own defense but Muñoz put a hand on him, calming him down. He accompanied his colleagues to the door as Noah congratulated, "Good one, doc."

"Excuse me," Frank said, and Bobby murmured, "Uh-oh."

The three men were talking on the sidewalk and Frank called Hunt's name. Dimmler swore under his breath. Muñoz said, "Lieutenant, I'm —"

She held up a hand. Hunt was a good head taller than Frank, bigger and meaner. Under his chin, close in to break his swing if he wanted one, she said, "I can't tell if you're stupid, psychotic or both. Even a dumb cowpoke like you has got to know you just bought a CUBO, maybe a suspension. If you've got a union rep, you better call him."

Thumbs hooked in his jeans, he laughed, "Thanks for the tip."

"I'm glad you think this is funny," Frank smiled, " 'Cause it's going to get a whole lot funnier."

"Whatever you say," he mocked.

"Take him home," she ordered, not leaving his face. Dimmler hustled him away, but Hunt wouldn't break his derisive stare. And Frank wouldn't let him. Even after his buddies got him into the back of their car he kept his eyes on her. Craning his neck, he flicked his tongue from the rear window. Frank watched the car drive around the corner, stood there after it was out of sight.

When she reclaimed her chair at the table, Johnnie speculated, "I wonder how Hunt's new asshole feels."

"You should know," his partner jabbed back, and the boys

started one-upping each other over who'd gotten the worst reaming by Frank. Gail's drink was empty and Frank asked, "Can I get you a refill?"

Gail shook her bob and Frank finished her soda. She was tired of cops and men, their noise and banter. Glancing at the doc, Clay's advice came to her.

"Hey. You like Italian food?"

Frank had to lean close to ask, and she picked up Gail's peachy shampoo again. "Doesn't everybody?"

"Want to get out of here?"

"I'm right behind you."

The doc drove behind Frank to her favorite restaurant, and as they settled heavy linen napkins in their laps, Frank told Gail she was great with Hunt.

"God, what a *creep*."

"You should lodge an official complaint. The guy's got some serious problems. I'm going to take care of it from my end but the more stuff that goes in his file the better."

"You're damn right I will. What an *asshole*. Or am I just an asshole magnet? First his beefcake friend, then that other guy? Maybe it's my pheromones."

Frank tried to suppress a smile, but Gail insisted, "No really. Christ, I get so tired of all these gorillas running around thumping their chests. And if one more man ever says to me at work, what's a nice girl like you doing in a place like this, I'm going to lay him out on the table! I swear I am."

Frank let her rave, then Gail said, "You must get that a lot too, huh?"

"Not really."

Gail looked puzzled, then laughed. Frank was handsome, especially when she was relaxed. Wheat-blonde hair usually held back by a pair of ray-Bans or a ponytail fell straight to her shoulders. Her eyes were deep and dark, like international waters. She had strong features and a long, fit body. Frank could have been a knockout, but her bearing clearly discouraged male attention.

"I'm sorry. I have to put up with apes like that all week, and the last thing I want to do is deal with them on my own time."

"I understand. Believe me."

The waiter glided to the table. Greeting Frank by name, he asked if she'd like to start with a carafe of wine.

"Not tonight, but the lady might like something."

Gail declined and the waiter recited the specials. After he left, the doc smiled coyly.

"I like the way you said, 'the lady' like there was only one of us here."

"I don't consider myself a lady."

"Why not?"

"Ladies are . . . hmm. How best to put this without being offensive."

"I was going to say, you're on some pretty thin ice."

"Ladies are beautiful and gracious," she said carefully.

"Neither of which you are?"

"I don't see myself as beautiful, nor gracious."

"Really?"

"No. I mean, I'm not ugly, but I'm not winning any beauty contests either."

"Well, I think you're very good-looking. And gracious to boot."

"Well, thank you. Now can we change the subject?"

Gail laughed and picked up her menu. Noting the red bumps on her hands, Frank said, "I see you you're still wearing latex."

"I'm always running out of the vinyl gloves and then I forget to order them."

"You can get them at a drugstore, can't you?"

"Yes, but I forget to do that too. I'm not horribly organized."

"I know. I've seen your office," Frank teased.

"I remember that day you came barging in when you were working on the Delamore case."

Frank winced slightly, but Gail didn't notice.

"I thought you were the rudest person I'd ever met."

"See?" Frank said. "Not gracious at all."

"You weren't that day. So RHD ended up breaking that case. Did you help them with it?"

"Hey. I'm sure we can find better things to talk about. The oso bucco's to die for."

Gail's mouth dropped open.

"You eat veal?

"Sure. Why?"

"Do you know how they raise veal calves?"

"In tiny little cages with no exercise or food, only milk to keep them tender."

"And you can still order it knowing that?"

"If I don't order it will they stop making it?"

"No, but how can you participate in such cruelty?"

"Guess I shouldn't order the lamb, either," Frank joked, but Gail's outraged expression didn't change.

"I know you're not a vegetarian. I saw you slam that roast beef the other night."

"No, I'm not. But at least cows and pigs and chickens have some sort of a normal life."

Frank conciliated, "Would you be happy if I got pasta?"

"You can get whatever you want. It's your conscience, not mine."

Don returned, asking if they'd decided.

"Certainly not the oso bucco," Frank mumbled.

"I should certainly hope not," Gail shot back. Without even opening the menu, Frank said, "I'll have the butternut ravioli, Caesar salad, and a glass of the Baileyanna chard with dinner."

Gail smiled into the menu, saying, "And I'll have the veal Marsala —"

"— hey!"

"Just kidding," she laughed, ordering the eggplant Parmigiana. Don whisked the menus away and Gail smoothed the perfectly flat tablecloth.

"So. Does this count as our second date?"

The question startled Frank enough that she chuckled out loud.

"I'm not sure. Do you want it to be?"

"I'm not sure, either," Gail offered. "I figured that's why I'd better check."

"Then how 'bout we just say it's dinner and call it good?"

Gail grinned, "That'll work."

Dinner was excellent, and as they shared a crème Brule, Gail mentioned that one of her doctors was execrable. Frank smiled.

"You know what I like about you, doc?"

"Tell me."

"You use big words like didactic and execrable."

"I've got to put eight years of college to use *somehow*"

Watching Gail swipe her spoon at the last of the Brule, Frank asked, "Are we done here?"

"Oh God, I am so full I can barely breathe. That was exquisite."

They both reached for the tab but Gail snatched it.

"This one's mine."

"I won't argue," Frank said.

"Smart," Gail said, pulling out a credit card. "I like that in a woman."

Frank walked Gail to her car, making sure she got in safely. The doc teased Frank about being gallant.

"Wouldn't look good if I let the County Coroner get assaulted."

"Are you always on duty?"

"Gets to be a habit after a while. You pick up a sixth sense for stuff you couldn't filter out even if you wanted to."

Through the rolled down window, Gail smiled up, telling Frank she had a lovely evening.

"I'm glad it was just dinner. It's nice getting to know you."

"Yeah," Frank agreed, oddly touched by their candor. She quickly scanned the doc's streetlit features. Angular shadows accentuated the high cheekbones, the narrow, emerald eyes, and the pert, upturned nose. Her complexion was ethereal in the twilight. A part in her bangs revealed two creases. Smaller lines parenthesized her mouth and radiated from her eyes. Frank wondered what it would be like to touch them, realizing she'd never gotten that chance with Maggie.

Frank straightened, slapping the Pathfinder's roof.

"Look. You be careful driving home. I'll see you next week."

Frank left Gail staring behind her.

Chapter Seventeen

At the cemetery, Frank spotted Bobby standing a discrete distance from Placa's funeral.

"What are you doing here?" he murmured.

"Thought I'd take in the action," she whispered back.

"Shoot, if I'd known you were coming I'd have stayed home. It would have saved me grief with Leslie."

"How's she doing?"

"All right," Bobby smiled, then blurted out, "She might be pregnant."

"No way."

"Yeah. She's going to the doctor on Tuesday."

"Hey, I hope it works out."

Bobby's wife had miscarried twice before. They wanted lots of kids and were in the process of adopting a little boy.

"Anybody around?"

"Not yet. I thought for sure I'd see a couple Playboys by now. I hate these gang funerals. It's like waiting around for sharks to find a school of bleeding fish."

Frank took a look at the assembled crowd. She recognized some of the older folks, the Estrella relatives, but most of the mourners were kids Placa's age. They were all dressed in their finest, the boys in large shirts with sharply pressed baggies, and the girls in divulging tops over skintight skirts. Tattoos were as common as pimples and Frank watched two groups of boys greet each other with bold hand signs, openly announcing their gang affiliation.

Several *ranflas* slowly cruised the street, no doubt Playboys or another set waiting and watching. The sharks were beginning to gather. Propping herself casually against Bobby's car, eyes and ears wide open, Frank told him about Claudia's reaction when Frank had mentioned dealing junk.

"Maybe it wasn't a Playboy," Bobby said, eyeing the crowd behind his dark glasses. "Maybe it was a deal that went bad. A kickdown."

"Maybe. We need to get with Narco, see if we can't pin down exactly what sort of action they're into."

"Okay," Bobby said, his eyes lingering on a knot of young men smoking at the entrance to the cemetery. Their tats identified all of them as Kings. Frank recognized some of them and Bobby asked, "Want to hit 'em up?"

"May as well. Why don't you take Rojo and I'll take my namesake over there."

"Roger."

The cops walked toward the boys, watching blunts get flicked away.

"Hmmm. Smells *good* over here," Bobby said.

"Yeah," Frank said, "and most of you are probably on parole, aren't you? Hey, Frankie. Walk with me a minute."

A thick-set older boy did as he was told, but not happily. Frank walked with him, close enough that her shoulder brushed his heavy arm. She stopped and crowded him.

"Okay. I know you're a smart guy. You wouldn't come to a funeral without protection, right?"

He didn't want to answer that, and Frank said, "Don't make me prone you in front of everybody. Just show me what you're carryin'."

Frankie sighed and looked sideways, lifting his long shirttail. A nickel-plated Tech-9 rode in his waistband.

"Nice. Now let me ask you some questions. You tell me something I can use, I don't talk to your parolie, okay?"

"Wha' you wanna know?"

"What's the word on Placa? Who hit her?"

"Seem like a Playboy."

"Yeah? Who's claimin' it?"

"Ain't nobody I know of. I heard some people say it was Ocho Ruiz. The ride that pulled on her was like his but ain't no Playboys ownin' it."

"And nobody else is. Don'tcha think that's kinda funny? Now if a King did this, you wouldn't be telling me that either, would you? Kinda makes me wonder if this was inside, you know what I mean?"

Frankie stopped walking, eyes hard and dark on Frank's.

"Wasn't no King done it," he warned.

"How do you know?"

"I just know. Placa was down. Ain't nobody'd have the guts to do it. And Placa was like, *loca*, man. You jus' didn't mess with her. She put a hex on a dude I knew. Made him think he was a chicken. You didn't mess with Placa 'cuz if she didn't put that freaky *malojo* on you then her sister would. That whole family's crazy. They's like witches or somethin'."

"Really? You believe that?"

"Yeah, man! I saw that *vato* get on his hands and knees and start eating dirt. He was just like a chicken."

"I'll be damned," Frank murmured. "All right, Frankie. I'll

147

believe you. But if I find out it was a King, I'ma come find you and you'll be back at the Hall before you can kiss your mother goodbye. *No es mentira.* You change your mind, or you hear somethin' before I do, call me. Don't lose this," she said slipping her card into his hand.

Frank turned around and said, "Okay. Who's next? Shadow. How 'bout you?"

A skinny little kid, with bones where muscles should have been, whined, "Why me? I ain't done nothin'!"

Frank just wiggled her finger and Shadow threw his hands up.

"Aw, man."

"Come on," she coaxed, "take it like a man."

"*Pero, mierda*, I ain't done nothin'."

He was shorter than Frank and she wrapped an arm around his ropey neck.

"Okay. Frankie showed me that pretty Tech-9 he's got, now I want to see what you're holding."

"Nothin'!" Shadow protested.

"Hey, easy, easy. I'm not on your case, man. 'Sides, if I was, I could probably get you for associating already, and that ain't air freshener I'm smellin'. I could take you in on just that."

"I'd be out in an hour," the kid bragged.

"Not if I pat you down and find you're holdin'. You don't want me to do that, do you?"

Frank twisted her head, "Besides. Aren't you sixteen now? Bust you this time you're going to County with the big boys. I hear they got a whole new block full a skinheads." She grinned, "I bet they'd love some puto-ass homeboy coming in on possession. Hm-hm," she said licking her lips.

"Fuck that," Shadow spat. He pulled a snub-nose .38 out of one pocket and a .22 out of the other.

"Man, what are you a Boy-Scout? You come prepared. Okay."

Frank gave him and another King the same spiel, getting much the same answers. Bobby's tack was different but he

148

ended up with what Frank did. Zip. Nobody had heard anything.

Propped against Bobby's car again, Frank said, "Okay. Tell me what this means."

Bobby picked a leaf off a tree and started folding it into what looked like an origami shape. Frank was about to add, "Before I get gray hair," when he said, "Well. It could mean a number of things. Could be a Playboy not claiming because he's afraid of payback. Could be a King not claiming for the same reason, somebody trying to rise in the clique. But that'd sure be a way to make a name for yourself. If it's one of those, somebody'll talk sooner or later. That kind of stuff doesn't happen alone. It could be a completely different clique, different gang. Maybe Lydia did it alone. Maybe it was getting too dangerous, or maybe Placa was playing her."

"With who?"

Frank waited patiently, then Bobby lit up.

"The guy who left the sperm in her."

Frank smiled, and Bobby said, "Ocho?"

"Could be. Maybe she was playing them both."

"Pretty dangerous, and for why?"

"Don't know. But look at our body count here. All of Julio Estrella's family, plus the uncle. Then Luis ODs. Supposedly."

"You've got nothing to say he didn't," Bobby warned. Despite Frank's misgivings about it, all her detectives were eager to put the Estrella shootings onto Luis.

"I'm just saying it's a big coincidence," Frank defended. "And now someone's capped Placa. All this within a week. And she wanted to talk to me about something. I'm saying this isn't over yet. That Placa knew something about what happened to her uncles, about what happened to Barracas, and that whoever killed them shut Placa up too, before she could talk. This is a lot of killing, for what? And Claudia knows something, and the drugs make her nervous. Let's say there's some action being run out of that house that we don't know about. Let's say the Estrella's are cutting into Ruiz' action, which might be cutting into somebody else's action. Let's say that somebody's fucking tired of it."

"You're saying Julio was cutting into Ruiz' turf?"

"I don't know. I don't know what the connection is yet, if there even is one. But we've got a car like Ruiz' at the scene. He's on the fly. Let's say he took out Placa. Why? Coincidence? Maybe Luis did kill his family, but we've got no motive for that either. All I'm saying is that maybe they're all tied up. Maybe Ruiz is the link, maybe he's not. Just keep in mind that this could be bigger than a banger thing."

"But if we pin Ocho to that party . . ."

"Then we got shit," Frank conceded.

Mourners started drifting from Placa's gravesite and Frank scrutinized every movement, thinking if there was going to be trouble, this was when it would start. Bobby flicked his leaf away, watching too.

"Well we know it wasn't an accident. Whoever shot her took a lot of trouble to do it. It wasn't just some wild-ass drive-by. That the car was parked, tells us she was probably in it with the shooter, or that whoever was driving it was friendly enough with her that they could take the time to park. So it had to be someone she knew."

"Kid spent her whole life in the 'hood so that doesn't exactly narrow the field for us."

"Yeah," Bobby agreed. "And dig this. Why would you come home and then leave after a few minutes? Toñio said she came home around six-thirty, quarter to seven. She was only there for a couple minutes then she left. He remembers because she kept walking in front of the TV and he was trying to watch Hercules. But why come home at all if you're not going to stay?"

Frank twisted her invisible ring, caught in the irresistible lure of chasing a homicide.

"To change clothes."

"Okay. Do we know what she was wearing at the park?"

Frank shook her head and said, "Find out. What else? How about to get something to eat?"

"Toñio said she didn't go in the kitchen. Just into her room then out, like she was getting something. Maybe she was getting strapped. Maybe she came home to get a stash and went out to sell it."

Closer to the truth than she knew, Frank nodded, "There's something about the drugs. I'll call Narco on Monday, see what I can find out. Maybe we can get a warrant. I'd like to search the whole house Monday. I'll set up the paper and have it good to go if Narco gives us anything."

"What are you looking for?"

"Anything. I want to check her personal effects, pictures, notebooks, backpacks, scrapbooks, pockets, drawers, anything that might indicate who she's been hangin' with, or where. Maybe she's slangin', who knows?"

"If there's incriminating stuff like that don't you think they'd have thrown it out buy now?"

"Maybe," Frank admitted. "I probably should have asked for a consent that first night, but I was too focused on Ruiz. Bad move on my part."

"I think we were all leaning to him. It seemed like a grounder."

"Yeah. Well, look. Get home to Les. Better not piss her off anymore than you already have."

Bobby smiled, "No, she's all right."

Frank started walking away, then called, "Hey!"

Bobby turned, and she asked if he'd ever brought the Estrellas donuts. He thought carefully then answered, "No."

"All right. Check with Nook would you? See if he took them any?"

Ever meticulous, Bobby made a note of it right there. Frank drove away, aware the donut she'd had with Claudia had long since worn off. A hole-in-the-wall off Crenshaw made incredible catfish and greens, but the place only had two tables, so Frank called in an order. She added a side of corn-bread, and coffee and bean pie for dessert.

At the tiny restaurant a large man, whose name she couldn't remember, greeted her with winking gold teeth. Black vats of oil simmered behind him and he gleamed gunmetal blue in the close kitchen. Frank poured hot sauce and salt on the greens then propped the containers open in the passenger seat. She went south on Van Ness to get back into Figueroa territory, then meandered east on 52nd. She drove slowly through the residential streets, eating with her fingers, enjoying the sweet, greasy fish and hot, sharp bite of the greens.

Even on her day off, her eye caught the three kids slinking into the alley too fast, the woman in the too-tight outfit near Tripps Market, the crackhead jerking toward a cluster of young men at the corner and their defiant perusal of all traffic. But none of that bothered her right now. With the sun warm through the window and hip-hop on the radio, she rolled through the shadows of tall palms and billboards advertising Hennesy and Alize, Virginia Slims and Camels, Whitney Houston and Ice Cube.

Strikes and tags boldly proclaimed which gang's turf she was in. Van Ness Gangsters and P Stones Jungles, Rollin' 60s and Rollin' 50s, Barrio Mojados and 38th Street. Where the boundaries met, rival names were repeatedly crossed out. Fresh names were painted over, then they too got crossed out and repainted. Frank made note of new tags and recognized old favorites. She turned onto a stretch of Denker that Placa had sprayed regularly. She didn't see anything recent, but paused at a tire yard fortified by brick walls and steel gates.

On the north wall, below the concertina wire and above a garbage-strewn lot, Placa and Toñio had painted a hauntingly beautiful memorial. Clasped black and blue hands, tattooed with three dots, prayed to a Grim Reaper rippling overhead. A weeping Madonna and Virgin of Guadalupe, skillfully robed in blue and yellow and orange, flanked the hands. The mural was circled with the names of fallen Kings. The inner ring had been completed long ago. As more kids died, their names had created a second, and then a third ring around the figures.

Sure she could have painted her way out of south-central, Bobby had barraged Placa with scholarship forms and program applications. Frank didn't know if she'd ever filled them out. Too late now, she thought, finding Placa's name flowing in blue script, a temporary tail on the outer circle. Chuey's name was painted near the beginning of the first ring and Frank wondered if Toñio's would be up there someday, and if so, who'd strike it for him?

Putting the old Honda in gear, Frank continued resolutely down Placa's unfinished canvas.

Chapter Eighteen

Later that evening, it took time for a ringing telephone to penetrate Frank's hard sleep. She rolled off the couch in the den, and jogged to the kitchen, answering, "This is Franco."

A CRASH unit had caught Ruiz taking a leak against a building just a block away from Lydia's apartment. They'd requested back up and taken him in. Frank had called Nook and Bobby and they'd met her at Figueroa. Ruiz had been waiting in the cramped interrogation room.

Nookey suggested, "Let's do good cop — bad cop. I'm little like him, so you," he nodded at Bobby, "can be the Intimidator. Besides, he might be more willing to talk to a gook than a spook."

"Well, when you put it that way," Bobby grimaced.

"Yeah. Try that," Frank agreed. Meanwhile, she banged out a warrant to impound Ruiz's T-bird. By three AM she was standing in Judge Levine's living room watching him sign it. Back at the office her detectives worked Ruiz. Nook was nice and bought him a Coke. He offered him cigarettes. He praised the Playboys and ragged on the Kings. He told Ruiz he was their prime suspect because of the car, but that if Lydia's alibi held up it would clear him. He wheedled, he cajoled, he joked. He made out like he was Ruiz' best friend. Then Bobby, three times larger than Ruiz, loomed over him, believably menacing. Nook interjected. He defended Ruiz and apologized for his partner's behavior, seeming to whisper behind Bobby's back that he was a monkey. But it was okay. The kid could trust Nook.

Frank watched all this from the small viewing window. Her boys put in a valiant effort but Ruiz wasn't buying the old "I'm your friend" routine. It was amazing how many idiots did buy the tired ruse, admitting sins mortal and venal that no one in their right mind would tell an interrogating police officer. But Ruiz was one of the cagier perps. He wouldn't open his mouth even after Nook confided that Lydia had copped to the party in Eagle Rock. For a second Ruiz had looked alarmed. Bobby had hammered him, but the boy sat with his lips clenched and fists in his lap.

After a quick briefing at 6:00, Noah followed Frank back to the window in the box.

"Does Ruiz know you?" he asked.

"I don't think so."

"Maybe you should put on the bra. Doesn't look like they're gettin' anywhere with him."

Frank stroked her chin.

"Too early. They're just getting started."

"How long's he been in there?"

Frank glanced at her watch.

"About five hours."

Frank returned to her office and made phone calls. She

organized the T-bird's removal to the print shed and instructed Johnnie to wait at the car until the police garage truck came.

By noon Nook and Bobby still hadn't cracked Ruiz. Ike had been hovering near Frank, watching his colleague's lack of progress, and she had him bring Nook out.

"I'm tired," he yawned. "This little fucker's wearing me down. I don't know why he won't tell us anything. Unless Lydia's lying about somethin' Saturday."

"Noah thought maybe I should put on the bra. What do you think?"

"Yeah, sure. What the hell. Couldn't hurt. We're not getting squat from him."

"All right. Why don't you two order some lunch. Eat in front of him. If he doesn't bend, back off."

"Got it."

Frank watched them for a moment, then headed downstairs. Planting a hip on the desk of a large, heavily made-up black woman, Frank grinned, "Donna. I need a make-over."

When she returned from the locker room, Frank's detectives jostled for space around the viewing window. She was going into the box. Cracking the door, she peered into the room.

"Oh, I'm sorry. Somebody told me Detective Taylor was in here. Have you seen him? Big tall, black guy?"

Ruiz sulked, "He was here 'bout half a hour ago."

"Oh, dear," Frank said, clearly distressed. She was wearing a Dolly Parton wig and Donna had artfully applied mascara, liner, shadow and lipstick. She'd said she couldn't help with the foundation. Frank smoothed her short skirt, absently giving Ruiz a great profile of her tight, hugely stuffed sweater. She made as if to leave, then frowned, and said, "You've been in here a while, haven't you, honey?"

"I guess," Ruiz mumbled, "Since about midnight."

"Midnight!" Frank screeched. "You poor thing! They give you anything to drink?"

"The *chino* brung me a Dr. Pepper."

"And that's all?"

"Yeah."

"Oh, you poor thing," she repeated. "You must be starving. You stay right here. I'm going to be right back."

She ducked out for a minute to low wolf-whistles and cat-calls.

"Where's the candy?"

Nookey produced two Snickers bars and a pack of M&M's with peanuts, as Frank had requested.

"Don't you guys have work to do?"

"Damn," Johnnie gloated, "this is better than the Comedy Channel."

Frank put her hand on the door knob, composing herself.

"Here we go," she said, bouncing into the box. She gave Ruiz the candy and he ripped a bar open. Frank sat on the opposite side of the table, leaning over it to show the cleavage from her taped breasts.

"I hope you like peanuts. I got candies with peanuts because I figured they had more nutrition."

Ruiz nodded and Frank shook her head, "Poor thing, look at you. You're starving. What have they got you in here for anyway?" she asked indignantly.

"I don't know," Ruiz said with his mouth full. " I din do nothin'."

"Then why don't they let you go?"

"I dunno. They think I had sumfin to do with shootin' some girl," he said through the caramel.

Frank sat back with a gasp.

"You shot a *girl*?"

"No, I din' do it, but they don' believe me."

Ruiz poured the M&Ms into his mouth and Frank pressed her fake breasts against the table.

"Well, don't you have an alibi? Why don't you just tell them where you were?"

"I can't. I was with my friends. We was kickin' it up to Dog Town."

Frank looked confused.

"You mean the pound?"

"No," Ruiz chuckled, showing brown teeth.

"That's a place up to Eagle Rock."

Feigning a daffy moment, Frank shook her head, then insisted, "Well, for heaven's sake, just tell them you were with your friends."

"I can't."

Frank cried, "Well, why not, *silly*? If you tell them that they'll let you go. They can't keep you if you have an alibi."

"I can't," he said again.

Frank reached across the table, and patted his hand.

"Honey, why not?" she implored.

"Cause I'll get 'em in trouble. We done some things," he said vaguely, "and they don't want to be talkin' to the po-lice. So I can't say nothin'."

Frank clucked, "Poor thing. I think that's very noble to defend your friends like that. They're lucky. Was that girl, the one that got . . . um . . . shot," Frank said delicately, "Was she a friend of yours?"

"No. She was from another gang."

"Oh, dear. How old was she?"

"I don't know. Maybe sixteen, seventeen."

Frank tsk-tsked, "Poor girl."

Ruiz shrugged matter-of-factly, "You claim and that shit happens. Oh. Sorry, lady."

"That's okay. I hear language like that all the time from the goons around here," she said, indicating the door.

"Goons," Ruiz grinned. "I like that."

The sugar was kicking into his empty system and he started bouncing his leg up and down. Ocho was only eighteen and Frank caught a glimpse of the little boy he once was. Continuing with her bimbo imitation, she asked, "What's claiming mean?"

"When you say who you're representin', you know, what *clica* you're with."

"Oh."

Pretending confusion she asked, "Are you a Blood or a Crip?"

Ruiz snickered, "You ain't been here long, have you, lady?"

"Why?" Frank asked innocently.

"Cause Bloods and Crips are black gangs. Mexicans don't claim with them. Well, maybe some of 'em do, but we don't."

Frank asked which gang he was in and he proudly flashed, "Fifty-first Street Playboys."

She was slowly gaining his trust and wanted to get him bragging.

"Aren't you afraid? Isn't it dangerous?"

"Naw, I ain't afraid," he boasted. "There ain't nobody scares me. They're scared a *me*," he confided.

"Why?" Frank breathed.

"See this?"

Ruiz put his hand on the table and pointed at a blue teardrop above his thumb.

"That means you don't mess with me. Cause I'll fuck you up. Sorry."

"*How*?" Frank whispered.

"However I got to. No one can be disrespecting my click. It's tough out there," he asserted. "You gotta protect what's yours. You gotta fight for everything, and protect it, even your name."

Frank nodded, open-mouthed.

"Have you ever *shot* anyone?"

Ruiz struck a casual pose.

"Maybe, maybe not. But I scare the *sokas*. They're scared a me. And my *vatos*. They know we mean business. They respect us."

Glancing over her shoulder at the door, she quickly leaned closer to Ruiz, whispering, "Have you ever *killed* anyone?"

She knew she was pushing her limit. Bragging was part of the art of establishing and maintaining status within a gang, but no self-respecting banger would ever admit to murder inside a police station. And Ruiz knew that too, shrewdly repeating, "Maybe, maybe not."

"Your friends, the ones in that gang, I mean, they wouldn't shoot that girl, would they?"

"Placa? Not unless I tol' em to."

"Told who?"

"The Playboys. My *clica*. The Kings don't mess with us," Ruiz boasted. "We mess with them."

Then he said unexpectedly, "But you know. Placa was a girl and everything, but she was down, you know? She was *carnal*."

"Carnal?"

"Yeah, you know. Down. She was all right."

Frank shook her head, and with grudging admiration, Ruiz explained Placa's unusual status.

"Wow," Frank said. "So who do *you* think killed her?"

"I don't know," he grinned, "But the *goons* think I done it."

Frank's eyes narrowed with concern, and she put her hand on Ruiz's.

"But you didn't have anything to do with that."

"Naw. I got better thin's a do then get in a war with those punk Kings. I got business to take care of. If I'da shot Placa, then my homes would be gettin' shot at and then we'd have to shoot back. It'd be stupid. Ain't no money in it."

"All right," Frank said mustering a motherly pat and a sigh. "Look, honey, I better get back to work. My boss is a goon too. Look, you're a sweet boy. Just tell the detectives you were with your friends and I'm sure they'll let you go. Now, you stay out of trouble, okay?"

She stood and deliberately tugged at her skirt. When she caught Ruiz noticing, he looked away. At the door she turned and said, "What's your name, honey?"

"Octavio Ruiz."

"That Mexican?"

He nodded and she said, "Well, you take care, Octavio. It was real nice meeting you."

Ruiz kind of waved and said, "Thanks for the candy."

Frank yanked off the wig and was pawing at her lipstick just as Foubarelle came around the corner. He stopped dead in his tracks.

"What the hell?"

Johnnie was leaving the show and he mumbled, "Frank in drag. Scariest thing you ever saw."

Frank raised an eyebrow at her detective and he snickered. She motioned for Fubar to follow into her office.

"What's going on?" he demanded.

"Just running a con on Octavio Ruiz. We brought him in late last night."

"Who's he?" the captain asked and Frank stifled a sigh. She explained that Ruiz was their prime suspect in Placa's murder, but that he wasn't talking. She'd just gotten him to offer partial confirmation of his girlfriend's alibi. It was becoming increasingly and uncomfortably possible that Ruiz might not be their man.

"Then who is?"

Behind the thick make-up, Frank's stare was cold and flat. How the man was able to command a fork to his mouth, much less an LAPD division, was still a mystery to her. "Don't know."

"Well, get on it, Frank. Not having any suspects is just unacceptable."

"You're right," she agreed, making the little man's day. He was a pompous idiot, but he was easily manipulated and Frank appreciated that in a supervisor.

"By the by, I'm officially on call this weekend, but I was wondering if you could take it for me. Something's come up that I need to attend to in Palm Springs."

Yeah, Frank thought, the Pro/Am classic.

"That'll be three in a row," Frank said.

Fubar flashed his media smile. "I know," he said unctuously. "I owe you one."

Frank made a peace sign.

"Two."

"All right," he chuckled, caught, "Two."

She let him get halfway down the hall, and said, "Oh, yeah. Something else. We got a uniform downstairs, guy named Hunt."

Frank told the captain what he'd done to Gail, and his jaw fell. Men in Fubar's circles didn't whip their dicks out in public. At least not in crowded bars with witnesses. Frank added that the doc had easily defused the situation, but someone else might think a lawsuit was more in order. She knew that would rattle the captain into action. Fear was Foubarelle's weakness and Frank plied him with it mercilessly.

She followed him downstairs, letting him rant that she'd gone over his head in initiating Hunt's CUBO. She knew if she hadn't, he wouldn't have taken action, so she contritely and happily accepted his remonstration.

In the locker room, she forgot about Foubarelle. Washing her face clean, she reflected that people liked to talk, out of conceit or for solace. They either wanted to brag or confess. Ruiz had done neither as far as Placa's murder was concerned. He had played with Frank, and was silent with the detectives. The boy was hard core and they weren't easy to break, but Frank was beginning to think that they didn't have anything to break him against.

Back upstairs, she called Northeast Division and talked with a duty sergeant. He reported Saturday had been quiet except for a shooting at a gang party and a stabbing in a liquor store. Frank asked where the party was and he told her an address that matched the one Lydia had taken them to. Frank asked him to check the logs for any arrests related to the two assaults, and while he was at it, to send her a list of any Major Incidents that occurred that night or early Sunday morning. He put her on hold, then disconnected her. She called back and was put on hold again.

While she was waiting, she wished she'd asked Ruiz how he got there. It was a considerable ride from south-central to Echo Park, and Hispanic bangers were notorious for not shitting in their own backyards. Ruiz and his homes could have done something anywhere on the route, which might be why he was holding out. Worse, it might give him a solid alibi.

Another sergeant came on the line and Frank had to re-explain what she wanted. He offered to FAX Frank the information she wanted. Said it'd be quicker that way and she groaned inwardly.

"How many you got?" she asked.

"Not that many, Lieutenant, but we're short-handed this morning and it'd save me some time."

"You're Sergeant Willis, right?"

"Yes ma'am."

"Fine, Willis. I'm standing by the FAX machine."

If Willis had any sense he'd know the LAPD was still hopelessly out-dated and that the whole station shared one FAX machine downstairs by Donna. When it wasn't out of paper it was usually out of toner. Rather than disturb the secretary again, Frank went downstairs to make sure the machine was running. On her way she stopped at the box. Her detectives looked exhausted. She knocked on the door and Bobby swung it into the hallway. She motioned him to come out.

"Anything?"

"No. We've hit him with GTA and everything. Says it's only a matter of time before he gets back in the house anyway. May as well get it over with." Rubbing his eyes, he said, "I hate these fatalistic ones. He's not giving anything up."

"Did you throw names at him?"

"Oh, yeah. I said we'd bring them all in one by one if we had to, and that somebody would tell. He just said whatever."

"I talked to Northeast. Seems like La Reina forgot to tell us someone got shot at that party. The sarge I talked to didn't know much about it, but he's faxing the log records and MIs for that time period. I'll see what we can get off that."

Bobby nodded and twirled his head around, trying to ease his stiff neck.

"What do you think?" Frank asked him.

"What you got from him backs Lydia's statement, but he won't deny or confirm," he answered, eyes closed. "How about the car?"

"SID's going to start it after lunch. I told Noah to call as soon they had anything."

Putting an ear to each wide shoulder, Bobby asked, "What do you want us to do?"

"Keep at him."

Chapter Nineteen

The squad room was dark except for a light from Frank's office. She'd spent two hours with Claudia and Gloria Estrella. Now she was updating her notes. When she was done with that she was going to compare them to Nook and Bobby's for discrepancies. Schubert tinkled from her ancient boom box and Frank paused to arch in her old wooden chair. The muscles in her shoulders complained and Frank promised herself a serious work-out when she got home.

As if she had no control over her own thoughts, they spun back to Placa and the weekend spent with Octavio Ruiz. The kid never did break. They told him two of his homes put him at a party in Eagle Rock. They'd taken blood and hair samples then kept him on his felony charges, hoping a tour in lockup might get his tongue moving.

Sunday night was spent with paperwork and then Monday morning Nook and Bobby hooked up with a senior officer from Northeast CRASH. Three Dog Town bangers tentatively put Ocho, Lydia, and half a dozen other Playboys at a party in Eagle Rock Saturday night. Northeast busted up the party after someone got shot. Apparently a Playboy shot a kid from Toonerville for drinking the last Corona. The Tooner was still in the hospital, but he was going to be okay. CRASH and Violent Crimes were still looking for the Playboy.

When Frank had confronted Lydia about the shooting, the girl pleaded ignorance, claiming she'd passed out in a lawn chair. They pulled Ruiz out of County and told him the same homes had ratted on him about the beer and the Dog Towner. Still Ruiz didn't open his mouth. By all accounts, Ruiz was getting bombed in Eagle Rock while Placa was trying to dodge bullets.

Frank fiddled with the plastic hula dancer that Noah had given her. Nothing about this case was going easily. It was after seven and here she was in the office, still banging her head against their lack of evidence when she should have been home banging on her Soloflex and getting some sleep.

Hearing unfamiliar footsteps through the music, she waited to see who they belonged to. She was surprised, and pleased, when Gail appeared in her doorway.

"Hey, doc. What are you doing here?"

"Just passing by. I thought I'd drop this off on my way home. The sergeant told me you were up here," she said offering an interdepartmental envelope.

Frank opened the flap, pulling out Luis Estrella's toxicology report.

"I knew you were anxious for the results. That mig and a half of morphine pretty much clinches the final report."

Frank scanned the bile results. Luis had a 1.7 milligram

percentage of free morphine in his system, the by-product of a heroin overdose.

Draping a leg over the edge of Frank's desk, Gail asked, "How late are you going to work?"

"Don't know," Frank answered, reading that he'd also tested positive for significant quantities of Librium and ethanol.

"Have you had dinner?" Gail pressed.

"Nope."

"Want to run by the Alibi, get a hamburger?"

Frank looked up at the ME, taking in nice slacks and a blouse, dangling gold earrings and necklace. She postponed the answer by asking, "What are you all dressed for?"

"I was in meetings with Orange County Health all day."

"Must be tired."

"Not too tired for dinner."

Frank veered off course.

"So that's it? OD plain and simple."

"I'm afraid so. What else were you looking for?"

Frank shrugged. She wanted something suspicious-looking. She was having a hard time buying that Luis' death was accidental. It was too convenient.

"How are the evidence reports coming along?"

"Slower. The spectrometer's backed up. I've got three microscopes down and Sartoris won't cut me any money for repairs. Bastard," she groused. "I'll let you know as soon as I get something."

Gail asked about dinner again.

"If I had any sense I'd go home and catch some Z's."

"Admit it," Gail teased, "you're not long on sense."

Frank's lips reached for a smile, almost made it.

"Maybe. Hey. Thanks for dropping this off. I appreciate it."

"You're welcome. I'm sorry it wasn't what you wanted. Well," Gail said rising, "if you're not going to take me up on dinner, I should let you get back to what you're doing."

The doc cocked her head, asking, "What are you listening to? It sounds familiar."

"Schubert, Trio in E flat. They used it in a movie called *The Hunger*. Did you ever see it?"

"Did I? Good God, I camped in the theatre for three weeks."

That produced a genuine smile from Frank and Gail tried one more time, "Are you sure you don't want to go out for a bite? I promise I won't keep you long."

Frank glanced at the cartons stacked next to her desk. They were full of Placa's schoolbooks, diaries, photo albums, clothing, the contents of her dresser drawers ... so much to go through and so little time. Taking advantage of Frank's hesitation, Gail coaxed, "You've got to eat sometime."

Frank took in the doc once more. She was pretty easy on the eyes tonight and Frank could use a nice view for a while. As if on cue, her stomach rumbled and Frank caved.

"What the hell. You're on."

Nancy waved at the women sliding into the booth. Gail was harping about Sartoris again, her administrative equivalent in the coroner's office.

"We just got a brand new mass spec so he thinks all of our equipment is state of the art. He accused the techs of mishandling the equipment and I said, 'Yeah, if processing test results 24 hours a day is mishandling, then yeah, we are.' God! He has no clue what goes on in the rest of that building. Crocetti used to have fits about him and now I see why."

They paused to order from Nancy and as she walked away, Gail said amiably,

"She's cute."

"And available."

"Is she an ex?"

Frank smiled, "Nope. You won't find many of those in my closet."

"Pun intended?" Gail asked.

Frank smiled, mentally hurrying Nancy along with the drinks. She was beat and knew the scotch would give her a temporary lift.

"Did you have a quiet weekend?"

"Not really. Worked most of it."

"Don't tell me you're a workaholic," Gail cringed.

"It's possible," Frank admitted. "First step to recovery's acknowledging it, though, right?"

"Did you get called in?"

"Nope. Worked mostly on Placa's case. We found our primary suspect Saturday night and worked him in the box for twenty-four hours —"

"—God, no wonder you're tired."

Frank shook her head at the table, "Nook and Bobby did the hard part. But none of what we have is adding up, which makes me think I'm going to land back at Go with no money. There are things about this case that I can't square."

"Like what?"

"Like my best suspects have valid alibis. Like why is Placa's mother so antsy every time I bring up drugs? I know they know something, but they're not talking. And the graffiti around the 'hood — it's as good as a daily newspaper. Bobby and I checked it out today. There are a couple memorials up for Placa, her brother did a really beautiful one. He's got his sister's talent with a can. Anyway, the memorials show a lot of respect, but the curious thing is that none of them are striking out a rival gang — and that's standard procedure on a memorial. The curious thing is, we're seeing strikes with LAPD struck out. Two of them are fresh ones we're pretty sure her brother did, and they both say 187 LAPD."

Frank explained that tacking the California penal code for murder onto a rival's name was a common death threat.

"So the brother's mad at the police?"

"Yeah. Like we're responsible somehow for his sister's death."

"Maybe he's just mad that you're not doing anything about it."

Frank smiled at Gail's innocence. She wasn't sure how the woman could be Chief Coroner of one of the world's most brutal cities and still be so naive.

"What?" Gail asked in response to Frank's amusement.

"Nothing. I don't think that's it," she said sitting back, so Nancy could set her drink down. "Bangers don't look to the law to solve their problems. The law *is* their problem. They'll take care of any justice or punishments in their own way."

"Street rules."

"Exactly."

"Which gives me job security."

"Both of us."

Stirring her drink with a fingertip, Gail said idly, "Maybe it's a cop."

"Maybe what's a cop?"

"The missing link. The person, persons, you're looking for."

Frank frowned, "Why would it be a cop?"

"Well, all that 187 LAPD graffiti, and the older man — what was his name?"

"Barracas?"

"Yeah, he was LAPD, right? Narco?"

"Retired."

"Still it's kind of interesting he was taken out too. And this courier business the boys supposedly ran sounds kind of flimsy. It's a perfect front for running drugs."

"Great," Frank nodded. "Now you're into LAPD bashing like the rest of the world."

"I'm not bashing anybody. It's just an idea."

"Hm. Better stick to your day job, doc."

"Whatever. You don't have to get so defensive."

"I'm not defensive," Frank clarified into her drink, "it's just hard enough to put up with the thrashing the department gets from the outside, then when my own colleagues start it gets a little tiresome."

"I'm not bashing your beloved institution," Gail argued, "but you have to admit the LAPD's hardly a bastion of ethics or morality."

"Granted, but by the same token most of its cops aren't out committing multiple homicides."

"Of course not," Gail agreed. "But you're a huge department. Rogue individuals turn up. It doesn't mean the whole institution's suspect. I'm not casting aspersions upon you personally."

"Better not be," Frank warned, as another waitress brought their dinner.

"Or?" Gail asked archly.

"Or else I won't stick around for dessert."

Stabbing at her salad Gail moped, "And now I've probably gone and pissed you off so much you won't answer my question."

"What question's that?"

"L.A. Your name. What's it stand for?"

Swallowing a huge bite of club sandwich, Frank answered, "Law And. My mother forgot the O."

"Come on. Tell me."

"Departmental secret. If I told you I'd have to kill you."

"It's something really sappy, isn't it? Like Lilith Ann or something absolutely not in character with a tough cop image. Am I right?"

"Yep. That's it," Frank agreed too easily.

"Can I call you Lily?"

"Call me whatever you like."

"Come on, tell me," Gail pleaded.

"Can't. Classified material."

Nancy came over to check on them and Frank circled a finger over the table. "Another round?"

Gail shook her head, narrowing her pretty green eyes at Frank.

"Don't think you can ply me with liquor, copper. I've got a memory like an elephant. And friends in high places."

Popping a French fry into her mouth, Frank grinned, "Good luck. It's legally L.A. Changed it years ago."

"You brat," Gail complained, and Frank was having such a good time sparring with the doc that she actually laughed.

Chapter Twenty

"Think about something, Bobby."

He and Frank were en route to the Compton PD to pick up a suspect.

"We're dealing with a family with a long history of banging. I mean, hardcore, hope-to-die OGs. It's a family tradition. These people don't scare lightly, but they're scared about something around Placa's murder. You can tell. They *know* something and they're afraid. They're not moving on this. If it was some *vato* who capped Placa, Gloria or Toñio'd be on him like stink on shit. But nothing's happened. Let's consider it's got nothing to do with a banger. Nor any sort of kickdown. Why would that scare them? That's their element. I think they're dealing with something out of their control here, something they can't or won't fight. What could that be to a bunch of OGs?"

Frank studied a clutch of women laughing outside a whipped hair salon. Bobby was quiet a long time and Frank let him drive slowly down Florence. Near a Tam's, she said, "Pull over. Want some coffee?"

"No," he said, absorbed in his quandry, engine idling. When Frank got back into the Mercury with a large cup, Bobby proudly announced, "The Eme."

The Mexican Mafia, with their long arms in the heroin trade. Frank had talked to Narco and they'd substantiated Ruiz' purported ties to the Eme, but the problem was linking Ruiz to the Estrellas. Short of Placa's involvement in her fight for his territory, there was no other link. And Ruiz' corner franchise just wasn't big enough to involve offing whole families. Much as she didn't want to, Frank was letting go of Ruiz' involvement in any of the homicides. He was a street banger, plain and simple, not an organized hit man.

What had surprised Frank was the paucity of information that Worthington, the Narco lieutenant, had provided. It was common knowledge that you could always buy smack from an Estrella, every beat cop knew that, yet Frank couldn't remember a recent drug charge on any of them. Frank had thought that odd but Worthington had written it off as not having the resources to worry about small timers who sold within the hood. While she'd been chewing on that, the dinner conversation she'd had with Gail kept whispering in her head.

She was willing to admit that the LAPD probably had more than their fair share of bad cops. That was obvious enough. And it was possible that one of them was shaking down the Estrellas. She'd reluctantly entertained the possibility, and the more she examined it, the more plausible it seemed. She still didn't like that a cop might be involved, but the more she played with the idea, the more sense it made.

"Good guess, but no. Think about the tags," she prodded. "Who's Toñio been Xing out?"

174

Bobby still hadn't driven out of Tam's little lot.

"We sitting here all day?"

He shoved the car into drive, hunching over the wheel. Finally he turned to his boss.

"You can't mean a *cop*?"

"Why not?"

"No way. No sir," he insisted adamantly.

"Just calm down for a minute. Don't get squeamish on me. Tell me how long that family's been dealing."

Bobby heaved one of his gargantuan shoulders, "Forever. So?"

"So when was the last time any one of them got busted?"

"It's been a long time," he admitted. "So you're talking about a shakedown."

"It's possible. It fits. Like Claudia claiming you brought donuts. It wasn't you or Nook. But Alicia said *some* cop brought donuts. Why? Who? Why would she say that? Why all the LAPD strikes all of a sudden? I mean there's always been *some*, but why this sudden proliferation at Toñio's hand? And it would absolutely explain why they're not talking, not retaliating, why they're afraid."

"I don't like it," Bobby maintained.

"I'm not asking you to like it; I'm asking you to consider it. Shit, I don't like it either, but this isn't lifting a bottle of Scotch or a leather jacket. It's not even lifting eight pounds of coke from a locker, man, it's murder. Wholesale murder."

"*Maybe*," Bobby corrected, as Frank always did when her men mistook supposition for fact.

"Maybe," she agreed. "That's all I'm saying. It's a possibility. And we shouldn't look the other way because we don't like what we see."

"Isn't that being kind of hypocritical?"

"What do you mean?" Frank asked carefully.

"We looked the other way on Willie Larkin."

Frank took in an iron works shop and the metal recycling center next door. They passed a body shop, then a sunroof and

175

alarm store before she answered, "That was different and you know it."

A small-time hustler, Larkin'd been working the block since he could walk. His felony charges used more ink than the editorial section of the Sunday *Times* and at nineteen he'd already danced on two murder raps. One was an old bag lady, Crazy Sadie. She only weighed 90 pounds with all her clothes on, but Larkin had strangled her because she wouldn't give up her Walkman. The second charge he'd waltzed on was the shooting of Travis Jones. Larkin and his homes were hanging out at JayZ's poolhall while eight year-old Travis pedaled slowly down the street. One of the homes bet Larkin couldn't shoot the bike out from under him and Larkin bet a bottle of Olde English that he could. He took aim with his .44 and the boy went down, shot through his femoral artery. Larkin looked around for high-fives while the kid bled to death in the street. The homes who'd bet the 40-ouncer reneged and Larkin beat the shit out of him.

Eighteen months later the owner of JayZ's called in a 240, assault in progress. Sergeant Eric Venedez was first on the scene. By the time he got there Larkin and his wrestling companion had put away their knives, but both were still in flight after pounding 40s all day, and thought Venedez looked like some fun standing there all alone.

Witnesses claimed Venedez approached the men first. Venedez said they came to him. After a short, confusing scuffle, the outcome was a DOG, Larkin's foe turned ally "dead on ground". Witnesses said Venedez shot without provocation. Venedez said Larkins's buddy pulled a gun. No one in the bar had seen him with a gun, only a knife, but backup units and Nine-three detectives found a stainless steel .38 next to him. Everyone in Figueroa knew Venedez carried a stainless steel .38 drop gun and even the boots knew why. Venedez' frequent and vociferous rationale was, "I'm not about to let twelve people who aren't even smart enough to

176

get out of jury duty second-guess what I should or shouldn't do out there. *My* ass is on the line, not theirs."

Venedez carried his luck with him that day, but Larkin left his at home with his brains. When he was patted down for his ride to the station, they found a 9mm on him, a 9mm he should have ditched the minute he saw Venedez pull his. Yet there it was, Venedez' defense riding in Larkin's waistband. Not one cop, Frank included, asked Venedez where his backup piece was. After inconclusive ballistics tests and autopsy findings came in, and not withstanding that no one in the bar had seen the dead man with a .38, Larkin went to the bing for a mandatory twenty-five.

In Larkin's case, the law was absent while justice stepped forward. Larkin killed in cold-blood; Venedez had killed in self-defense. Larkin belonged in jail; Venedez didn't. The logic was simple and Frank had succumbed to it, but not happily. Despite it's frequent and egregious errors, Frank believed in the system as a whole. Because homicide was the ultimate offense, she wasn't against bending the rules now and then to close a case. But no matter how justified Larkin's setup was, it dismayed her that she could so easily leap to the other side of the law.

"Looks like a double-standard to me," Bobby argued softly.

"Then you're looking at it wrong. Venedez is one of the best uniforms we have. He does good work out there. What happened that day was an accident, but he'd have been left twisting in the wind for it. Whoever's bumping off the Estrellas isn't doing it by accident. This is cold, it's calculated, and it's deliberate. And where's it going to stop?"

"I still think you're barking up the wrong tree," Bobby muttered.

Sipping around his braking and accelerating, Frank countered, "Maybe, Picasso. But in case you haven't noticed, we're running out of trees to bark at."

They were working south on Hoover, toward Compton.

They were obviously in Blood territory, because the project wall on Frank's right dripped, "Bompton Krip Killas" in bright red paint. Frank considered the rash of anti-LAPD graffiti in Toñio's hood.

"Just play with it for a sec. Assume for the sake of argument that we're looking for a cop. Where do we start?"

"Damn," Bobby swore his strongest oath.

"Where do you start?" Frank repeated patiently.

"I don't know. Surveillance?" her detective said reluctantly.

Frank hoisted an eyebrow.

"On *your* spare time, Nook's, or mine?"

"All right. We bug the house. Put in a camera."

"Possible, but improbable. Unless we did it illegally."

Bobby took a sideways glance at his lieutenant.

"It wouldn't be admissible anyway, so who'd know if we did it off the record."

"Off the record," Frank smirked. "You're starting to sound like a reporter. If you were shaking them down would you be going to their house all the time?"

"Risky," he conceded, his teeth sinking into the query. Frank knew once he bit down on it Bobby wouldn't let go until he'd thrashed out every possible answer. He was like a pit bull.

"Get Narco in on it," he suggested.

"What if it *is* Narco? We don't know that. We still haven't looked too closely at Barracas. I gotta get his file. Maybe he's got some sticky fingers here. And that courier service. What the hell kind of front is that? Did you subpoena his IRS records yet?"

Bobby shook his head.

"We don't get Narco on this. Too risky. Next plan?"

Bobby negotiated a maze of blocks that had once been a proud neighborhood. Now the houses were crumbling and disintegrating. Trash spilled from them, blowing from yard to yard. Cracked, uprooted sidewalks glinted with broken glass.

A weedy lot with burned furniture and bullet-pocked appliances had become the local dump.

"How about we bust a move on Claudia and her kids? Hit them with what you know. Or what you *think* you know."

"Now you sound like a cop," Frank praised. "But let's not do anything yet. In fact don't even mention it to Nook. Just think about it. Kick it around some while I run with it a little, okay?"

"You're the boss."

It was after three by the time they returned to the station. Bobby processed their suspect while Frank went upstairs to generate the avalanche of reports and forms on him. This wasn't her job as a Lieutenant, but they were so short-handed that she pitched in whenever she could. Besides, what would take her a couple hours would take the finical Detective Taylor a couple of days. Ike and Noah were still there, typing and talking on the phone. Noah grinned and flapped a big hand at her. Ike just glanced at her. She hung her linen jacket behind the door, glad there were no more meetings today.

The phone rang and she picked it up. It was Fubar whining about her write-up for the monthly newsletter. Assuring him it would be on his desk tomorrow morning, she absently poked through one of Placa's cartons. Nook had sent the clothing off to the lab. There was white powder in most of her pockets and they wanted an analysis, even though it was probably just antacid residue. Placa had stubs of Tums rolls everywhere — her pockets, drawers, backpack. That was a lot of bellyaches and Frank had been meaning to ask Claudia if Placa had an ulcer.

Foubarelle ranted about sundry things, and Frank answered in monosyllables as she went through the backpack. Two notebooks, school papers, a math and history text. A Dallas Cowboys cap. She fished out Tampax, half a pack of generic cigarettes, crumpled napkins and match books, a handful of bus schedules and tokens, six open Tums rolls.

Frank had to offer the captain more assurances before

he'd let her go, then she pawed through the litter in the bottom of the pack. Discarded wrappers, crumbled tablets and loose tobacco concealed an assortment of hollow-point bullets and an envelope of razor blades. A zippered flap held an ugly switchblade.

Frank shook the pack onto a section of newspaper without finding anything else. She wet her finger and tasted the powdery residue coating everything. Sweet. Tums. Flipping through one of Placa's notebooks, she placed a call.

"Hey sport. You get the stuff I sent you about Custard Pie?"

"Yeah, thanks."

They chatted for a minute, Frank fending off the anticipatory jabs, like Kennedy accusing Frank of calling because she missed her.

"Horribly," Frank answered, "but as long as I'm here, I was wondering if you could do me a favor."

Kennedy said something obscene and as steeled as she was, Frank was glad Kennedy wasn't there to see her face flush. Sex with Kennedy had been exhilarating and Frank wished for a moment she could accept the young woman's indecent proposal.

" 'Fraid nothing that exciting," she said levelly. "But while you're still on the desk, check out this family for me."

Frank gave Kennedy all the Estrella's names, asking her to dig up whatever she could on them. When Ike strolled into her office it gave Frank an excuse to hang up before Kennedy could launch into her customary harangue.

"Wus up, Pink?"

Running a bejeweled hand down his silk tie, he bared perfect white teeth.

"Hittin' them Estrella's hard, huh?"

"Tryin' to."

"You getting anywhere?"

Frank rocked a flat hand back and forth.

"What can I do for you?"

The dapper detective seemed to chase his thoughts around, then said, "Anthony Richards. Queenie's offering to drop him from 2nd-degree to vehicular manslaughter if he pleads guilty. And drop the kidnapping because he never intended to take the kid."

Frank thought over laced fingers. Richards had jacked a car parked in front of an AM/PM. The owner of the car had run in to buy a soda and a pack of cigarettes, leaving the car running with his 4-year old son in the car seat. Richards had shoved the boy out, but the car seat got tangled in the seat belt and never detached from the vehicle. He drove up the One-Ten at over 80 miles an hour before being stopped just south of the Coliseum. The kid was still strapped into the remains of the car seat. The DA didn't want him getting off on technicalities so she was lightening the charges to get him at all.

"I'll call her," Frank said.

"His arraignment's tomorrow," Ike warned. He was resplendent in a tailored three-piece navy pinstripe, diamonds winking, and mustache perfectly groomed to department standards. Even though he bristled each time, it was impossible for the guys to resist calling him "Gangsta".

Frank reached for the phone and it rang just as she touched it.

"Homicide. Franco."

"Hi. It's Gail."

"Hey." Frank was pleased, but didn't show it. "Hold on." She lowered the mouthpiece.

"Anything else?"

"No. Don't forget, though."

"I won't," she promised, waiting until he left before asking into the phone, "What's up?"

"Bad time to call?"

"Not at all."

"I just wanted to let you know I got Placa's tox results."

"Anything stand out?"

"Not really. At least not to me. Alcohol, lots of antacid residue, cannibinol. The usual stuff. Anyway, I've got to go. I just wanted to let you know it's here. I'll leave it with Rhondie."

"Good. I'll stop and get it on my way home."

Placa's toxicology report was incentive enough for Frank to leave the office at a reasonable time and at the Coroner's office she took the stairs two at a time.

"Hey, Rhondie," she greeted Gail's secretary. "The boss around?"

The older woman nodded toward the doc's office, saying, "I think she's busy."

"I won't bug her then. Just tell her I said thanks."

"I'll buzz her if you like, and let her know you're here."

"I don't want to interrupt."

"Hold on."

Rhondie called the doc who said on her speaker phone to send Frank in. She was bent over a computer on a wheeled stand, surrounded by a flurry of sketches and diagrams.

"Hi," Gail grinned, "Check this out."

She demonstrated a vividly animated reconstruction of a stabbing, showing exact placement of the wounds and points of entry.

"Pretty cool, huh?"

"That come with an R rating?"

"It should. Did you get your report?"

"Yeah. Thanks. Hey look, I really appreciate you getting these to me so quickly."

"Pays to know the Chief Coroner, doesn't it?"

"In spades. And I was wondering if the Chief Coroner would let me buy her dinner. The lowly homicide cop's humble way of saying thank you."

Gail glanced at the thin watch on her wrist and Frank admonished, "When are you going to get some vinyl gloves?"

"I'm hopeless," Gail shrugged. "But I'd love dinner."

Chapter Twenty-One

Across the street from the USC complex, the Marengo Grill was a modern clash of dark wood and mirrors, soulless, but functional. The waiter tried to seat them at a table in the center of the room, but Frank was uneasy with her back to the entrance. She told the waiter she wanted the empty bench seat in the corner and he obliged, efficiently taking their drink orders.

"I took your suggestion to heart," Frank said, settling a napkin onto her lap.

"Which suggestion is that?" Gail asked, doing the same thing.

"Considering that a cop might be involved in the Estrella business."

"Really?" Gail asked, surprised.

"I don't have any better leads right now," Frank allowed, "and some of the things you said made sense. I don't have a suspect but it's an interesting idea to toy with. It would explain a couple lose ends that have been bugging me."

"Like what?"

"Odds and ends."

She explained what she'd already told Bobby, adding, "There wasn't one spent shotgun shell at the Estrella's. Whoever did them picked up after himself. Or herself. I should be impartial 'til I have a fact. Anyway, you saw Luis Estrella's room. It was a pigsty."

As a junkie's habit worsened, so did his personal hygiene, and from the looks and smell of the garage room, Luis had been pretty heavily into his addiction. Frank went on to explain the incongruity of an oil-burner like Luis meticulously shooting six people and carefully picking up each ejected shell.

"Yeah," Gail agreed. "Especially after just having killed his *family*."

"And the dog," Frank added, the line having become the black joke tagged on to any mention of the Estrella body count.

"And we know Placa took five rounds, but only one casing was recovered from the scene."

"Maybe she was being shot at from inside the car."

"Not likely. It doesn't make physical sense to fire a handgun inside a car. If the shooter was in the vehicle, in all probability he had his hand out the window. So where are the other four jackets? Item: only one out of eleven cartridges was found. Item: all the Estrella's were killed with one, well-placed shot. The shooter wasn't firing in a panic or a frenzy. He was coolly, deliberately aiming for maximum effect. He was doing a premeditated job."

"The same for Placa," Gail added and Frank nodded.

"Let's say it was the same shooter. He got three of the five shots in the ten spot. That's damn good placement for a moving target. Whoever shot her's either extremely lucky or has had some serious practice with a handgun. Plus another item: the shot to the back of her head? One hundred percent fatal — you're random shooter doesn't know that. These idiots spray bullets everywhere and half of them glance off the skull bone. This guy, or gal, but I don't think so, went out of his way to place that shot. It was worth it to him to risk the extra time it took to make that shot. Why would somebody be that afraid of her? Was it somebody with a lot to lose? A reputation, a career, a family?"

Frank was drinking beer tonight and she traced a bead of condensation down the side of her Guinness bottle.

"Who knows. Anyway, this is absolutely just between you and me."

Nodding her complicity, Gail said, "See? I might not be such a bad detective after all."

"Maybe not," Frank granted.

After coffee and Armangac, they sauntered back to Gail's office, enjoying the silky night air and easy conversation. Frank waited while Gail prowled around in her purse for keys.

"Tarrah," she said holding them aloft. She caught Frank reflexively checking Gail's empty, dark car, and chided, "Always the cop."

"Should make you feel safe."

"I feel a lot of things around you," Gail admitted. "That's one of them."

Frank didn't know what to do with that and she examined the pavement at her feet.

"So what do you think?" Gail asked. "We've had a couple dinners now. How would you feel about a real date?"

"What do you mean a real date?" Frank hedged.

"A planned event. Not something accidental after work or at the Alibi."

Frank nodded, seeking refuge again in the solid ground.

"Gail," she struggled, "I really enjoy your company. I like being with you. But I'm moving through some stuff right now," Frank faltered. "Let's just say it probably wouldn't be wise of me to get into any kind of a romantic involvement."

She paused and Gail asked, "What sort of stuff?"

"Old stuff. Stuff I should have dealt with a long time ago, and that I'm just now getting around to."

"I see. So does this *stuff*," Gail stressed, "preclude something as innocent as a movie, or going for a walk together?"

"No," Frank allowed with a thin smile. "I just don't want to mislead you. I don't think I'm up for anything more significant than a fine friendship right now. And you might want more. I don't know."

Holding a grin back on her lower lip, Gail said, "I've been single all my life, Frank. I'm not asking you to marry me. I just thought it would be nice to look forward to doing something together. Would that be so awful?"

"Not at all. But I remember you saying something about being ready to settle down . . . and if you had that intention with me, it's probably not such a good idea."

"Fair enough," Gail said letting the grin loose. "So do you think you'd be up for a hike Saturday morning or would that be too involved?"

"A hike?" Frank asked like she'd never heard the word.

"Yeah, you know." Gail waved a rashed hand, "Up on the Angeles Crest or something."

"I've never been hiking," Frank answered, pulling on her chin. "Sound's like something Boy Scouts do."

"What do you mean you've never been hiking?"

"Which part of that didn't you understand?"

"How can you have never hiked?"

"Hey. I grew up in New York City," Frank insisted, "And now I live in L.A. Where am I supposed to have done all this hiking?"

"All around," Gail cried. "God, we've got some of the most beautiful country in the world right in our own back yard. We've got the Santa Monica's, the San Gabriel's, San

Gorgonio. These places are beautiful. Anza Borrego in the spring, God! I can't believe you've never been! Let me take you Saturday," Gail pleaded. "We won't do anything strenuous, just a short hike. I know a pretty little trail right outside of Altadena. What do you think?"

"Would I need hiking boots?"

The doc answered with the low chuckle that Frank found so attractive.

"No, silly. Just tennis shoes. We're not scaling Everest."

"How long would it take?"

"As long as we wanted it to. Unless you really don't want to do it. You're enthusiasm's hardly overwhelming."

Frank considered, finally relenting, "All right, Nature Girl. Show me."

"You be at my place Saturday morning at eight o'clock, and I'll show you."

"I don't need a backpack or a walking stick like those guys on the cover of "Outside"?"

"It's a two-hour hike, Frank, not a forced march across the Himalayas."

"All right," Frank smiled. "See you at the Alibi Friday?"

"Probably not. I've got to get a good night's sleep for this *arduous* trek."

"Good idea. See you Saturday then."

"Okay."

Gail opened her door, but Frank said, "Hey. Do I need pitons and rappelling ropes?"

"Yeah. For when I throw you over a cliff," Gail laughed. "Don't get too drunk Friday."

"Can't. On call again."

"Are you on call *every* weekend?"

"Nope. Just building up favors. Never know when you might need them."

~ ~ ~ ~ ~

Frank did as instructed, showing up at Gail's condo at eight AM sharp on Saturday morning. The doc drove them out to the mountains behind Pasadena and they hiked until the day got too warm. Other than mistaking every stick in the trail for a rattlesnake, Frank had a good time. It was easy being with Gail and when they got back to the condo, Frank ventured, "You got a hot date tonight or would you like to come over to my place? I'll throw some steaks on the grill, maybe rent a movie . . . you know, a planned event."

"Oh, my. Are you sure you're ready for such a big commitment?"

"Pretty sure," Frank replied. "I've got to go into town. Get some work done. How's six-thirty sound?"

"Divine. What can I bring?"

"Nothing. I got you covered."

A couple hours later, after a quick, hard run on the treadmill, then a shower, Frank started the coals for the barbeque. She didn't have to rush though, because Gail was late. Half an hour later, she added more charcoal and lowered the temperature on the potatoes in the oven. Compulsive about being on time, it tweaked Frank that the rest of the world thought six-thirty meant seven or seven-thirty. But when Gail finally arrived, her color high from the morning sun and her eyes still holding all the warmth of the day, Frank forgot her irritation. Pouring her a glass of wine, they moved out to the patio and listened to the steaks sizzle.

"I was taking my boots off after I got home," Gail was saying, "and it dawned on me that Luis Estrella's shoes still had blood in the grooves. A lot. Don't you think that most of it would have caked off after he'd been walking around in the chaparral for a while?"

"You'd think," Frank nodded. "So either he wasn't walking or he wasn't wearing those shoes."

"Well he had to have been wearing some shoes. There was

no evidence that he was barefoot. But maybe he wasn't walking in them for very long."

Frank clacked the barbecue tongs open and shut.

"Yeah," Frank mused. "Maybe the latter. I went into the canyon where they found him and had a look around. He had to have gone through some relatively thick brush to get down there. I was walking around in broad daylight, straight, and I still snagged my clothes and got scratched up. I can't imagine how he got down there in the dark, and half OD'd, without any more scratches and rips than he had. It's almost like someone carried him in. And what was he doing up there in the first place?" she mused, warming to the intrigue.

"Who knows? Maybe he was on the run. Maybe he wanted to go someplace where he could be alone, think about what he'd done."

"I can't imagine a junkie being that reflective. And I can't see him heading for the hills if he was scared. He wasn't a nature boy. He was a city kid, like me. He wouldn't run into the boonies for comfort. He'd go underground. Either in south-central or some other city where he could blend in, and not be too far from skag. He only had a couple hits on him. It doesn't make sense that he was up there unless someone *brought* him up there. Brought him up there and dumped him. That would explain his shoes, and his clothes being so unmarked. See, none of this is adding up to an accidental OD."

"Then how'd he get all that blood in his shoes unless he was there when his family was being killed?"

"Maybe he was a witness. Maybe whoever did it needed something from him and couldn't kill him right away. Maybe it was a buy that went sideways. I don't know," Frank admitted.

"Maybe we'll know more when we get the rest of the lab work back."

"Hope so," Frank said. "This is a goddamn who-done-it,

and no matter how bad the boys want to clear six names, I still don't think it's Luis."

"It's that rogue cop," Gail winked.

"I'm starting to think you're right, Detective Lawless. Let's eat."

Frank had cleared the dining room table of all its junk. They ate on linens and china arranged around the flowers Frank still brought home every Friday night. After the steaks, they lingered over tiramisu and coffee. Frank poured grappa, but after Gail's first sip she made a face and pushed the glass away.

"Yuk. It tastes like kerosene."

Frank smiled.

"Let me run some ideas by you. See what you think."

She started by explaining that buses were often the primary transportation for south-central residents, so she hadn't thought much of it when she'd pulled the bus schedules out of Placa's backpack. Then she'd been thinking about them on her way into the office that afternoon. Placa had been riding these buses all her life; where would she be going that she didn't already know routes and times?

When she'd gotten to Figueroa, Frank had pulled the four schedules out of Placa's pack again. They were worn and greasy from use. She unfolded one to see dates, times, and circled stops, in red pen, blue pen, black ink, pencil. One in green crayon. She opened the other schedules. Same thing. Frank felt like she'd found treasure maps and the first thing she'd done was make copies of them.

Drugs immediately sprang to mind; Placa must have been serving all over LA. Why else would she have been in Westwood, Brentwood, Bel Aire? Even Pasadena. All nice places, places where there was money. And maybe some cop was pimping her, finding the clients and sending Placa off to them.

Then Frank remembered Placa'd had sex with a man only

hours before she died. Maybe some cop was literally pimping her. Maybe that was why she'd come home — to change clothes from a trick. That might explain why she wasn't strapped and why she didn't tell anyone where she was going that day. Placa was smart enough to pull it off, ambitious enough too. She wanted to go to college. Maybe this was her tuition. But they hadn't found any clothes that would support the theory. Frank couldn't see Placa tricking, and certainly not for chump change. She'd make them pay and Frank doubted there was a big market for men aroused by girls in shapeless T-shirts and baggies.

Gail had been listening carefully, but now she interrupted.

"Well, I'm not a detective, but I *am* a doctor. Let me shoot some holes in that story before you go any further."

Bending a finger for each point, Gail said, "She appeared to be reproductively able, but she wasn't using an obvious form of birth control. There was no abortion scarring, no sign of STDs. No apparent vaginal or anal traumas. Unless she just started turning tricks yesterday, I'd expect to see some evidence that she was promiscuous, and there is none."

The doc was right. Given the age of the bus schedules, Placa had been at this for quite a while.

"All right, so here's another idea. Let's say she was pimping Ocho's girl."

"That's disgusting," Gail shuddered, and Frank was thrown off track, charmed once again by the ME's naiveté.

"Happens all the time," Frank continued. "Women don't have a lot of options, or protection in the 'hood. Drugs, religion, children, death. That's about it. And Placa was too smart for any of that. So let's say she wouldn't hook herself, but how about she gets Lydia on her side? Like I said, not a lot of options in the 'hood. Placa was a ghetto star, maybe burning brighter than Ruiz, I don't know. Gang girls try and hook their wagons to whichever star's rising. They don't want to crash and burn when their men do."

Trying to hide a yawn, Gail said, "You're saying Lydia hitched her wagon to Placa's star? Don't you think that's a little implausible?"

"Not really. Placa was a charmer when she wanted to be. And smart. Throw in a hope-to-die OG and I can see her getting a huge kick out of pimping her rival's girlfriend. I can see her laughing now."

"What would be in it for Lydia?"

"Protection, money, maybe affection. I don't think Placa would have tattooed Lydia's name under her twat unless she cared about her."

Gail grimaced at the rough noun and Frank said, "Sorry."

"Why would Placa have sperm on her if Lydia was the hooker?"

"Good point," Frank said swirling the clear brandy. None of this speculation tied in to the shooter being a cop, but Frank played with the ideas anyway. It was mental gamesmanship and Frank enjoyed toying with even the weakest of leads; playing with ideas either strengthened or eliminated them. Despite the obvious weaknesses, she didn't want to overlook any possibilities. She'd already done that when she'd assumed Ruiz was the shooter and that had put the case back to square one. And while the idea of a cop's involvement was intriguing, it was also disturbing. There'd be hell itself to pay if a cop was the shooter. Before committing herself to that disquieting tack, Frank wanted to make damn sure she'd exhausted every other option, no matter how ridiculous it might seem.

"Maybe Placa wasn't above cutting off a slice now and then."

"Do you ever hear yourself?" Gail asked in amazement.

"What?"

"The way you talk. You sound like some of those wife-beaters."

"Sorry. Guess I'm not known for my sensitivity."

"I guess not. You're so cold-blooded sometimes."

"Comes with the territory. Murder's a pretty cold-blooded business."

Balancing her hands like full scales, Gail said, "The tender Frank, the brutal Frank. The warm Frank, the frosty Frank. Sometimes it's difficult to reconcile your two personalities."

Frank joked, "You should try living with them."

"Hey, I'm sorry. I know what you put up with every day. I see the results of it on my tables. I know you have to find a way to deal with that, but I hate to see your finer qualities subsumed by the heartlessness of your work."

Gail paused, seeing a grin start on Frank's face. "What?"

"Nothing. That just sounded so . . . Shakespearean."

"Well see? You talk like a wife-beater and I talk like a British Lit professor. Maybe brutal's better."

"No," Frank corrected, "I love the way you talk. It's like listening to Mah-stuh-piece Thee-uh-tuh."

Gail laughed, and Frank felt uncharacteristically self-conscious under the doc's scrutiny.

"Can I ask you something?"

"Already told you what L.A. stands for."

"I know," Gail smiled. "I was thinking of something else."

"Shoot."

"The stuff you said you were working through. Can I ask what it is or would I be prying?"

Playing with her snifter, Frank considered, then said, "You'd be prying. And I can tell you. Be good for me. Make my shrink proud."

Gail's brow crunched in disbelief.

"You have a *shrink*?"

"Richard Clay. At Behavioral Sciences. They're mostly a bunch of quacks over there, but Clay's a good guy. I've worked with him, and I had to see somebody after I shot Timothy Johnston. He's all right."

It was amazingly easy to tell Gail about Maggie and how she died, then about Kennedy and Delamore, and how she was finally dealing with the whole literally bloody mess.

"Impressive," Gail said when Frank was finished.

"How so?" Frank asked, draining the last of her grappa.

"There's a lot more substance to you than I originally thought."

Frank smiled, "More than just a wife-beater, huh?"

Gail returned the smile, her eyes lingering on Frank's. Looking away, Frank said, "I saw you hiding a yawn a while ago. Maybe we should call it a day."

"Probably," Gail said. Frank cleared the dessert plates and Gail helped. When she started rinsing the dishes in the sink Frank stopped her.

"Leave 'em. I'll get 'em tomorrow."

"Wow. You cook *and* do dishes. Are you sure you don't want a girlfriend?"

"Pretty sure. But if I change my mind, you'll be the first one to know."

"Promise?"

"Absolutely," Frank assured, walking Gail to the door.

"Thanks for dinner. It was wonderful. And I had a great time today."

"Me too. Maybe we can do it again."

"Really? Even the hegira?" Gail chuckled, and Frank thought, *damn*, that's the sexiest sound.

"See?" Frank pointed out. "There you go again."

"There I go what again?"

"Hegira. I've never heard anybody use that word in conversation."

Gail laughed and Frank made sure the doc drove away safely. For a long time she stayed under the red Pasadena sky, searching the darkness where Gail had turned the corner. When she finally went back into her house, she whispered as if trying to convince herself, "Pretty sure."

Chapter Twenty-two

Frank hated Mondays. Not because she was going back to work, but because meetings ate up the day; press meetings, the lieutenants meeting, community building meetings, district attorney meetings — meetings ad nauseum. She didn't catch Nook and Bobby until quitting time. Flapping the bus schedules in front of them, she asked what they thought.

"Busy girl," Nook said.

"Busy doing what?" Bobby said, taking the words straight out of Frank's mouth. She loved watching her detectives chew on a problem, and she sat back, letting them run with it. Slanging was their first thought too and they kicked it around, deciding it was a family thing. Their points were that Claudia, Gloria, and Chuey had all had possession with intent to distribute charges. They weren't rolling in dough but were obviously living better than they could on AFDC and food stamps. Claudia probably handled the business end and the kids had done the running. Claudia's offhand remarks about dealing here and there belied a sensitivity to the issue. It was likely there was someone else involved, someone bigger than Claudia who could put the screws to her, maybe even cap her family when necessary.

The cops felt like they were getting part of the picture but not the whole screen. Frank considered asking Nook's opinion on the shakedown theory, but kept quiet, still wanting to flesh it out more. It was a serious charge, and not one that Nook or anyone else in the department would take lightly.

When she asked if they thought Placa could have been hooking, Bobby stared at her deadpan. His partner snickered, "That girl had her hustle on, but not like that."

"I don't know," Frank said, stretching her arms over her head, "I think it might be worth nailing down."

"Yeah, well, Les and I've got a doctor's appointment at 3:30 . . ."

"I'll take care of it," Frank said. "It's a silly idea, but if I can find Lydia I'll run it by her. See if I can't pin her down some more about the dope."

"I'd go with you," Nook said, "but I've got an appointment too."

"Yeah, with your Lazy-boy."

"I'm not young like you two," he balked. "Time for the old dogs to move over and let you pups have a try."

Frank baited, "Don't tell me you're retiring, Nook."

He hissed at the "r" word, mumbling retirement was for losers. His old partner had retired in January and that was when Nook had put in for transfer. He was right. Homicide at Figueroa wasn't for old dogs. Frank usually worked at least a twelve-hour day. When they rolled on a fresh case, 24, 36, even 48-hour days weren't uncommon. The job was physically, emotionally, and intellectually demanding. Joe Girardi had called homicide the decathlon of police work, and Figueroa the Olympic arena.

After they left, Frank reveled in the silence that enabled her best work. She stopped for a moment when she heard footsteps shuffle and click in the squad room. Ike was the determined click and Diego was the Vibram-soled shuffle. Frank went out to tell Ike that McQueen wouldn't budge on her charges.

"Whatever. I did my part."

"That's all you can do you," Frank commiserated. It was hard enough finding the bad guys, but then when the district attorney's office let them go with a slap on the hand it felt like fighting a losing battle.

"How's it going?" she asked Diego

"Okay," he answered, filling Frank in on their day. When he was done, she said to Ike, "Aren't you late for the track?"

"That's were I'm headed."

Every afternoon he could be found at Hollywood Park, putting money on the last races of the day.

"Damn, Pinkie, I don't know. Peep you, dipped like a baller, got your bling on . . . those ponies must be ridin' bank to you."

Ike's mouth turned down. He was no Rhodes scholar but he hated street slang. All you had to do to send him into a fit was say "ebonics."

"Yeah," Diego grinned, slipping Frank some skin, "Gi' my dawg mad props. He be da illest one-time hoedin' it down fo' da Nine-Tray."

"Assholes," Ike grumbled, straightening his tie. He was the only detective Frank knew who *tightened* his tie after work.

"Gang-stuh," Diego kidded, watching his partner preen. Frank unperched from the desk, saying goodnight. She was tired of being inside all day and figured she'd try to find Lydia or Toñio. Driving north from the station, she absorbed the surrounding graffiti and street action. The ratty section of Hoover Street that she was on was probably how most people envisioned south-central. Neglected houses pocked with bullet holes and defaced by taggers served as shooting galleries and rock houses. Empty windows yawned behind the black teeth of iron bars. Dirt yards fronting the street were strewn with garbage, rusted engine parts and busted furniture. Banana trees and bougainvillea struggled in the impacted soil, creating the look of an impoverished banana republic plunked down in the middle of one of the wealthiest cities in the world.

The Estrella's street was neater and cleaner. Frank noticed their tired Buick wasn't in the driveway and was pleased when Toñio opened the door.

"Hey. *Quivo?*"

"My mom's not here," he answered through the steel mesh.

"That's okay," Frank answered easily, "How 'bout your sister?"

"She ain't here either."

Frank asked where they were. Toñio said he didn't know, they'd been gone when he got home."

"Where you been today?"

"You know. School."

"This the one day a week you go?"

"Huh?"

"Nothin'," Frank grinned, picking up the stink of stale malt liquor. "You look like you been hangin' out. Smokin' some Phillies, crackin' some Eights."

"I wun doin' that."

"Hey. I ain't your PO. I don't care if you're flying all day long. Looks like I woke you up."

"Yeah."

"What you so tired from?"

Toñio pitched a thin shoulder. A crude Virgin of Guadalupe was tattooed on his bicep. On his left arm he wore the same gang insignia his sisters had, and on the right he had KV2. He was wearing boxer shorts and a dingy tank-T. Frank noticed a faint blue mist on the shirt. She glanced at his index fingers, finding more of the tell-tale blue, the King's favorite color.

"Been out strikin'?"

He flicked his shoulder again.

"You do that one at the PikRite? It's pretty good."

"Nah, that was Tiny. He's way better'n me."

"I don't know. There's some pretty nice tags out there for your sister. I know you done some of 'em. You do that one on Denker? That big one? It's pretty good."

The boy sheepishly scratched his belly, confiding that Placa had done most of the mural.

"You should be in art school or something, I mean, I can't even sketch a crime scene. Where'd you learn to do that?"

"Don't know," he answered, bashful all of a sudden.

"Placa teach you how to make those curvy letters?"

"Yeah, she taught me some."

"She was pretty good, huh?"

He agreed and Frank said, "Tell me, how you get them so high? You carry a ladder around or something?"

The boy guffawed and Frank grinned, "Is that how you do it?"

Frank was trying to build Toñio's confidence, his trust.

"No way," he snorted. "You gotta make somethin' to step on, you know. You stick screwdrivers into the cracks. Or branches off trees. You can step on 'em."

"Man, that's dangerous."

The kid shrugged dismissively, "You gotta be careful. But I don't weigh so much. Some of these guys, they can't do it, you know? They're too big."

"Do you ever fall?" Frank asked, seemingly in awe.

Twisting his back, he pointed proudly to a large, bruised scrape.

"I did that last week, doin' the one on 58th Street."

Bingo, Frank thought. Toñio had done the hard part for her.

"Oh yeah, I know the one you're talking about. That's a good one too. But why you'd strike out the LAPD?"

Toñio's enthusiasm was quickly replaced with sullen wariness. He just stared at the porch floor.

"Is it me? 'Cause I'm hanging around so much? Is that it?"

When he didn't respond, Frank sighed loudly, and hung her head too.

"I'm just trying to figure out who did this to your sister. I want the *maricon* did this caught and put in the 'Dad for a long time. And I hope he's real pretty and that all the guys like him. A lot."

Frank dropped her voice, appealing to Toñio's Latino pride.

"I know you know who did it. I can't blame your mom and Gloria for not talking. They're women. They're scared. I understand that. But you're different. You're a man. You're not a coward. You're not a little boy anymore either, even though your mama tries to protect you. I respect you, Toñio. And I respected your sister. She had a heart like a man."

In the barrio, where masculinity and strength were admired above all else, that was high praise. Toñio was still staring down. His features were fine and sharp, offering no hiding place for his distress.

"She called me a couple days before she died, wanted to meet with me. Said she had something to tell me. It must have been hard for her to call. I could tell from her voice that she was scared. But she did it anyway. She didn't give in to her fear, she didn't let it beat her. Whatever Placa was afraid of, she was facing it like a man. Are you? Would she be proud of you, Toñio? Are you respecting her memory?"

She gave him time to consider, then gently slipped her card into the door frame.

"Keep that. You're Placa's baby brother, but I think you're just as brave. Tell your mom and Gloria I said hello."

Next, she cruised southeast, into 51st Playboy territory, keeping an eye out for Lydia. The girl didn't have a phone so Frank couldn't call her, but wouldn't have anyway; announcing her visits gave people time to think of answers or disappear. There was no reply when Frank knocked on Lydia's door. A thick, older woman taking out garbage, eyed Frank suspiciously, then said, "The tramp ain't home. I seen her go out about lunchtime."

She wheezed on a cigarette and Frank asked if Lydia had left alone.

The woman hacked up a lung, adding, "She was with those hoodlum friends of hers. They're none of 'em no good. Robbin' old ladies and children."

She spit in the hallway, narrowly missing Frank's expensive loafers.

"I seen you here before," she said, taking in the ID clip and badge on Frank's belt. "What did she do?"

"Afraid I can't tell you that," Frank played up, "But let's just say it ain't good."

The old lady nodded, snorting, "That don't surprise me."

Frank returned the nod, adding, "Yeah. And I'll bet you've seen a lot."

"Oh!" the old lady coughed, flourishing a chubby hand, "I could write a book."

"You ever see her with a real tough looking girl? Got her gang tattooed on her forehead, a devil on her arm?"

The old lady was nodding before Frank even finished.

"You ever see them go out together?"

"No, I only seen that other one going into her apartment. *That* girl was trouble."

"How do you mean?"

"Well, just look at her!" she sputtered. "That girl couldn'a been up to no good. Uh-uh."

Then she went into the diatribe Frank knew by heart. How this used to be a nice place to live until the gangs started taking over and why didn't the police do anything about them? Always disposed to recruiting snoopy neighbors, Frank sympathized for about two minutes before taking a firm but graceful exit. She tried a few more places where she thought she might find Lydia, then tried the apartment again. Frank's luck was good because Lydia was just slipping the key into her lock.

"Hey."

Lydia jumped. She relaxed slightly when she saw it was just Frank, but didn't finish opening her door.

"Got a couple questions for you. Want me to ask out here or some place private?"

Lydia grumpily clicked the lock, allowing Frank into a dime-sized but tidy apartment.

"How you afford this?"

"Ocho pays for it."

"Damn. He pays for the place where you're knockin' boots with an off-brand. You got some nerve," Frank praised. "Let me ask you something personal. Did you and Placa ever do business together?"

"What do you mean," Lydia asked, her dark eyes narrowing to slits.

"You know, like hustlin', going somewhere to do business outside the 'hood?"

Lydia cracked her gum, eyeing Frank with obvious disdain. She made a grunting sound, "You mean like those low-class *putas* that hang out on the corner?"

"No, not like those skanks. I mean real nice, high-class work. None of that strawberry shit."

"We don't gotta do that," she said, her disgust becoming disbelief. "Why you askin' that for?"

"It's just something I heard. I just-"

"Who you heard that from?" Lydia cried. "I'll lay that

fuckin' *chingona* out on the sidewalk. Who tolt you that? Don't nobody know *nothin'* about me and Placa."

Lydia's indignation was real, and Frank calmed her, lying, "Hey, it's no big, just some trash I heard from a kid in lockup. Did you ever meet her anywhere outside of here? You know, where no one would see you together?"

"People can see you anywhere," Lydia said angrily. "I tolt you, we hooked up here."

"Nowhere else?"

"No."

"What happened when you two saw each other on the street?"

"We'd flash each other. We'd dis each other, but not too much. We didn't want to start no trouble."

Frank nodded, "Tell me again about the drugs. Did she ever tell you who she sold to, or where? Anything like that?"

"I already tolt you that too," Lydia explained.

"I know. I'm stupid. Tell me again," and she did so, exaggeratedly patient, like Frank was a slow child. Frank again asked where Placa was going when she left her that last day. Lydia again said she didn't know.

"She did that sometimes. Just said she had to go somewhere. She'd get real sad and mad like. I asked her once or twice but she never tolt me. Said she couldn't, so stop askin'."

Lydia was wistful when she added, "She was different like that. Cholos always be talkin' about what they done and what bad-asses they are, but me and Placa, we din' talk about where we been or where we are. We liked talking about where we wanted to be."

"You knew she wanted to go to college, right?"

Lydia's animosity softened, "Yeah, that was her dream. She used to say she had to get out of here. She said she'd take me with her when she left and that we'd leave this *vida loca* foolishness. One time," Lydia smiled behind her hand, "she said she wanted to be a cop and come back and arrest all the P51s."

"What was your dream?" Frank asked.

"To go with her," Lydia whispered.

"All right," Frank said, feeling a pang of tenderness. "You be careful out there. Don't make me have to be asking questions about *you* someday."

"I can take care of myself," Lydia huffed.

"Yeah, I know. That's what Placa used to say."

Chapter Twenty-three

Frank had been determined to get to the Estrella's, but the 93rd pulled a new case before briefing was even over — a Korean store owner beat to death at dawn while rolling up his metal storm door. Tensions between black and Korean communities ran high in south-central. The blacks accused the Koreans of sabotaging their neighborhoods by operating liquor stores on every corner. The Koreans said they had every right to run a business where there was opportunity. Frank had called Fubar before they even rolled and he arrived as the coroner techs were loading the vics body.

The brass knew crime scenes were off-limits even to them, yet they consistently ignored the yellow police tape.

Foubarelle stepped under it and Frank was grateful he hadn't arrived earlier to fuck up the evidence collection.

"What have you got?" he asked, his chest puffed like a fighting cock.

Frank indicated three separate people talking to detectives. Smoothly guiding her supervisor back under the tape, she said, "We actually have wits to this one. The old man was walking up the street. Saw a tall, muscular, black male, shaved head. He was arguing with the owner. He thinks the suspect's name is Luther Moore. Everybody calls him Mr. Em. Styles himself a Muslim but the old man says he's a bum. He got a little closer and he heard this Em saying he just wanted a pack of cigarettes. The vic, name's Ruk, he owned the store, but he wouldn't open up. Old man says Em kept arguing. Says Ruk seemed frightened and was trying to get into the store but Em was in his face. Em grabbed the vic by the arm and slammed him against the building. Then he picked up a garbage can," Foubarelle frowned at the garbage still coating the sidewalk, "and threw it at Ruk. Ruk went down, then Em picks up the can again and starts beating the vic with it. That's what the other two described too."

"Shit," Foubarelle said. "It *had* to be an African-American."

Frank smiled, knowing he was worried about the reporters pacing the area, cat-calling questions at him.

"Have fun," she offered, but he grabbed her sleeve.

"Do we have any idea where this Mr. Em is?"

"Nope. Old man thinks he lives a couple blocks south. Might be an Eleven-Deuce Crip."

That was LASD jurisdiction and Frank confirmed their notification. Inglewood and Watts PD, along with Southeast Division, had an APB too. Noah walked by, clucking, "And they say smoking's not addictive."

Frank put her whole squad on Ruk. They spent the next twenty-four hours searching for Luther Moore, amid howlings of the media, black and Korean business and community directors, deputy chiefs, the Chief, even the mayor. Frank could see them all churning this into another riot and pressed her crew mercilessly.

At approximately two o'clock the following afternoon, Southeast got a complaint from a woman who said there was a man sleeping in her garage. The responding officers found Luther Moore curled up in an Impala on blocks, snoring loud enough to scare Christ away.

Frank called Gail from the Alibi's payphone, exhausted, but exhilarated that their suspect was in lock-up.

"Been a long week," Frank said. "I'm glad it's Friday. We gonna see you tonight?"

"I don't think so. I've had a long week too."

"Look," Frank yelled, a finger in her other ear. "I've got an idea, if you're not busy tomorrow."

"I should chain myself to my desk until I can see the top of it again," Gail sighed. "But I'm sure your idea's better. What is it?"

"It's a surprise. I think you'll like it."

"Another *hegira*?" Gail teased, making Frank smile.

"Not what I intended. Just be ready for me to pick you up at nine AM."

"Where are we going?" Gail asked.

"If I told you it wouldn't be a surprise. Just wear something comfortable and plan on being gone all day. Can you do that?"

"I think I can handle it," then, "What are you up to?"

"Just trust me. Go home. Get some sleep. I'll see you tomorrow. Okay?"

"Okay," Gail said fondly, then threw in, "You're a nut."

"Yeah. See you in the morning."

Frank returned to the nine-three table, vaguely amused with herself, and eager to contribute her share of damage to the fast-emptying pitchers.

~ ~ ~ ~ ~

When Gail opened the door to her apartment, Frank announced, "I've got lattes and croissants waiting in the car."

"Let me get my purse."

She checked Gail's clothing while she waited. Nice jeans, scoop neck T-shirt, green like her eyes. The color reminded her of the way sun came dappled through the tall oaks on her street. Funky earrings, the gold knife and scissors Gail liked.

"Do I get to know where we're going yet?"

"Nope. Get a jacket or a sweater and let's go."

Frank angled toward the 101 Freeway while Gail described the week from hell. They drove further and further west until Gail finally whined, "Where are we *going*?"

"All right," Frank relented, pleased to see the city behind her in the rearview mirror. "Good morning lady, sans gentleman. Thank you for choosing Air Frank today. We know you have many other options and are pleased you've chosen us for your travel needs. The weather for our flight today is beautiful, highs in the low eighties, wind 10-15 miles off shore."

Gail tilted her head back, laughing. Her neck was smooth and creamy white, and Frank suddenly wondered what it would be like to kiss her there. The thought surprised her but she squelched it, continuing her patter.

"We'll be cruising at an altitude of approximately 40 miles above sea level at a speed of 65 miles per hour. During our flight, you'll be able to see the Pacific Ocean on your left and the San Gabriel Mountains on your right. Approximate travel time is 45 minutes, and we hope you'll enjoy your flight to Santa Barbara. If you have any problems or questions please feel free to contact the hostess. And again, thank you for choosing Air Frank. Click."

"Santa Barbara?" Gail asked happily.

"Yeah. I thought it'd be fun to get away for a while. You ever been to the botanical garden?"

Gail shook her head, and Frank said, "They're supposed to be incredible this time of year. You said you wished you had a garden and this is one helluva garden. We'll do that first, then have lunch at Citronell. Exquisite food at exhorbitant prices but well worth it. After that, maybe walk off a few pounds on the beach, or check out the antique stores. You like antiques, right?"

Gail nodded, "You've got a good memory."

"Helps in my line of work. So we'll do that. Maybe grab a drink somewhere then head for home while the sun's setting. How's that sound?"

"You really want to know?"

"Yeah."

"It sounds very romantic. Was that your intention?"

"No-o," Frank said slowly, "I just wanted to get away for a while. Been a rough week. Thought it'd be nice to turn our pagers off and get the hell out of Dodge."

"It's *very* nice and you're sweet to think of it."

"All right then. Just sit back and relax. If you still remember how to do that."

"I do, but I'll bet *you* don't."

"Ah-h, I might surprise you."

"You seem to keep doing that," Gail observed.

Walking through the Santa Barbara Botanic Garden in spring was like walking through a museum of uncased jewels. Gail zig-zagged from flower to flower, while Frank watched indulgently, charmed by the doc's simple and obvious pleasure. Later they ate appetizers and salad for lunch, with an outrageously good bottle of wine, then puttered through the antique stores downtown. Frank people-watched while Gail hunted unsuccessfully for deals.

With the sun heavy to the west, they started the drive back, bogged down in the weekend traffic. Frank fiddled with the radio, pausing on what sounded like the mournful opening to *Tristan and Isolde*.

"You like opera?" Gail asked, snuggling against the door

"Kind of. I don't know much about it. Maggie used to listen to it all the time and I got used to her favorites. They're about all I know."

"We should go sometime," Gail said, closing her eyes.

"Wine catching up to you?"

She nodded with a sleepy smile. Frank reached across Gail and locked her door. "Always the cop," Gail murmured.

Frank was trying to decipher the colorful strike on the truck next to her, when Gail jerked up, exclaiming, "Oh, shit!"

Snagging her big purse from behind the seat, she pulled out a large envelope and offered it to Frank.

"I forgot. It's Luis Estrella's lab results."

"You've been carrying that around all day?"

"Well, I figured if I put it in my purse I'd see it and remember to give it to you but you haven't let me pay for anything."

"Shit," Frank muttered, tearing open the envelope, "That'll teach me to be generous. How'd you get these so quick?"

"Do you know Suzie? In the lab?"

"She that chunky little butch with the glasses?"

"She's a little crusty," Gail admitted, "but she's a sweetie."

"Probably got a crush on you."

"I doubt it. She's got three grandkids and a husband who just retired. I told her I'd take her out to lunch if she could get that to me ASAP."

"Must want to have lunch with you pretty bad," Frank maintained.

"Oh, stop," Gail said, taking a swat at Frank, who was already scanning the material. Interestingly, there was no blood on his pants, but the blood on Estrella's sweatshirt matched samples from the rest of his murdered family, as did the samples from his shoes. A wad of old gum had trapped some fibers. Brown and tan polyesters that appeared to be automotive textiles, then an odd fiber. A horse hair. The soles also contained minute traces of what appeared to be alfalfa, oats, and horse manure.

That made Frank's forehead crease. The Sentra behind her honked and Frank eased up to the bumper in front of her.

No blowback on his hands. Odd. After having just shot that many people, at that close a range, Luis should have had blood and flesh spatter on his hands. But there was none. No gunshot residue either. Frank grabbed a pen and wrote "gloves?" But that didn't make sense. Luis lived at the homicide scene. His prints were all over. Why would he bother to put on gloves?

She read more. Bits of organic debris shaken from his clothing were consistent with his location in the canyon. A man tripping around in the dark would have certainly put his hands out to brace himself, but there was no mention of organic debris in the nail scrapes. There were also more alfalfa, oat and horse manure traces. Was he in a barn somewhere? A stable? *Why?* Frank wondered.

The lab found the same brown automobile fibers in all his clothing and in his hair. Frank remembered the interior of Luis' car was brown. There were other fibers as well — navy, gray, and black wool. Clothing fiber. A couple others turned out to be more horse hairs.

"Jesus," Frank breathed, her mind speeding with the sudden possibilities. She glanced at Gail dozing with her mouth slightly open. Frank was glad the doc wasn't awake to see the notes she was scribbling on the back of the report.

Chapter Twenty-four

Frank paced around the dining room table in shorts and a T-shirt. A couple empties stood upside down in the sink and she scowled when the phone rang. Fubar was on call and she hoped it wasn't him. When he caught something he often asked Frank to "help". And she had to admit, she'd spoiled him because she usually did; it was easier to take the case from the beginning than clean up his mess later.

"Franco," she answered.

"Hi. It's Gail. I didn't wake you up, did I?"

"Nope. I was just sitting here thinking about Luis Estrella's lab results."

"Well, Santa's heard you've been a good girl and he wants to give you an early Christmas present. Is it too late to drop it off?"

"Damn. Santa's working overtime," Frank smiled into the phone. "Come on over."

When Gail arrived, Frank got her a beer, asking what she was doing out so late.

"It's Tuesday," Gail made a face. "Rounds until ten. Here. Before I forget and you yell at me again," she said, handing Frank another envelope.

"I didn't yell at you," Frank objected.

"Yes, you did," Gail sulked. "And here I was just trying to be nice. I'm wondering if Santa got his information mixed up about you."

Frank grinned, "Who's the one that took you to Santa Barbara and bought you that great lunch?"

"Well, that's true."

Frank fished out lab results for a beating death the nine-three caught had caught a couple weeks ago.

"I like this personal service," she noted, scanning the data. Gail was propped against the table sipping her Corona.

"How'd you get that scar?" she asked, giving Frank's knee a nod.

"Old football injury," Frank murmured.

"I'm serious."

"So am I. I was playing with my cousins and I fell on a broken bottle."

"Ouch. How about that one?" she asked, leaning to swipe a finger over a jagged line on Frank's forearm.

"That one . . ." Frank said, trying to analyze a 2x4 pattern on the victim's cheek, "came from a chain link fence. I was chasing a punk and when I hit the fence I impaled myself on a busted link, I didn't realize it, so I ripped half my arm off when I went over."

"How many stitches?"

"I don't remember."

"Do they bother you?"

"No. Can't feel a thing. They were both a long time ago."

"No, I meant aesthetically."

"Nah. Scars are like wrinkles; they're war wounds. I've earned every one of 'em."

"That's a good attitude."

Frank didn't look up when Gail volunteered, "I've got a scar."

"Oh, yeah?"

"Yeah. A mastectomy," the doc said without a missing a beat. Frank lowered the report. She looked for a joke in Gail's face but didn't see it.

"Full or partial?"

"Full. My entire left breast."

"When?"

"A little over two and a half years ago."

"Been clean since?"

"Knock on wood," Gail answered, rapping on the envelope.

"You can't tell," Frank said.

The doc flashed a quick grin.

"I'm flattered you've looked."

There was a weighted silence, in which Frank wasn't sure what to say. Gail finally admitted, "I don't know why I told you. I've never told anyone outside my immediate family. I guess it's good to practice on a friend."

"I'm glad you did."

"Yeah," Gail said, "now you know better than to date me."

"Think it makes you any less attractive?"

"I've rationalized in my head that it doesn't, but on the other hand I haven't had a date in two and a half years, so go figure. Anyway, I like what you said about a scar being a badge of honor."

"Wear it proudly. Not every one gets the chance to."

"You're right," Gail said, setting her beer down. "You have such a healthy perspective sometimes."

Rolling her eyes, Frank said, "Tell Clay that."

"It's getting kind of late," Gail said shoving off from the table. "I've got to go in early and prep for testimony."

"I won't keep you," Frank stood. "You shouldn't have come out of your way."

"I don't consider you out of the way," Gail tossed off, then suddenly she wheeled.

"Hey! Now this isn't fair. Here I've gone and shared my deepest, most intimate secret with you and I *still* don't even know your first name!"

"Ahhh," Frank said, "Tit for tat, so to speak?"

"You're terrible," Gail laughed, that sexy chuckle.

"This my price for such incredible personalized service from the coroner's office?"

Gail held her palm out.

"Pay up, sister."

"Okay," Frank gave in. "Here goes. You have to understand that my mother was always into fads and cults. Whatever the latest trend was, she was into it. Rebirthing, Zen, EST, Christian Science — you name it, she tried it. My dad used to call it her faith-of-the-month club, and when she was carrying me, she was into Wicca. Thought she was a witch or something. It was pretty harmless. I mean, I don't remember her sacrificing goats in the living room or anything. Anyway, she got this idea in her head that a really great name, one that would confer a lot of power for a little girl, would be — are you ready?"

Gail nodded eagerly and Frank enunciated, "Lu-ci-fe-ra An-ge-li-na."

"No-oo," Gail breathed.

"Yep. My dad had a fit. Tore up the birth certificate. Told

my mother to give me a decent name. But she never did. That was the name she wanted. Even after the Wicca stuff faded. She was the only one who ever called me that."

"Thank God," Gail said, repeating the name. "What a mouthful. Was your dad as trippy as your mom?"

They'd walked outside to Gail's car and Frank's soft smile was almost concealed by the modest city darkness.

"No. He was a rock. My mother was out there, but my dad held it all together. I think he wanted a boy, but he made do with me. Sometimes on Saturdays he'd take me on his route. He delivered bread, and sometimes we'd stop at a hotdog stand for lunch. He took me to Giants games when he could afford them. Took me with him to the bar almost every night. I'd sit next to him, drinking a Coke and eating peanuts. He and my uncle Al would be talking to their friends. Lots of politics, war stories, bullshit. My uncle was a cop and I loved his stories the best. Sometimes he'd tell a really gory one and one of the guys would say, 'For Christ's sake, Al, the kid.' My dad'd rough up my hair and put his arm around me. I loved the weight of it, so heavy and solid. It was like nothing bad could happen as long as he had his arm around me."

Frank fell silent, thinking it would be a short slide from good memories to bad ones. But she felt Gail's eyes gently tugging her along.

"Look. You need to go home. Gotta look sharp in front of that jury tomorrow, right?"

"Right," Gail smiled. She finally got in her car but before she closed the door, she said, "Thanks for the beer. And for the pep talk."

"Anytime."

"Promise?" Gail asked.

"Promise."

~ ~ ~ ~ ~

Back to back homicides at Figueroa were telling Frank what the weatherman hadn't, that summer had arrived. Now she was sitting in the Alibi knocking back stouts. Johnnie smacked the table and she thought her crew was probably generating more noise then the rest of the bar combined.

"Blam! Blam! Blam! Just like that. Three in a row! Jesus Christ!"

Frank listened to their bitching with half an ear. She could do her own but didn't. She'd only managed to get to the Estrella's twice this week. Once she'd encountered only Gloria and the kids, the other time it was Claudia alone, but her pager had gone off after only a few minutes. She was tempted just to drag them all down to the station but didn't want push to come to shove. Something told her that might make the family clamp down even harder, and Frank had a new approach she wanted to try. She promised herself more time with them this weekend. Quality time, she thought sarcastically, especially with Toñio.

Diego vacated his chair and Noah slid into it, nudging Frank.

"So where's the doc?"

"Now why would I know that?" she asked.

"Come on," Noah winked. "I heard you two went to Santa Barbara last weekend. And you told me you were working," he chided.

"I did. Worked all day Sunday."

"I want to know what happened Saturday."

"No big. Went for a ride, had lunch, saw some flowers. That's it."

"That's it," Noah repeated.

"That's it."

Noah wagged his head. "I used to have more respect for you, Frank. That woman's hot for you and you're just sniffing *flowers*."

Frank smiled slightly at the innuendo, allowed it because it came from No. He was straddling the chair and she leaned close to his ear

"I know you pride yourself on your match-making skills, buddy, but maybe the girl ain't as interested as you think. Might want to give this one a rest."

"You mean she's not one with the Amazons?"

"I mean we're just friends. Period."

"Why? Did you try something?" Noah pushed. "You know for sure?"

"Sure enough."

"Ah," Noah whispered, "Then no wonder you're hangin' with her. She's *safe*."

Frank sat back, folding her arms over her chest. A sharp rejoinder leapt to her tongue but she bit it back, acknowledging instead, "Maybe that's what I need right now."

Diego was approaching them, so Noah stood up. Patting Frank on the shoulder, he nodded, "True, dudess. True."

The next morning, after punishing her hangover with a grueling workout, Frank headed into town. She caught Gloria and Toñio eating cereal and watching TV with the babies. Claudia and Alicia were in church. Frank asked a few questions and Gloria waved them away like they were gnats. No, Placa didn't have an ulcer. No, she didn't know where her sister went on the bus all the time. No, they didn't know anyone who owned a car with a tan interior. No, they didn't know anyone in the service.

Both of Claudia's children were surly and uncommunicative, until Frank asked Gloria why her brother was making strikes against the LAPD. The question sparked the young woman into a full-blown rage. She slammed her cereal onto the table, spilling most of it onto the floor and demanded Frank leave her house. Frank stayed on the arm of the couch, so Gloria turned her fury on Toñio, ordering him outside in his underwear. Scooping up the babies and dressed only in a

218

sheer nightie, she followed her brother through the front door. Frank sighed, leaving a card near the dripping bowl. There was no one outside and Frank assumed Gloria had gone to a neighbors house. Toño's bike had been locked to the porch when she came in, now it was gone. She drove around, unsuccessfully trying to find him.

Frank dropped by Lydia's on her way back to the office. She was lucky enough to catch La Reina sitting on the apartment steps with her home girls. They were pissed when Frank told them to leave and Lydia complained, "Now what you want?"

"Nothing. Just tell me who you know that drives a car with beige or tan carpet on the floor."

She couldn't think of any Playboys that did. Most of their rides were GTAs anyway, hot cars wired just for a spree then left abandoned. Frank made a note to check the GTAs twenty-four hours prior to Placa's death.

"She ever tell you about any cops?"

"She told me about you once. How you and that black guy used to be real nice to her when she was little. How the black guy always was wantin' her to go to art school."

"She talk about anybody else? Any other cops?"

Lydia cracked her gum, wagged her head.

"Tell me who she was dealing to."

"I already tolt you I don't know. She never said nothin' to me about that."

"I got a lab report says she was handlin' shit right before she died, and she was with you before she died."

"Well, she musta been playin' with it before she seen me, 'cause I don't know nothin' 'bout no dope."

"I understand your man's out."

"Yeah," she shrugged.

"That's not good news?"

"S'okay."

Frank almost smiled at her ambivalence. She was begin-

ning to see how this spunky girl would have appealed to Placa.
La Reina was a tough kid, not to be underestimated, but she
wore her heart on her sleeve.

"Did you love Placa?"

Lydia's head drooped and she mumbled, "I don't know.
She was different from the boys. She was nice to me. She'd
treat me respectful like."

"I knew her since she was this big."

Frank's hands made a shape the size of a basketball.

"I loved her too," she said simply, watching amazement
grow in Lydia's eyes. Slipping her another business card, she
said, "Call if you think of anything."

Driving back to the office, a nasty thought skipped around
in Frank's head. After she'd read Luis Estrella's lab reports,
she'd done some subtle snooping around on Hunt. Going
through the old Figueroa news letters, she found the issue
profiling Hunt's rodeo exploits. He was a champion team
roper and kept a stable of horses in Simi Valley. The article
also mentioned John Knowles, Hunt's equally successful
teammate in the Professional Rodeo Cowboys Association, and
his old partner at Hollywood.

Hunt was a good old boy from up north, an Okie who'd
started out with the Fresno PD. He'd hired onto the LAPD at
Hollywood, then been demoted to Shootin' Newton after a
handful of unsubstantiated unnecessary force charges. His
transfer from Newton came after another unfounded charge
that he'd beaten a handcuffed prisoner badly enough to send
him into ICU, followed by clouded allegations about his and
Knowles involvement with a kilo of coke missing from the
Newton evidence locker.

She'd snooped around about Knowles too. He was as ugly
with his fists as Hunt, and because of it had been busted back
to regular patrol. Frank played with the idea that Hunt and
Knowles had walked off with the key, and that they were still
partners, not in law, but against it. She had a list of things to

check — Knowles whereabouts on the night of the Estrella shootings, whether Hunt knew Barracas while he was at Hollywood, what kind of car Knowles drove . . . she knew she was grasping, but it was about all she had to go and oddly enough her leads were all tying in somehow to Hunt and his partner. Even while she told herself that she was working a SWAG, just some wild-ass guess, the evidence continued pointing toward Hunt. So she followed it.

At the station she made coffee, figuring it was time to sweat Toñio hard, make him pop a name or too. She didn't even consider Gloria. Even with kids, she still hadn't mellowed. She was tough, like her sister, and Frank knew she'd relish going against Frank. No matter what Frank did to her, it would be Gloria's personal triumph not to break. Claudia seemed the most afraid and the one who knew the most, but she wasn't breaking either. Toñio was just a boy. Where he wasn't savvy, he was the most gullible, and Frank had already seen she'd been able to get to him. She pulled his thin rap sheet from Placa's murder book. It was mostly minor stuff. A B&E, petty theft, public intox.

The phone rang and she answered absently.

"Hi," Gail said. "I tracked you down."

"Hey," Frank said, putting down the rap sheet to give Gail her full attention. "Missed you last night."

"I just wasn't up for the full compliment of Neanderthal's. Present company excluded, of course. Did anybody get set on fire or handcuffed to the urinal?"

"Nope. They were good children last night. What are you up to?"

"Working on my histopathology lecture for next week," then after a pause, "And wondering if I scared you off."

"What makes you say that?"

"We haven't talked since Tuesday night. Since I told you about the mastectomy. I was just wondering if it put you off."

"Not at all. I've just been busy following your lead."

"My lead?"

"The cop theory. I like it more and more. I even have a sketchy suspect."

"That's terrific. I probably can't ask who, can I?"

"Nope. But once more I stand indebted. Might have to buy you dinner again."

"I don't think so. If anybody's buying it's me. I can't remember the last time you let me buy a meal."

"How about tonight?"

"Really? Do you have time?"

"I'll make it. What do you feel like?"

"I don't know. Do you want to go back to La Perla? That was awfully good."

"Long as you don't get the veal," Frank smiled into the receiver.

They arranged a time and Frank sat back, tapping a pencil to Ella belting out a Johnnie Mercer tune. The pencil beat a mean rhythm as Frank hummed along, eyes closed. She'd gotten to that funky point in a case where there was just a tangled ball of leads in her head. Concentrating on it was confusing and exacting, and she knew if she could just let it alone for a while that the ball would unravel itself. Eventually the leads would fall out into somewhat of a straight line and that line would point her in the right direction. It was hard not to force the unraveling, but when the music clicked off Frank crammed her notes into the briefcase and hit the freeway.

She drove with one arm hanging in the sun. Ella's sophisticated arrangements had given way to Dre and Snoop's thugged out bass lines. Banging her hand against the door, Frank realized she was happy. Brick by brick she was building a case against Placa's killer, a killer who might very well be a cop in her own house. She didn't like that her best suspect was a cop, and dreaded the inevitable backlash of theory becoming reality. Still it felt good to have a name to bite into and it didn't bother her that the name was Hunt. She had to move delicately on this, but at least she was moving and that was a feeling Frank lived for.

Not only that, she was on her way to dinner with a beautiful woman. Frank wasn't sure which development was more pleasing, but decided not to worry about it. Her relationship with Gail was fun and friendly, and that was all. It was nice where it was and didn't need to be poked or probed or prodded. Best, she thought thumping out the beat, to save that kind of effort for Hunt.

Chapter Twenty-five

Frank answered the phone to hear, "Dang, girl. You're harder to get aholt of than a greased pig in a stockyard."

"Who is this?"

"Don't sass me, LT."

"Whassup, sport?

"I done checked around like you asked me too, about the Estrella's. Lots of little stuff, but not a felony rap since the mid-nineties. Before that there was a whole rash of them, the whole family had 'em. Like measles or something."

Kennedy's awful drawl faded as she warmed to her info.

"I thought it was weird that they'd stopped so I talked to

a guy who used to work Narco at Figueroa. He said not to worry about it, that it wasn't my problem. Of course that just got me more curious."

A thin smile creased Frank's face. She felt sorry for any dumb bastard who thought he could give Kennedy the brush-off.

"I kept at him and he got really pissed. Told me to keep my goddamn Parker nose out of Figueroa business. He said the Estrella's were pocket change, and that they had better things to do with their resources. And so what if a bunch of spics were just serving to other spics?"

"So there's still action but everybody's looking the other way."

"That's my take on it. But if they're that obvious, why not bust 'em for easy stats?"

Frank squeezed more notes onto a crowded sheet of paper headed COP.

"You done good, sport. I owe you one."

"Yeah, and I'll make you pay, believe me."

"Don't doubt you for a moment." To sidetrack her, Frank asked, "How's our favorite waitress?"

"Fine. I ain't busted her heart yet, like you told her I would."

"Yet's the operative word."

"You're just too cynical, Frank. You don't trust anybody. You know that's true."

"Absolutely," Frank agreed, the ensuing pause prompting Kennedy to forge ahead undaunted. As usual she knew exactly what Frank needed, and as usual it involved a complicated gymnastic routine in the bedroom. Frank again agreed, glancing at the wall clock. It was already noon and she was determined to talk with Toñio before the day was through. She told Kennedy she had to run and ducked out of the office. In a few minutes she was at Claudia's, but Toñio wasn't home. She cruised his most likely hangouts and eventually found him rolling dice in an alley. She made him get in the car despite his sullen protests.

"You arrestin' me?"

"Nope. Just want to talk."

"What if I ain't got nothin' to say?"

"Too bad. Get in."

They drove around in what seemed like circles until Frank parked across from the 52nd Street School. Pointing at a small, elegant tag on a concrete piling, she asked, "*Es tuyo?*"

Toñio glared the other way. She cut the engine and slouched down, propping a knee against the panel board. Casually pulling a pack of Camels out of her shirt pocket, she lit one, careful not to inhale too deeply and get dizzy. Frank was going to break Toñio, even if it meant spending the night here and getting hooked on nicotine all over again. But halfway through her cigarette, Toñio's impatient youth got the better of him.

"What are we doin' here?" he griped.

"Nothing so far. But I got all day."

The boy made a disgusted sound and turned back toward his window. Frank puffed, tapped ash.

"You smoke?" she asked, knowing he did. She pushed the pack at him.

He sneered, " I thought kid's just supposed to say no."

"Hey, the way your family's been catching bullets lately, you'd be lucky to live long enough to get cancer."

Frank saw his slight move toward them, then how he caught himself. She studied his slice of profile.

"I can't remember. You and Placa have the same father?"

"No."

"You look a lot like her anyway."

Frank flicked her stub onto the road. They watched a paramedic truck scream past the windshield.

"Wonder where they're going," she muttered.

Toñio's hands flew angrily in the air.

"What you want?"

"You know," Frank said in a friendly tone, almost chipper.

"I don't know who did it," he grunted stubbornly.

Frank made no rush to speak.

"What if I told you I knew it was a cop."

He looked at her like he hoped she wasn't playing a really bad joke then he turned his face back out the window. He lost some color and his chest started rising a little faster. Excellent, Frank thought, a direct hit.

"I don't know *which* cop — or cops —," she said slowly, "but I got a pretty good idea. It's only a matter of time now."

Toñio whirled unexpectedly toward her.

"It ain't a *chota*," he insisted, and like a bloodhound, Frank picked up the scent of fear. "It ain't no fuckin' *chota*!"

His vehemence confirmed his involuntary physical responses.

"Why are you *covering* for him? Or them. That's what I don't get. What do they have on you?"

"Nothin'! Ain't no one got nothin' on me. You hear? *Nothin'!*"

He was screaming, almost in tears. The weeks of continual harassment were finally taking their toll, finally wearing him down. Watching him desperately trying to hold himself together, she knew this was where he could go either way.

"Give me a name, Toñio. This is your chance to be a *man* about this. Don't be like a dog, running with its tail between its legs. Stand up for your sister, your *familia*. They need you, Toñio. This is your blood. You're all they got left."

"I can't," he choked, letting the tears fall. "I can't. He'll kill us. Like he's killed everyone!"

Frank's blood was itchy, her veins suddenly walled with fiberglass.

"*Who'll* kill you?"

"*He* will! He killed everybody and then he killed Placa because she was gonna tell, and now he's gonna kill us if we tell! Don't you see? I *can't* tell."

227

Slipping into his vernacular, she assured, "He ain't gonna know you told me. *Te promete*."

"*No! I can't*," he pleaded, his face wet, fists balled.

Frank moved a light hand onto his shoulder.

"Yes, you can," she whispered, leaning into him.

"I can't, I can't, I can't."

She squeezed gently, afraid of losing his attention.

"Toñio," she crooned, finding his huge eyes, "*Digame*."

"If I tol' you, you won' *believe* me."

"*Te juro*. On your sister's grave, I swear I will."

"You can' tell *nobody*. Not the other cops, that, that black dude, Taylor, and, and that *chino*. Nobody. You can't tell *nobody* 'cause if he find out he'll kill us."

She believed him. Completely.

"There's only me. Right here, right now, just between you and me. Tell me his name."

An acrid, bitter smell wafted off Toñio and he gulped air like he was drowning. Frank wooed him, her voice velvety and soft, "What's his name?"

He rocked back and forth in the seat, like a much smaller boy. She was afraid of losing him, and stroked him again.

"Tell me his name, Toñio."

The boy said one sharp word. Frank reared back, slapped. The air jammed in her lungs.

"What did you say?" she finally managed.

Toñio heaved, "I *tol*' you. I tol' you you wouldn' believe me!"

Frank closed her eyes, torn between back-handing him or choking him with his shirt yanked tight under his throat.

"Just tell me again," she said quietly, forcing herself into the still spot that she knew was inside her, the place where it was cool and hard and nothing could get to her.

He repeated the last name.

"What's his first name?"

After a second, he told her that too.

Frank looked at the sky overhead. It was blue and clear.

She could see all the way to the San Gabriel's today. It was pretty up there. It would be quiet. She remembered that from her hike with Gail. She thought about how she'd like to be there right now. Looking down on the city, watching the few cotton-ball clouds billowing by. The breeze through the window was sweet and she imagined how it would feel up there, the sun hot on her skin, the wind a cool tickle.

She propped her elbows inside the steering wheel and took a long time massaging the ridge of bone over her eyes. She lit another cigarette, dragged deeply, and passed it to Toñio. He grabbed it.

"That's what Placa was going to tell me," she stated.

Toñio's shoulders bowed over his scrawny chest. Drained and defeated, the words came pouring out.

"Yeah. And about how he kilt my uncles and *sobrinos*. And about the dope. We been runnin' it for him since I was little. He and my mother's uncle was in business. Mostly my uncles ran it but my mom and Gloria did too. Then when Gloria had the babies Placa had to do it. But she hated it. She didn't wanna do it no more. She was smart. She wanted to stay clean, go to college. But he wouldn't let her quit. He used to slap her around, punch her a little. She *hated* him. She used to tell me what she was gonna do to him."

He paused for air then plunged back into his confession.

"Placa was gonna tell you. My mom and Gloria, oh man, they was so mad when you tolt 'em Placa was gonna meet with you. They don't mind it, you know? They like the money. They hate him but they like the money. But Placa, man, she hated him like nothin' I've ever seen. She used to fight with them all the time. They'd fight so bad. And she made me promise to never carry. She wanted to get out so bad. She was gonna go to school and live in Beverly Hills and she was gonna take me with her."

Toñio broke down into his hands and Frank sorted though his words.

"How do you know he did it?"

"He come by the night he kilt my Uncle Julio. He tol' us about it. Said it looked like my Uncle Luis done it and wasn't it too bad that he'd kilt hisself over it. My mom was all busted up but she wouldn' do nothin'. Just said we had to do whatever he tol' us. Then he found out Placa was gonna talk to you and he kilt her too. He was really mad after that. He was laughin' when he tolt us about my uncles, but he was real mad about Placa. He said he'd come after the babies if we made anymore trouble. So we couldn't say nothin'. Now I done it. I tol'," he sobbed.

Frank watched a latte-skinned woman tug three children in front of the car. She had another one in her belly. Ike called Mexican women milk makers. That was the nicest thing he called them. Lighting another cigarette, she said dully, "You did the right thing."

She smoked, giving them both time to calm down. When she started the car, he looked alarmed.

"Where we goin'?"

"I'm taking you home."

"Wha' you gonna do?"

"I've gotta think."

Toñio turned toward her, all the fear back.

"You *promised* you wouldn' tell nobody."

She studied him, seeing so much of Placa in the high cheekbones, the pretty mouth.

"*I* won't," she responded.

When she walked him into the house, Gloria was on the couch watching a *novella* with her friends. Their kids tumbled on the floor like puppies. Claudia came out of the kitchen, wiping her hands on a dishtowel. She looked at her son, then at Frank.

"Where you been?" she asked with unusual concern.

He waved an arm at her and started shuffling down the hall, but Frank grabbed him.

"Uh-uh. Gloria you might want to ask everyone to leave."

"*Fuck* you. This is *my* house."

"Whatever. Your brother wants to tell you something."

His chocolate-colored eyes filled with fear again. Gloria saw it, and said, "Tell me what, *pendejo?*"

He turned to Frank, pleading, "You *promised* you wouldn' tell nobody!"

"I'm not."

She turned him toward Gloria, who was rising off the couch, coming toward him.

"*Hijo?*" Claudia asked.

Gloria was shorter than Toñio, but wider, thicker of arm. She stood under her half-brother's chin. "*Chingado,*" she warned making a fist. "*Que lo dijiste?*"

"*Nada,*" he quavered. "I didn't tell her nothin'. *Esta loca, ella.*"

"Tell them, Toñio."

Gloria growled in Spanish at her friends. They grabbed their babies and left in a hurry. She turned back to her brother and shoved him. He stepped backwards and she followed, shoving him again.

"*Que hiciste?* "she shouted at him.

Putting his forearms up as if to block a blow, he insisted he hadn't done anything. Claudia came between them, staring up at her son. She said something Frank couldn't hear and Toñio answered, "Mami, I had to. She *knew!*"

"*Hijola!*" Gloria screamed, launching herself at him like a heavy-weight contender. She slapped his head with arms like windmills and when he tried to defend himself she pummeled his belly. Dazed, Claudia walked back to the kitchen. The kids froze in their play, mouths loose and eyes wide. Frank followed Claudia. She was sagged over the sink.

"Why didn't you tell me?"

"What could you do?" she shrugged, resigned always to the worst.

"I could have helped you."

"Like he helped?" she hurled. "Like any *jura* ever helped us?"

"Maybe no other cop's helped you, but *I* did. I cut you plenty of breaks, you know that's true. I've never jacked you, Claudia, or any one in your family. I've always been *firme* with you."

"You're still a cop. Just like him."

Gloria screamed into the kitchen, raging at Frank, "There! Are you happy now? You got your answers, eh? Are you happy? Eh? Eh? Is that what you wanted?"

For a crazy second it looked like Gloria was going to swing at her, but before she could, Claudia snapped, *"Bastante!"*

She ordered her daughter to leave them in peace, to go from the room. Eyes rabid, Gloria backed out. The two women stood alone in the kitchen. All the babies were crying and they listened to Gloria soothe and scold them at the same time.

"What you gonna do now ?" Claudia asked tiredly.

"I don't know yet. This is all your word against his. I've got to check some things out."

"He'll kill us if he thinks you know."

"Claudia, if this is true, I don't want him to know. But I need your help with that. I have to know *everything* you know. I can't help you — or protect you — unless you talk to me."

Frank pulled out a chair. "Tell me everything. From the beginning."

Chapter Twenty-six

A sleepy voice answered, "Hello?"

"Hey, Joe. It's Frank. Did I wake you up?"

"Matter of fact you did. It's . . . four o'clock your time. What's up? Must be serious for you to call me."

"It is. Listen."

She told her old boss who Toñio had implicated as his sister's murderer, continued after he'd whistled.

"I was with Claudia and the kids all night. This started years ago, when he was with Narco. He had the contacts, Barracas had the dope, and Claudia and her brothers ran it. Claudia'd send the kids out on deliveries. Gloria did it until she had the babies, then Placa had to do it. Over the years he and Barracas got pretty big — Christ, I don't even want to know how big. By now Barracas knew the contacts and he wanted to muscle our boy out. That ended with Barracas and his family dead on ground.

"So now all the running's left up to Claudia and the kids. Well, to Placa really. She was doing most of it. She hated it and he's made it pretty clear what'll happen if they didn't say 'How high?' when he says 'Jump.' But she was gonna rat him out. She was always so fucking proud."

"Tell me something."

"Yeah?"

"Why do you believe them? How do you know they just aren't throwing shit at you?"

She told Joe how she'd been at the Estrella's until two in the morning. They were whipped, even Gloria, who'd cried, then lashed out at Toñio again. In a monotone, Claudia narrated what had been happening all these years. As she talked, Toñio or Gloria would throw in a detail. Frank hadn't wanted to believe them, but everything fit, and after a career spent weeding truth from lies, she was convinced.

"Got any wits?"

"No. That's the bitch. Seems she'd just gotten home Saturday from making a big delivery for him when he calls and says he's got a client in Hollywood who needs dope*pronto*. Placa was pissed. She'd just gotten home and now she had to go out again. Claudia gave her the stash and she slammed out of the house. That was the last they saw her. He must have picked her up on the way to the bus stop. She probably knew right off she was fucked, but she got in anyway. First mistake. Should've run then. But she didn't. He drives her where he wants her. Takes her .25 away. Fucks her. Then somehow she gets away from him but she's a loose cannon now and he knows it. Grabs the .25 right there. Pops her. Just another drive-by. Only two wits saw he was parked there. Couldn't make the car, but they said it had a round back, not a square one. Guess what he's driving this year. A brand new Lincoln."

Frank paused.

"He called her out of the house, Joe. Premeditated."

"You can't prove that."

"Not yet," she repeated. "I pulled a search warrant. Bobby and Nook confiscated a bunch of her stuff. They went through some of it but got derailed by a redeye last week. I came back to the office after I got done with the Estrella's. I've been going through the rest of it. She had two notebooks from school. They've got hexes and curses all over about 'the fucking pigs' and 'chotas die, 187 LAPD, the LAPD struck out. Then I saw this really heavy impression on one of the pages. I shaded it real light with a pencil. His name was all over the page. She was furious. She had the motive to cheese him out, and knowing her, she would have. And the motherfucker knew," she sighed.

Frank explained how Claudia had produced two photos of him taking money from Placa. Toñio had taken the pictures and though the quality was poor, both subjects and their activities were clear. Gloria had found them under her sister's underwear, snuggled next to a .22. When she'd found them she'd come screaming to her mother, threatening to kill her brother for being so stupid. Toñio hadn't wanted to take the pictures, but Placa made him, calling it their seguro, their insurance.

"I'm thinking that was what she wanted to show me Sunday morning. If they were insurance she was keeping for a rainy day, they'd have been hidden somewhere safe, not right next to her gat."

"Okay, okay. Maybe you can get him on extortion. How's that prove he capped her?"

Frank squeezed the bunched muscles at the base of her skull.

"It doesn't. I don't have anything to pin his balls to the wall with. Not yet."

Joe didn't say anything and Frank asked, "Still there?"

"Yeah, yeah. Have you told anybody about this yet?"

"Only you."

"Good, good. Don't. This is some deep shit you're wading in, my girl."

"Don't I know it."

"And as far as you know, this is just him?"

"From what they're telling me, but who the fuck knows what this could open up."

"All right. Let me think for a minute."

She heard the faint click of Joe's Zippo then a long drag on a cigarette.

At length Joe said, "Okay. This is what we do first."

At the briefing that morning, Frank pulled Bobby and Nook off Placa's case. The squad looked at her curiously. Frank frequently worked cases with her detectives but she'd never taken one on alone.

"This isn't going anywhere," she shrugged. "We're just beating a dead horse right now and you have fresher cases to work. The end of the month's coming up and I want to concentrate on cases with better potential. I'll keep working Placa. I'm not going to let it die. You guys keep an ear out, pass on anything relevant, but right now we're focusing on more promising books."

"Whatever," Nook sighed, but Bobby shook his head silently at the ceiling. Amid some grumbles and protests, she reprioritized a few other cases. When the meeting was over, Bobby followed Frank into her office and closed the door. He bent his massive frame over her desk. It was an old wooden piece with inlaid leather, eight drawers, and two pull-outs for extra work space. Frank had bought it at a yard sale and lugged it in on a Saturday morning. It was almost six feet wide and took up most of her tiny office, but when Bobby stood next to it, it looked like something a preschooler would use.

"I don't understand why you pulled us. We've still got some leads to work. There's the whole cop angle, and we haven't even begun to turn up the heat yet."

She'd singed his pride, and Frank felt bad. She waved a hand, looked disgusted.

"I talked to Toñio yesterday. Made him cry. I thought he was made of sterner stuff, but he got all blubbery about harassment, and leaving the family alone. I worked him for over two hours. I don't think he knows shit. Claudia does, but she's not talking. And I don't think I was right on the 187 angle. I pushed it some with Gloria last night but I didn't get a feel for any police involvement."

Frank tipped her chair back.

"And the bottom line is stats are down, have been the last couple months. Fubar's getting pinched from upstairs, got his jockeys all in a wad, now he's kicking my ass. That's why I want to concentrate on the cases with the best chance of closure. Get them under our belts so I can get Fubar off us, then we can go back to these colder ones, before summer hits us even harder than it already has."

Bobby stared at Frank.

"It's nothing you've done, Bobby. You and Nook have been great on this. But right now we're digging in granite. I'm just moving you around to softer dirt for a while."

"When you hit granite, you use TNT," Bobby said.

Frank asked playfully, "Got any on you?" He just held Frank's gaze and she said, "Look. I know you want this. So do I. We just need to step back from it a little. I'm still going to keep working Claudia, work the homes some more. But our personal involvement can't distract us from other cases. We've thrown a lot of time at this and we've dead-ended. For now. So we'll take a break, try and close-out more promising cases, then come back to this. I'm not going to let it die, Bobby. I promise. I just want to switch gears for a while."

"You're the boss," Bobby shrugged, leaving in obvious disgust. For a moment Frank listened to her squad working. She hated the lies she was telling them, the reason behind the lies. Frank sighed and fluttered a stack of phone messages. She returned the calls in order, first OSS at the Sheriff's department, then Morgan at Personnel, and somebody at Motor Transportation about gas allowances. While the MT clerk clicked through his computer, Frank frowned at the next message slip.

Detective Harris, Sheriff's Homicide, wanted her to return his call. Robbie Harris, better known as Bartlett, spoke maddeningly in quotations. The day was young but already wearing on Frank. She didn't feel up to dealing with Harris or his irritating quirk, but unlike most of the other LASD dicks, Harris was always affable and willing to share information. Probably, she imagined, just so he'd have a fresh audience. Frank gritted her teeth after finishing with the MT and called him.

"Ah-ha!," he answered. "You know what Nietzsche said about women don't you?"

" 'Fraid I'm about to find out."

"If a woman possesses manly virtues one should run away from her, and if she does not possess them she runs away from herself."

"Charming. Did you call just to tell me that or is there actually something I can help you with?"

"Brrr," Harris responded, " 'Thou art all ice. Thy kindness freezes.' Shakespeare," he sighed. "Say, Doc Lawless tells me you got a stiff missing some body parts, few weeks back. That so?"

Frank took a patient breath. When he wasn't speaking in quotes, Harris tended to sound like a cop from a 1940's B-movie.

"You mean the kid missing his liver?"

"Yeah, that's the one, sister. I got a vic over here missing

238

his heart. Thought there might be a link. You mind if I come over and look at your notes."

"Help yourself. I'll tell Briggs you're coming."

"Ah, Briggs. A man I'm sure who believes that work is the curse of the drinking classes."

"Anything else, Robbie?"

"Eliot said it, but it's so true in our case, that in every parting there is an image of death. Let me leave you with this — 'the individual woman is required a thousand times a day to choose either to accept her appointed role and thereby rescue her good disposition out of the wreckage of her self-respect, or else follow an independent line of behavior and rescue her self-respect out of the wreckage of her good disposition.' Whaddaya say?"

"Goodbye."

Frank returned one more call, then Foubarelle slipped into her office with a pile of make-work designed to make Figueroa look proactive in community relations. After that, Noah and Johnnie needed case reviews. Johnnie requested a day off to take his son to Disneyland on his birthday. Frank denied it, coldly pointing out that Johnnie should have thought about that before he burned all his comp time and sick leave on hangovers. Between phone calls from seemingly every other jurisdiction in southern California, she helped Diego prep for court, talked to lawyers and PDs, and signed off on dozens of forms, requests and reports. This went on until the squad room had at last quieted and emptied, until Frank's time was finally her own.

She was running through a list of things to do. First was to get his phone records. Second, she had to figure a way to get a saliva sample from him. Then samples from his closet and his car. Her father had taught her that if she had to hit somebody bigger than herself, hit them so hard they couldn't get back up. That's what she intended to do now; hit this son of a bitch with so much evidence he'd be buried alive in it.

The phone rang a couple times but she ignored it. If it was important, the desk would know how to find her. When she heard the quick clack-clack-clack on the stairs she sighed and put her pen down.

"I understand you've reassigned your case load," Foubarelle announced, walking into her office for the second time that day.

Frank nodded, wondering how the hell he'd gotten wind of that.

"And that you're working that banger girl on your own."

"Yeah."

"Would you mind telling me what that's all about?"

She gave him a version of the song and dance she'd given Bobby.

"I don't like it, Frank. If this was a high-priority case, or something very sensitive, then that would be different, but it doesn't look good that a lieutenant is actively working a run-of-the-mill drive-by. You're not a Detective Three anymore, Frank. You've got a squad to run and I don't want it to suffer because you're off pursuing leads that are best pursued by the men under you. I want you to give that case back to the detectives who originally handled it."

"I can't do that."

"Oh really? Please enlighten me," he said, spreading his hands expansively.

Frank massaged her ring finger. She wasn't ready to tell him. She wanted a lot more ammo than she had right now so she tried stalling.

"This isn't just a drive-by. I think it's something a little bigger, little more volatile."

Foubarelle tensed.

"How much bigger?"

"I'd rather not say yet. Until I have more facts I'm just shooting from the hip."

"How much bigger and how much more volatile?" he repeated, his bluster evaporating.

Frank chewed on the inside of her lip. She'd have to tell him sooner or later. She'd just hoped it was going to be later.

"I think it might be an officer involved incident," she gave up.

"*What?*"

Fubar was turning red and Frank wouldn't have been surprised if the top of his head flew off like a jack in the box.

"I don't have all the facts yet," she said calmly. "That's why I haven't told you anything. But I didn't want Bobby or Nook digging up any more on this. That's why I took it over."

"I see. Well that certainly casts the situation in a different light."

Foubarelle looked sick and Frank almost felt sorry for him.

"Is it an officer from Figueroa?"

"Yeah."

"Oh, Christ," he said. "We better call Langley."

He was referring to his boss, the deputy chief.

"I wish you wouldn't."

"Why the hell not?"

"Because I don't have a lot to go on right now, just circumstance and second-hand testimony."

"That's enough that he should be told about it."

Frank disagreed, suspecting Fubar just wanted someone to shoulder this heavy load with him.

"Just give me some time, John. Another day."

As he grabbed for Frank's phone he shook his head.

"Langley's got to know."

He got the DC's secretary, telling her he had "a situation" and to have Langley call ASAP.

"Tell me what you've got," he said, biting on his thumbnail. As she told him, he paced and kept repeating, "Oh, Christ." Frank declined to give the cop's name and Fubar didn't push it. He already knew more than he wanted to.

Two hours later she sat in Langley's office, telling the

story again. The DC listened intently, not saying anything until Frank was finished.

"Well," he mused, leaning back in his large chair. Silver-haired, tanned and trim, Langley looked like a Beverly Hills surgeon. Like Foubarelle, the DC was a political animal, but at least he'd spent some time in uniform. His understanding of what happened on the streets was better than the captain's, yet he too was disinclined to buck prevailing political winds. When he smiled indulgently, Frank felt her stomach roll over.

"Lieutenant, as you're well aware, lately the department has had some rather serious setbacks. Mind you, some of these difficulties we've brought on ourselves. Others are . . . *inadequacies* with public perception. Regardless however of who's at fault, it all adds up to give us a rather *tarnished* image."

The DC chose his words carefully and deliberately, as if choosing steps through a yard full of dog shit. It was his media speech, the let's-give-them-something-but-not-what-they-want talk and she knew what was coming next.

She barely listened as he said, "You must see, that with so little evidence we are in no clear position to proceed with these *allegations*. At this point your charges are *highly* speculative. Certainly if the officer in question has been involved in *inappropriate* activities he should be investigated. It's the department's responsibility to investigate all such allegations and take action dependent upon the outcome of said investigations. However, this is not a good time to bring certain of these *charges* to light, particularly with so little evidence to back them. Speculation at this stage is pointless, and should word leak out, the department could have a rather *inflammatory* incident on its hands. *Surely* you can appreciate the reaction to this?"

When Frank's reply wasn't forthcoming, he continued, "I appreciate the job you're doing, Lieutenant. Credit is due you for your diligence. Though I'm sure it has *pained* you to implicate a fellow colleague, you have pursued a difficult line of inquiry to its logical conclusion. At this point however, I would deem it more *fruitful* to follow a different path. Various of these allegations have merit, and I can *assure* you they will be brought to IADs attention."

Frank couldn't look at the DC as he continued with a thinly disguised warning that should this *somehow* become public knowledge, that would be *extremely* unfortunate. Did both the captain and the lieutenant understand that?

"Yes, sir," Fubar piped up.

Langley waited, his paternalistic urbanity, turning cool.

"Do you understand what we've discussed, Lieutenant?"

Holding her teeth together, she said, "Yes, sir."

"Very good," he said standing to end their meeting. Shaking Frank's hand he added with absolute sincerity, "Keep up the good work, Lieutenant."

Chapter Twenty-seven

Frank swore all the way back to her office. She had nothing on this bastard for the Estrella murders. She knew that. Nor could she substantiate Luis Estrella's murder. But with Placa she'd had a better chance. He'd been taken by surprise and forced to make mistakes. Still, even if he'd been caught kneeling over Placa and firing into her heart the department would be reluctant to pursue charges against one of their own. Such a reluctance might almost have been noble if it were a matter of a brother protecting a brother, but the code of silence wasn't about protecting a comrade; it was a sickening reflection of how many heads might roll if the truth got out.

Frank's stomach cramped through her anger and she tried

to remember the last time she'd eaten. Camped in traffic, she decided it was going to be a long night and that her first priority should be food and a drink so stiff it was rigored. She wasn't far from USC and wondered if Gail was still at work. It'd be nice to talk to someone sane for a little while.

Frank dialed her office and got Rhondie, who said she'd page Gail. Frank hung up. Maybe she'd just go on over to the Marengo Grill. If Gail couldn't make it she'd just eat without her. No big deal, she thought, swinging onto Cesar Chavez, but was glad when Gail called back a few minutes later.

"Hey. Interested in dinner at the Grill? I was close and thought maybe you could join me."

"You thought right," Gail answered. "Can you give me about forty-five minutes?"

"Is that Lawless time or real time?"

When Gail laughed the answer Frank knew how badly she wanted to see her. And it scared Frank. She'd gotten used to not wanting anything. It made life so much simpler. And duller, she admitted. Frank wondered what Clay would have her do, knowing the answer even before she finished the question.

"Jesus," she let out with a deep breath. It was just dinner. She warned herself to quit nutting up, rationalizing that she was just wired from the afternoon and all she still had to do. Frank had wanted that bastard nailed five ways to Sunday before even whispering his name and now three other people knew. She needed damage control pronto. Her best scenario was that Langley wouldn't follow through. But she doubted it. He'd pass something along to IAD just to cover his ass. Exactly what he offered and how far Internal went with it was unpredictable. She had to proceed on the assumption that her suspect would eventually know he was being investigated on extortion charges at the very least. That could either work against her or for her.

She slid into a parking spot at the restaurant and ordered a double scotch before the waiter had even finished seating her. Frank recognized a defense attorney at one of the tables and watched him laughing, thinking she needed to talk to McQueen. She could lay out what she had, tell Queenie it was hypothetical, and hope she wouldn't give Frank her withering, "You've got to be kidding" look.

That was the damn frustrating part. When Toñio had first told her, Frank didn't want to believe him. But all her little clues and circumstances had lined up to back his story and the more she thought about it, the more it made *sense*. But you couldn't prosecute a case on common sense and instinct. And Frank couldn't push like she would with a normal suspect. Truth was, if this guy was as smart as he should be, she'd never have enough on him. Langley was right. He could absolutely walk.

Frank seethed, wondering what the odds were of his even being fully investigated for trafficking. And then, the likelihood of prosecution and conviction if it got as far as that. Would he even get more than a slap on the wrist? The man was a decorated Vietnam vet and a great cop with citations and commendations to prove it. It was possible that what Langley told IAD would go straight into one of their files and sit there, until if and when they ever needed it.

Compounding her lack of credibility were Luis Estrella and Ocho Ruiz. On the surface, they both still appeared to be the logical suspects. Ruiz still hadn't fessed up to his actions on the night Placa died and she thought she'd have to get to him first thing in the morning. She needed supporting statements from him and Lydia and the homes that were in Eagle Rock with him.

Gail walked in just as Frank finished her first drink. The doc was only in scrubs but it was still nice watching her walk to the table. She had a sultry, long-legged sway, and Frank realized, not without some alarm, that this was the second time in less than an hour that she was glad the doc was around.

"What a nice surprise," Gail said, sliding into her chair.

She handed Frank an envelope, saying hello to the waiter and ordering a gin and tonic. Frank got another double. She allowed herself the luxury of staring at the doc, who arched a brow and stated, "You look like hell. What have you been up to?"

"Wading in shit."

"Placa's shit?"

"None other. How about you? How's your week going?"

Gail's eyes rolled and she frowned, "I'll tell you about that in a minute. Open that first," she said to the envelope.

"Another Christmas present?" Frank asked, extracting a sheaf of papers. It was Placa's lab results and Frank whistled, impressed.

"Damn. What'd this cost you?"

"I had to promise Suzie it was the last one I'd harangue her about for a while."

"Harangue," Frank repeated. "Big word."

Gail sipped her water, saying, "Look what was under her nails. The right hand in particular."

Frank flipped a couple pages until she found the section. Tan automotive upholstery fibers. Traces of horse manure and alfalfa. Human skin and horse hairs. Lots of wool fibers and a few silk.

The trace evidence created a clear picture for Frank. He and Placa in his front seat, he on top of her. The skin under her nails showed she'd have fought him first, then she'd have had to give in; he was bigger, stronger, and maybe holding her own .25 to her head. Her right hand had clenched into the debris on the floorboard. The samples from the left hand were cleaner. Only human skin and wool fibers. Meaning non-upholstered seats. The leather in the Lincoln.

"Have we compared these to Luis' samples?"

"Suze is working on it."

"How about DNA profiles? Do the skin and sperm match?"

"We ran PCR strips," Gail said, leaning over to turn pages. She found the strip pictures, showing a match.

"We've developing RFLPs too. That'll increase the accuracy of the match."

"Beautiful. I owe you big time."

"Yes you do," Gail grinned, but Frank was still absorbed in the technicalities of the various reports.

The waiter brought their meals, a healthy salad for Gail and a not so healthy cheeseburger with bacon for Frank.

Gail shook her head, scolding, "You're diet's reprehensible."

"Sound like Nancy," Frank said swirling her ice cubes. "Only she wouldn't have used such a big word."

"When was the last time you had your cholesterol checked?"

"Me? Never."

"*Never?*" Gail repeated, aghast.

"Nope. Why should I? I'm only forty."

"Hello? That's my point."

"You doctor's worry too much," Frank dismissed.

"That's because we know what can happen."

"All right then. How often do you get any cardio-vascular exercise?"

Gail pursed her lips and narrowed her eyes.

"Gotcha," Frank answered. "Still haven't told me how your week's going."

"Shitty," Gail said propping herself on the table with her elbow. She stabbed a cucumber, asking, "You heard about the mayor's daughter?"

Frank nodded. His twenty-two year old crashed head on into another vehicle at one in the morning on the 405. She was dead on scene and so were the three teenagers in the Jeep she'd flipped. None of them had been in seat belts and all three were scattered onto the highway.

Gail checked the room before confiding, "Between you and me? Hizonor is not going to be happy. His daughter had a *point three-six* blood-alcohol level."

"Hizonor might ask for a favor," Frank warned.

"No kidding," Gail said. "Why do you think Rhondie is screening all my calls?"

"What are you going to do?"

"Worry about it when it happens. In fact I don't even want to think about it right now. Tell me about your day. Why the circles under your eyes? And how many of those doubles have you had?"

"Very observant, doc. There's hope for you yet."

Gail waited for Frank to continue, and she finally conceded, "It's bad. I talked to Placa's brother. He dropped a name. A cop. I can't say much else. Probably shouldn't have said as much as I already have. Fubar found out I took Nook and Bobby off Placa. Came up to my office and wanted to know why. I had to tell him. He called the DC right away. Surprise, surprise, they don't want to move on it. Too *inflammatory*. Might further tarnish our already dulled image. Told me he'd pass it on to IAD. Time for me to drop the case and move along like a good little girl. Let the big boys handle it."

"*That's all?*" Gail squawked.

"That's all," Frank snapped her fingers. "Eight people and a dog. No big. We'll pass it on to IAD and fuck you very much."

Frank swallowed half her drink, not liking the bitter tone in her voice.

"Well you can't just *drop* it. Not a thing like this."

"Who said anything about dropping it?"

Frank rattled her ice cubes.

"This is just going to make it that much harder."

Chapter Twenty-eight

Frank had flicked off her pager but turned it back on as she finished her coffee.

"Thanks for having dinner with me, doc. You were a welcome, if only temporary distraction."

Gail flirted, "I could be more permanent, you know."

"So you've said," Frank nodded into her napkin. Gail chuckled at Frank's subtle discomfort, and Frank smiled, warmed from the scotch, the burger, and that sound. She fingered the check as Gail's hand closed over hers.

"You got the last one."

"Shoot bullets through me," Frank said, glancing at the

number scrolling across her hip. "Shouldn't have turned this back on so soon," she muttered.

"Who is it?"

"The desk. Probably a body I so do not need right now. We going to fight over the bill all night?"

"I'm not fighting," Gail said, her hand still on Frank's.

"Hate to, doc, but I've got to get going. Let me get this one and you get the next, okay?"

"Deal."

They settled the tab and walked outside together. Gail told Frank to call her and Frank agreed. She dialed the desk, watching Gail walk across the street. She liked watching Gail walk. Coming was better but leaving was pretty good too.

"Romanowski. Franco. What's up?"

"There you are!" the old sergeant boomed. "Everybody's been trying like fuck to find you."

Frank didn't like the sound of that, but waited patiently while he shuffled some papers.

"Somethin' about some boy, yeah, here we go. You got calls from half the squad about a kid named Toñio Estrella."

Frank's heart fell onto the pavement and split open.

"Guess he's at King/Drew and not doing so good. Looks like he got a pretty bad beat-on-sight."

"Room number?"

"ICU."

Frank swore and dialed Bobby's cell number. He picked up immediately.

"What's going on, Bobby?"

"Damn, Frank. Toñio's all messed up. Somebody kicked the shit out of him. Gloria brought him in about six AM. He was bleeding inside pretty bad. They did a splenectomy and his liver's pretty messed up."

"Who did it?" Frank asked, feeling her dinner sliding around.

251

"We don't know. Gloria and Claudia, neither of them are saying a word. The hospital called us in case . . ."

"In case what?"

"In case he doesn't make it."

"He's that bad?"

"Yeah. I guess he had some sort of clot right after the surgery, and went into arrest. They had to take him back in."

Frank ground her teeth together, squeezing out, "Who's there with you?"

"The whole Estrella clan. At least what's left of them. All the babies, a grandma."

"And nobody's saying how he got hurt."

"Gloria just said she heard some fighting, came into the living room and found him like that with the front door open. Sounds bogus to me."

"Is Nook with you?"

"Yeah."

"Who else? Any uniforms?"

"Yeah, why?"

"Listen, Bobby. I don't want anyone in Toñio's room, except you, do you understand?"

"Sure, but why?"

"Not Nook, not Foubarelle, not God. Understand? Just you and the doctors."

"Sure."

"You stay until I get there, okay? I'm on my way."

"Okay, Frank."

"And don't let Claudia or Gloria out of sight. I want Nook pasted to them. Is that clear?"

"Yeah, sure.

"Okay. Hang tight. I'll be there in a little bit. I'll explain everything then."

Growling, *"Motherfucker,"* Frank laid rubber in the parking lot.

~ ~ ~ ~ ~

She could hear Gloria screaming and cursing before she was even out of the elevator. Jogging down the hall, Frank saw her struggling with Nook and two uniforms, the other Estrella's crying around them, trying to hang onto Gloria.

"What the hell's going on?" she barked, causing all three cops to jerk around and lose their grip on Gloria. Bobby had just come out of the ICU ward and Gloria ran to him. The big detective blocked Gloria easily and Frank repeated her question. Bobby shouted over her head, "She wants to go in."

Jesus, Frank thought. She hadn't meant for him to keep the family out. It was her fault. Bobby had taken her literally when she said everyone. He was thorough like that.

"Is it okay with the doctor?"

"I guess," he shrugged vaguely. "They were in there earlier."

Frank put herself between Bobby and Gloria, telling her she could see Toñio, but only if she calmed down.

"Fuck that shit!" she screamed, spit flying. "I'll calm down when that *jodido maricon's* in his fucking grave!"

Claudia half-heartedly tried to calm her daughter but Gloria repeated, "Fuck that! What we gonna do? Let him come after us one at a time? Fuck that! We goin' after him. I'll do it myself if I have to! Uh-uh. I ain't playing no more."

"Hey," Frank soothed. "You stay away from him. Let me take care of this. That's *my* job."

"Yeah, like you been taking care of us so far?" she shouted. "We just gonna sit and wait for you useless *jodida* police to come and help us. This shit's gone too far. That *maricon* ain't comin' near my babies. I'ma get him myself."

Nook came up behind Gloria and asked, "Which *maricon*?"

Gloria told him to fuck himself. He made a helpless gesture at Frank.

"I want to see Toñio," she said, trying to push past Frank, who stopped her.

"You want to see your brother?" Frank asked.

"Yes! I want to see him."

"Then you gotta calm down," Frank soothed. "You can see him. You just gotta be calm. For his sake."

Gloria shot her hands through her hair and moaned, "Just let me in."

"He needs you to be calm. You gonna be calm for him?"

"I'm calm," she whimpered, "I'm calm."

Frank nodded her head and Gloria rushed past Bobby. Frank followed her through the ward, baring her ID as two nurses glared from the desk. Toñio was in a cubicle with barely enough room for his bed and the machines he was attached to. Gloria squeezed in beside him, smoothing his hair, cooing, "Niñito."

Claudia stepped quietly around Frank, taking a place on the other side of the bed. She found a way around the tubes and held her son's hand. Frank tried to shut the door but a nurse called out to keep it open. Frank cursed under her breath. She knew who the *maricon* was but wanted to hear one of the women say it. She let them have a moment with Toñio then stood next to Claudia.

"Did he do this?"

There was no response, as if Frank wasn't even in the room. She put her hand on Claudia's shoulder, asking again. She startled Frank by spinning around. She hit a tray with her elbow and sent it clattering to the floor.

"*Leave us alone!*" she said savagely. "You hurt us enough! Now just leave us be!"

Bobby loomed in the doorway and a nurse scurried in, hissing, "That's it! Everybody out!"

Gloria started crying but Claudia whirled past Frank. She followed her out to the noisy waiting room, motioning Nook over.

"Who have you talked to about this case?"

"What do you mean?"

"I mean who have you talked to about Placa's case since I pulled you ?"

"I don't know. I guess Johnnie, Ike, No. You know."

"I don't know. Think!"

"What's the big-"

Bobby had joined his partner.

"Just who have you talked to about this?"

"Well, Hunt and Waddell. They responded to that stabbing the other night. We were talking for a while. Muñoz and Lewis were there too," he added.

"Did you talk about specifics?"

Bobby and Nook exchanged a glance that said they had. Frank wrestled with her composure, furious where this was going.

"You were bitching about being pulled," Frank stated.

"Yeah," Bobby squirmed. "The case isn't even cold yet. There are still a lot of leads we can work."

"And you mentioned those leads specifically?"

Bobby pawed his Florsheim at the ground. Now he saw where this was going too.

"Kind of."

Frank nodded.

"To everyone?"

He looked up at the ceiling and Frank strangled the grip on her temper.

Nook said, "I don't believe it. You're *serious*. You really think one of *us* is involved?"

"Bartlett and some other deputy was there too," Bobby added glumly.

Frank's jaw muscles bounced and she couldn't resist asking, "Why didn't you just take out a full-page ad in the *Times*?"

"You *do*," Nook continued. "You really think it's one of those guys. And that's why you pulled us."

"It doesn't have to be one of them," Bobby answered, gamely holding Frank's angry stare. "They could have talked to anybody."

"I'll be damned," Nook shook his head. "You've gone over to the other side."

If looks could kill it would have been too late for Nook even though he was standing in the middle of the ICU. Frank walked away from her men, over to Claudia who sat as rigid as the plastic chair she was in. Kneeling in front of her, Frank beseeched, "Talk to me, Claudia. Help me."

The retort was a stinging slap. Frank's eyes watered, but she didn't flinch.

"Help *you*," Claudia hissed.

"I deserved that," Frank said quietly. Locking onto the livid brown face, she begged, "Please, Claudia. *Te promete* I'll end this right now. Just give me the last bullet."

Frank stood and held her hand out. Claudia stared at it a long time but Frank wouldn't retract it. Finally she stood, following Frank toward the elevator. Slumped in a corner, barely audible, Claudia told Frank what had happened. It was a simple, ugly story and it didn't take long. Frank wanted to touch Claudia, to comfort her, but she didn't. She said only, "Okay. We've got him now."

Frank was almost in three fender-benders on the short ride between the hospital and the station. Having made sure the Estrella's were relatively safe, her next goal was to kick Langley's ass into gear. Frank had already decided to move on this bastard and his actions over the last twenty-four hours only fortified her resolve; with or without the department's sanction, she was taking him down. But Frank wasn't a hero. She had seventeen years toward her pension and didn't fancy starting a new career at age forty. She was willing to take the risk but preferred Langley's backing. She had to figure how to get it without threatening or alienating him, no easy task when going against a DC.

Almost rear-ending an old Nova, Frank remembered to call Noah and Johnnie. They were next in line to catch but she couldn't get hold of either one. She left messages and paged them both. Noah returned her call just as she was pulling into the station lot.

"Dudess, word up?"

"Hey. You're on call. I pulled —"

"— I can't be! We're on our way to La Jolla, Les' playoff game."

"Sorry. I need you available."

"I'll call Ike or —"

"No! Do you know where Johnnie is?"

"Probably passed out in an alley," Noah whined, "I don't know! What's going on anyway? Why can't Bobby or Nook handle it?"

"They're out of rotation. Gloria Estrella got raped last night. Guy did it right in front of Toñio, in front of her kids, and Toñio went ape-shit on him. Then this bastard went even worse on Toñio. He's just a scrawny little kid. He's at King/Drew. They took his spleen out and his livers lacerated. Bobby and Nook are posted at the hospital until I find this cocksucker."

"You know who it is?" Noah asked.

"Look, I can't talk. I'm on the cell."

"Aw, *come on*, Frank."

"Just know you're on. I'll talk to you later," she said, hanging up. She hoped he'd have sense enough to go to the game anyway, and that nothing happened in the meantime. *If I could just get hold of Johnnie*, she thought taking the stairs two at a time, *he could cover*. Frank offered a silent thanks when she walked into the squad room and there he was, hunkered over late reports.

"Hey. Tried to page you."

Johnnie fiddled at his belt. His shirt was wrinkled and he hadn't shaved.

"It wasn't on," he grinned sheepishly.

"Work better when they are. I called No, too. You guys are up."

She raised her palm at his expected remonstrance, con-

257

tinuing, "You need to page him. He's at a game down south, let him know you'll cover 'til he can get his ass up here. Go downstairs and shave. You look like shit in a sack."

His initial protest silenced, he just slumped in his chair. He sullenly asked the same thing Noah did and Frank explained without detail. Johnnie blew his lips at the ceiling and she closed her door on him. A few minutes later she heard a phone ring, and Johnnie's dejected rumble.

Frank gutted Placa's murder book, laying out the autopsy protocol, the tox results, lab reports, Placa's pictures, sketches, Bobby's reports — everything, all neatly arrayed in front of her. Hunched in her old chair she sifted through the papers like a fortune-teller reading the cards. She weighed options and deliberated. She sighed occasionally, shifted a piece of paper, but mostly she just thought. After a while she picked up the phone

Foubarelle's wife curtly said her husband was busy. Equally curt, Frank told her, "Tell him another Estrella's in the hospital. He might want to know."

He called back in less than a minute.

"What's the problem?" he greeted shortly.

She told him. Then added, "I'm charging him, John."

"Now wait a minute."

She heard the panic in his voice and would have been amused any other time.

"Langley clearly said you're not to do anything with this, and I won't have you going against him, Frank."

"I have to. Even if this goes nowhere and the DA throws it back in my lap, he's at least got to know we're on to him, that *I'm* on to him. He can't keep getting away with this. I don't know how many people he has to kill before the department has the balls to move against him, but I'm not going to wait around and see. I'm charging him, John, with or without Langley's blessing."

"You can't do that," the captain protested, the whine and

the fear higher in his voice. He seemed to get it under control, because his next words were more authoritative.

"I'm ordering you not to do this, Frank."

"Sorry, John."

She wasn't.

"You realize the ramifications of openly defying your supervisor."

What should have been his boldest statement yet was couched with fear, and Frank played him as she so often did. It was like fishing, set the hook and reel him in. No wonder Joe liked it so much.

"Yes, I do. Do you want to call Langley or should I?" she asked needlessly.

She waited almost an hour for the phone to ring. Fubar nervously told her the DC was out of town. Frank was to meet him at Chief Nelson's house ASAP. Frank pulled her case together and started the long drive to Brentwood. She was shown into his study, where Nelson greeted her without cheer.

"Notoriety seems to be plaguing you personally as much as it is the department."

"Yes, sir."

Frank stood stiffly in front of his well-polished desk. A liaison from IAD and a department lawyer sat in leather wing chairs with brass studs. Foubarelle fidgeted behind them.

"Tell me, Lieutenant, do you actively seek out problems or do they just happen to find you?"

The big man wasn't happy and Frank responded, "I don't seek them anymore than the rest of the department, sir."

That seemed to placate him a bit and he said, "Well, show us what the furor's about."

Because she had so little to go with on the Estrella massacre, Frank focused entirely on Placa's case. She carefully outlined his motive, explaining how the business with Barracas had evolved and the subsequent showdown. She described Placa and her refusal to do the work, the confession from Toñio, and this latest turn of events wherein he'd found out the net was closing in. She acknowledged that her case for murder was weak but told them about the equine-related samples found on Placa, the sperm, and the fact that she hoped to obtain supporting DNA and fiber samples from the suspect. If the samples matched as she thought they would, they'd have a much stronger case.

The lawyer questioned and probed, finally opining that they could foreseeably prosecute various allegations, but not murder. Not yet. He cleared his throat and amended smoothly, "Of course should this matter go any further, we'd have to consult with the District Attorney directly."

Nelson nodded, boring coldy through Frank.

"The department has more than it's share of troubles right now, Lieutenant. I know you. I know your record. I'm still not convinced that the incident last winter wasn't an overreaction on your part."

Frank burned at the indictment but her exterior remained at zero centigrade. "Before we go any farther with this, there are a few things I need to know."

Nelson abruptly dismissed Foubarelle and his counsel, waving Frank into a wing chair. She sat in it, slightly repulsed by the leftover warmth. The chief took the other chair, pulling it close to her. Only inches from her face, he ordered sternly, but kindly, "Level with me, Franco. Tell me about this man."

An incredulous smile almost got away from Frank as she realized what the chief was up to. He was looking for something personal, a vendetta or agenda that would explain Frank's accusations, something he could twist to discredit her suspicions. She found herself in the paradoxical position of defending the bastard, wanting to laugh at the surrealism of the situation. Over the next half hour, Frank grudgingly admired the Chief's interrogation skills and was relieved when he told her to call the others back in.

"I've decided to give the lieutenant twenty-four hours to

come up with something more than this," he said tapping Placa's murder book. "That means," he said, casting Frank a piercing glare, "that what we have discussed today does not leave this room until further notice from me. Is that clear?"

It wasn't as good as Frank had hoped for, but not as bad as she'd feared.

"Yes, sir."

"These are serious charges against a fine officer and I won't have this department needlessly dragged through the mud. Is that clear, also?

"Yes, sir."

Nelson turned to the lawyer, asking if he wanted to add anything. He threw in a few standard caveats then Nelson adjourned their meeting.

"Sir?" Frank asked, reclaiming the chief's attention, sensing Fubar tensing next to her.

"What is it, Lieutenant?"

"Sir, should these charges be justified, this man poses an immediate threat to the surviving family members. I'd like to request their residence be under twenty-four hour guard surveillance by one of my teams and a radio car."

Nelson thought about it.

"One radio car."

"Yes, sir."

"See she gets it," he said with a nod to Foubarelle.

The red light on Frank's phone machine blinked maniacally. She stared at it, foggy-brained, wondering if she needed to know who'd called. She punched the rewind button, drowsing as she stood. Christ, she was tired.

Somebody wanting to know if she wished to renew her subscription to the *L.A. Times.* The second call was Bobby, telling her to call him ASAP. That had been while she was having dinner with Gail. Another call from Nook, Romanowski, then Bobby again. Fubar in full panic was the fifth call. She fast-forwarded to the next call.

"Hi. It's Gail. It's not too often I get to call people this late, so I thought I'd take advantage of it."

It sounded like she was chewing as she continued, "I just wanted to thank you again for dinner. It was sweet of you to call me. And thanks for sharing your bad day with me and letting me share mine. It makes them more bearable, don't you think? At any rate, I hope the rest of your night went well. Hope you get some sleep. Call me if you want. I'll be up until about midnight. I have a ton of e-mail to catch up on. Bye. Oh! I almost forgot. Do you like opera? Don Giovanni's at the Pavillion. It could be fun. Let me know. Bye."

Frank checked her watch, knowing it was well beyond midnight, but hoping she was wrong. Stripping her clothes off, she rewound the last message and played it again, falling naked into bed, almost asleep before she could get the covers up under her chin.

Chapter Twenty-nine

She left home again as the sky was graying to the east. The young day retained a hint of coolness and Frank sped down the highway with the windows open, the wind slapping her hair dry. Before the sun had crossed the horizon, she was walking up three flights of stairs, smelling dirty diapers, urine, and old grease. She knocked at Ocho Ruiz's apartment and an old woman opened the door, eyes snapping to attention when Frank flashed her badge. She protested, trying to close the door, but Frank held it open.

"Calmate," she soothed. Her accent was awful but it seemed to help and the woman quieted. In broken Spanish Frank told her she only wanted to talk to Ruiz. She wasn't here to arrest him. Sweeping her hand behind her she indi-

cated she was alone, *"No hay mas policia. Solo quiero hablar."*
Just talk.

The woman backed up, still frightened, and Frank spoke
in English, telling her to get Ruiz. She must have understood
because she went into a room down a narrow hall. After some
muttering, Ruiz appeared, equally fuzzy-eyed and disheveled.

Frank showed her ID again and told Ruiz she needed to
talk to him. He asked what about and she told him Placa's
murder. Exasperated, he pawed on a low coffee table for a
pack of cigarettes.

"Why you people comin' aroun' with that shit again? I
don't know nothin' about that bitch."

"I believe you," Frank said. Ruiz lit up, cocking a curious
eye at the lieutenant. Frank didn't think he recognized her
from the Dolly Parton interrogation, but she didn't give him
time to dwell on it.

"Look. You are *not* a suspect in Placa's shooting. I have a
suspect. But unless you can give me a really good alibi, you
look like the better suspect and the district attorney isn't
gonna believe it's this other person."

Frank explained she needed to know exactly where he was,
and who with, so that she could clear him. If he was innocent,
he had nothing to be afraid of.

"We know you were involved in that shooting at Eagle
Rock. Personally, I don't give a shit. The guy's okay. All I care
about right now is nailing this sonofabitch who killed Placa.
If you talk to me, give me a good alibi so I can eliminate you
as a suspect, I'll make sure nothing happens to you. I don't
want you for any of that other shit. I want to be able to say
to the DA, Octavio Ruiz didn't do it and here's why."

"Then I go to jail for shooting that punk."

"No. If you're being *carnal*, if you had nothing to do with
Placa, I'll make sure they can't touch you for anything related
to that evening."

"What about my posse?"

Frank needed Ruiz, so she said, "Them too," unsure how she could guarantee that. Ruiz fell onto the couch, considering the bargain. He was being cooperative for once so Frank maintained a persuasive rather than coercive tack.

"I don't want you, Ocho. I don't want your homes. I want the person that I *know* did this. Thing is, I don't have a lot of evidence, so the DA's gonna laugh me out of her office when I go to her and say oh it's this other person not Octavio Ruiz. But if I can prove it's not you, and none of your crew, she'll have to look at what I got. Then we can lay off you. I don't like wasting my time chasing after you any more than you like my detectives all over your ass. If you help, we both get what we want."

"No matter what we was doin' that night?"

"Except for murder, I don't give a flying fuck."

"How do I know you ain't lying?"

"You don't. All you have is my promise. Ask around to see if it's any good."

Frank and Ruiz maintained a stare. Finally Ruiz said, "I've heard a you," and started to talk. He stuck to the story he'd told her in the box, only this time he added it was a business trip; he and his *vatos* had gone there to sell some guns. A .22, two .38s and a .44.

Frank nodded.

"I need to know who the homes were."

Ruiz pouted and Frank assured him, "I ain't gonna bust nobody. I just gotta check out your story."

"Man, this don't fly, bustin' my *vatos*."

"I'm not bustin' anybody. I already told you that. But just hangin' with your homes doesn't make a very strong alibi. I want people that were there, that are gonna swear to me that you were there too. That's all. I get that, you never see me again."

Ruiz sneered. "Yeah, right. First it's me, them my homes. You fuckin' one-times are all liars."

"Hey. Whatever. You can believe me and have me out of your life or you can have me in your face and in your friends faces until I get my answers. And if I have to do it the hard way, I'm taking everybody down with me, and I'll tell them it's 'cause you were too fuckin' chicken-shit to cooperate."

"Ain't chicken-shit," Ruiz laughed around a drag on his cigarette.

"Then let's end this right now. It's on you, man."

Ruiz considered her from behind the curling smoke.

"You know if somethin' was to happen to me, I got people on the street reppin' me. Even if you was to fuck me, you couldn't fuck everybody."

Frank nodded submissively. Her acquiescence lured Ruiz into thinking he had the upper hand. He stared at her some more, hard, before saying, "This is fucked, man."

Then he gave her names. She wrote them down, and as she was leaving he said, "You got a sister?"

"Yeah," Frank lied. "She's a secretary at the station."

"I thought so. You better be tellin' me the truth here, you know what I mean, cuz she's a nice lady. You wouldn't want nothin' to happen to her, you know what I'm sayin'?"

"I hear you, man."

Frank made it to the station just in time for briefing. It was short and tense, with a lot of unanswered questions and accusations that Frank said she'd explain later. She rushed back out, eager to catch Ruiz' homies still in bed. Camped in rush hour traffic she reflected that letting Ruiz go was highly immoral, and illegal, but she needed every thing she could lay her hands on to nail Placa's shooter. She didn't like bargaining over felonies, but told herself it was only a matter of time before Ruiz got in trouble again. Sooner or later he'd get caught for something.

She further rationalized Ruiz' shooting wasn't as serious as Placa's murder. It was a simple accounting based on the rules of the street: one lesser crime was not equal to or greater than the crime of murder. The only flaw in this logic was the possibility that Ruiz' next crime might be murder.

But Frank was willing to gamble on that. Inching along, she consoled her conscience with the fact that the Estrellas weren't inherently bad. They were simply playing a bad hand as well as they knew how. They hadn't gotten a lot of opportunities and none of them, except Placa, seemed to have the wherewithal to change their lives.

On the other hand, there was no justification for the shooter. Here was someone who had it all, who was sworn to uphold the law and protect the public, but was instead using his position to create more power. Frank could excuse ignorance and she could understand avarice, but she couldn't bear his total disregard for a justice that she still believed in, still fought for and tried her best to maintain every day.

Clay had nailed it during their first session together. Work was all Frank had. It was her god, her muse, and her passion. And to do her work she had to believe that justice existed at some level. Whether it was meted out from the courts or delivered swiftly on the streets, she had to know that there was a reason why she did what she did every day. Sometimes she failed, that was true, but not for lack of effort. Sometimes the system beat her and it was easier to go along so she could get along. And like with Larkin, sometimes, she looked the other way. Her old boss had been right when he'd said sometimes law and justice didn't recognize each other on the street.

Frank could justify until the freeway cleared, but the truth was, she would use whatever she had to get this bastard. If that meant playing outside the law and on the streets, then Frank was in the middle of the road. Joe had asked her if she was willing to take on the risks of this case and she'd meant it when she answered yes. If she had to, she'd leak what she had and let public sentiment force Nelson into action. It would probably get her fired, but better to be fired she reasoned, than not be able to look at herself in the mirror.

~ ~ ~ ~ ~

An hour after the deadline that night, when she still hadn't heard from anyone, Frank called the chief. She hadn't dug up much since yesterday. This bastard's tracks were well covered, but Frank had sworn testimonies from Claudia and Gloria, as well as Ruiz, Lydia, and two home boys. Not the most reputable witnesses, but Frank was hoping she could parlay the quantity of wits for the quality. She'd forked over a small ransom to a source at the phone company who faxed her a years worth of phone bills. She'd highlighted all the calls to Julio Estrella's house, and then the sudden flurry of calls to Claudia's house after the massacre. It wasn't much but it was better than what she'd had. He sighed heavily and told her he'd call back. Frank paced while she waited, jumping on the phone when it rang. Nelson told her to proceed.

Frank shot her fist to the ceiling, and yelled a silent, *Yes!*

"But only on trafficking and extortion charges."

"*What?*" she yelled, unable to contain her dismay.

"The department's legal team and the DA's office feel that at this time those are the only charges you can substantiate."

Despite the over-riding sensation that she was in a bad free-fall, she picked up the chief's use of "you." It dawned on her as she listened to his self-serving rationale, that she was in this alone. All the way.

"The homicide charges aren't based on anything more than circumstance and hearsay. A bad attorney could laugh us out of court on that; in the hands of a good attorney . . . well, I don't even want to speculate on the repercussions that could invite."

Nelson said more politic things, then pointedly warned Frank from pursuing any investigations other than the ones he'd sanctioned. She hung up, dumb-struck. But she shouldn't have been.

The twenty-four hours had been to tear apart what little Frank had; the chief had only been stalling her. And she'd been an *idiot* to think he'd stick his neck out. Frank was furious with herself. She circled the empty desks in the squad room. It hurt, she thought. It hurt that she'd set herself up for a fall, that she worked for a man and an organization that wouldn't back her in doing the right thing. Their gross and abject failure was wounding. But what hurt the most was Frank's failure to protect Claudia and her children, the live ones as well as the dead.

Frank slammed a quick one-two at the wall, cracking the plaster board. She knew it was stupid but she welcomed the pain in her fists. It was better than the pain in her heart and she did it again. She bowed her head against the wall until she'd collected herself, then started making phone calls.

Chapter Thirty

She sat stoically behind the big desk. She had one card left and was waiting to play it. Her fingers beat a staccato on the chair's scarred old arms. Finally she heard him. Click, click. Those were his shoes on the stairs. Click, click. Through the squad room. Click, click, and into her office. He was handsome, even with the scratches on his face and swelling jaw. Of course he was as immaculate as always. He always rolled out beautifully. Tonight it was a tailored navy pinstripe with silk tie and French cuffs.

"Hey, what's going on?"

"You tell me," she answered.

Ike Zabbo's face screwed up.

"What are you talking about?"

Frank clucked and shook her head.

"You shouldn't have gone after Toñio, man."

Ike grinned in disbelief, "What the fuck are you talking about?"

"Landing him in the hospital like that? You fucked up. Cut his liver in a couple places. Busted his spleen. If he dies, it's a homicide with two witnesses."

She shook her head again, disappointed. "Sloppy work, Pink. "

"Hey, you called me in to roll. I don't know what's going on here but if there's no case, I'm leaving."

"There's a case, Ike. We're on it. This is it."

The detective squinted at his lieutenant.

"Are you drunk?"

"No." Frank sat calmly behind her desk, ready to play her trump card. "You shouldn't have lost it. Before this, you were pretty much home free. I gotta hand it to you. You panicked a little with Placa, but even there it was hard to pin you down. You'd have probably walked on her too. But after tonight . . ."

Frank made a who-knows gesture.

"I'm sure you've been calling the hospital. He's thrown three clots already. That's a lot and chances are good he'll throw another one. The doctor said his heart's wearing out. If he dies, Ike, you're fried and fucked. Twelve different ways."

"I don't know what you're talking about. I'm out of here."

He turned to go but she caught the sudden gleam of perspiration on his forehead.

"What I can't figure," she responded evenly, "Is how the fuck you thought you were going to get away with this. I admit though, the traces of horse hair and alfalfa really threw me off. Funny how after all this time my prejudices still color my judgment. I was thinking Hunt had done all this. Can you imagine? But you've got to admit he's the sort of asshole you'd *expect* to do something like this. Yet here you are, worse than that damn Okie," she grinned with teeth.

"Tell me how you thought you were going to get away with this. I mean I always thought you were a smart cop, but this," she threw up a hand, "This is pretty stupid, Ike. Toñio's rattled your cage and he's bringing you down. Some punk wet-back's bringing the great Ike Zabbo to his knees. Go figure."

Ike laughed, "No one's bringing me to my knees, babe."

Frank admired his confidence, as she asked, "You want to talk to me or walk out that door?"

"I'm walking."

Frank slid an arrest warrant across the desk. "You won't get far."

"What the hell's that for?"

"All I could get you on. But I'm not done."

Ike picked it up and read it, put it down.

"You're making a big mistake," he warned.

"How so?"

"I want my lawyer."

Frank pushed her phone toward him. When he was done talking to his attorney, he jabbed a finger at her.

"You're going down in flames, baby doll. And I'm gonna laugh while you burn."

"Did you get behind on the ponies? Is that what started this all? I like the way you hooked up with Barracas. That was good. He'd confiscate the shit, you'd report half of it or less, then you had all the contacts to sell it to. Your associates at the track. Then you guys got bigger and wanted to branch out so you bought that string of ponies. Trailer them back and forth to the races in Texas and Arizona, concentrate on the border states where it's easy to pick up a couple keys, stash it in the trailers. False bottoms in the tack trunks. I like that, too. Nice. Nobody looks twice. Run it back in. Get Jimmy's family to run it for you. You two probably have old buds in Narco that agreed to not sweat the Estrellas. And you never get dirty.

"Then Jimmy tried to muscle you out. He put up all the money for the ponies and he had all the contacts now. Didn't

272

need you anymore. Told you to take a walk. And you should've, Pink. Should've been smart enough to get out then. But instead you took him out. Took the whole family out. Set it up to look like Luis. You put his sweatshirt and his shoes on, didn't you? Must've been a tight squeeze but you got blood all over both them. None on his pants, though. No way you could've got into those. Oh well, close enough, huh? Then you drove over to Claudia's. Told them what you did. Told them they were your new partners. Did you do Luis before or after that? Huh?"

"Fuck you, Franco. You got nothing on me and you know it."

"Wrong, Pink. I've got you for this," she tapped a warrant, "and if Toñio dies, I got you for the rest of it too. Including Placa. You were good with the Estrellas and Luis. I admit, they'll be harder to nail you on, but give me time. I'll get you."

Ike laughed, "You're one delusional bitch. Yeah, so Toñio and I got in a fight. Little spic pulled a fucking knife on me. I was *defending* myself."

When Frank said that wasn't Gloria's version, Ike laughed again.

"Like a jury's gonna believe that cunt over me? I don't think so."

"They might when I pull some more rabbits out of my hat."

"Like what?"

"Like her PERK results. Same as Placa's. Plus I combed the back of your chair for fibers, sent them up to DOJ with the wool ones we pulled off Placa. Think any'll match? You really gotta lose those suits. Way too incriminating."

"So I got some gash. What's your problem, Frank, you jealous?"

"My problem," Frank said tapping her murder book, "is that phone records — and that was sloppy too — show you calling the Estrella's one hour and thirteen minutes before Placa died."

"Since when is it illegal to call someone?"

"My problem," she continued, "is that she was raped sometime within that seventy-three minute period. How do you think your DNA sample's going to match up to hers?"

She didn't give him time to answer.

"That was your biggest mistake wasn't it? You underestimated her. Thought you could cut off a piece then dump her somewhere and that your cum would've dried up by the time she was found. But she got away from you didn't she? You had no choice but to fire right there. Fortunately for you, you always were the best shooter in the squad. But again, that was sloppy. Two wits placed a round-backed sedan at the scene. It was convenient for you that Ruiz drove a T-bird. They look a lot like a Lincoln down a dark street. But his has a brown interior. Yours is tan. I looked when you rolled Monday night. Got a carpet sample for DOJ too. Should match the fibers under Placa's nails and maybe the ones stuck in Luis' shoes. What do you think?"

"I think you're losing it, Frank. You've had your head up too many asses lately and you're short on oxygen."

"My *problem* is you set her up, Ike. You knew she was going to tell me. You heard it all at the Alibi that night. Even offered to go with me, which I thought was overly generous of you. You must have gone over to Claudia's the minute I left the bar. Bought yourself some time 'til you could think what to do with Placa. But you underestimated her again. She got away from you, didn't she?"

"I can't believe you're serious," he said in amazement. Frank's smile yawed like an arctic crevasse.

"Dead serious," she said dangling a phony search warrant.

"They're in your crib even as we speak. What are they going to find?"

"Nothing," he said, which was exactly what Frank expected. Even Ike wasn't stupid enough to have kept the guns or have a stash in his house. He leaned menacingly across the desk.

"You know what I don't get, is why you and half this ass-kissing squad give a fuck about these goddamn beaners. So somebody took out another milk maker and spared L.A. another dozen babies on welfare." His hands flew up, "Big fucking deal."

Frank sucked on her bottom lip, savoring the sensation of wrapping her belt around Ike's thick neck and pulling until he was blue and his eyes bugged out.

"Yeah, it's a big fucking deal, and if you were a halfway decent cop you'd know that."

"I'm more cop than you'll ever be."

"Not by the time I'm done with you," she answered.

The phone rang, startling them both. Ike stared at it, then at Frank. She answered, listened. She chewed her lip, glanced at Ike.

"Bring Claudia and Gloria in for formal statements." Then, "No, that's okay. Just come back to the station. I need to talk to you. And Nook."

Frank hung up, saying nothing.

"Let me guess," Ike snickered. "That was Bobby conveniently calling to tell you poor Toñio threw another clot, only this one killed him. Am I right?"

Frank pushed the phone at him.

"Bingo."

Ike doubled over, "There is no *way* I'm falling for that. Fuck, I'm insulted!" Smoothing his hand over his slick hair, he chuckled, "Thinking you can run a scam on me. Give me a break, Frank. I'm not some moron off the street."

"No, you're not. That's why beating Toñio to death surprised me. What do you weigh? About 200? A two-hundred pound cop kicks the shit out of a 14-year old that weighs 120 if he's wet. And you think a jury in L.A.'s gonna *smile* at that? You better hope Johnnie Cochran's your lawyer, man."

Smiling viciously, Ike punched a number into the phone. "Give me intensive care."

Neither cop took their eyes off the other.

"This is Captain Foubarelle, LAPD. Let me talk to Detective Nukisona."

A pause that filled years, then, "Hey Nook. It's Ike. What's going on with that Estrella kid, man?"

Frank was sure Ike could hear her heart and she prayed, *Come on, Nook! Come on!*

"He did, huh? What of? Oh yeah. What time? Really? Nook, man, I hate to say this but it sounds like you're bullshitting a bullshitter. What the hell's going on over there?"

He stared at her, listening. An icy drop of sweat splashed onto her ribs and she had to remind herself to breathe.

"You levelin' with me? 'Cause it doesn't sound like you are, man. Let me in. What's going on?"

Ike's face split nastily and he faked surprise when he said, "She told you to tell everyone that, huh?"

Frank depressed the phone button.

"Okay. You get round one. But your worst nightmare's just starting."

Ike cackled, slamming the handset down, "Oh *baby*. That was a good one! You actually thought you'd get me blabbing didn't you, spilling my guts like some punk-ass bitch. Thought I wouldn't notice I hadn't been Mirandized. You're incredible, baby, just incredible."

Hanging over Frank's desk, he went on, "Let me tell you, Frankie-girl, don't waste your time. I am Mr. Teflon and you are not going to get *anything* to stick on me. You hear me? *Nothing*. Now, is there anything else before I go outside for a smoke?"

"Go ahead," she said, "Go get your smoke. The condemned man having one last cigarette — I like it."

"You're the one that's condemned. Your career?" He dove his hand toward the floor. "Crash and burn, le Freek. Film and pictures at eleven."

He laughed all the way out of the squad room. Frank stared at the blank rectangle of her open door. She wondered idly if she was going to throw up or slam the wall again. Neither seemed like a good option. She'd had her shot and she'd blown it. Frank just stared at her phone for a while. Finally she reached for it. It was time for Nelson to set his dogs loose, muzzled as they were.

Chapter Thirty-one

Frank had put too many people in jail to appreciate an unexpected knock on her door. She put her beer on the counter, glancing at the 9mm holstered on the table.

"Who is it?" she bellowed over the stereo.

"It's me. Gail."

Checking through the peephole to make sure someone wasn't holding a gun on the doc, Frank thought, I am becoming one paranoid asshole.

"Hey. Why aren't you home in bed?"

"I wish I were," Gail groaned. "I had a date with the mayor."

"Uh-oh."

"I wanted to call you but I didn't want to wake you up in

case you were sleeping. So I drove by and when I saw the lights on . . . do you mind if I come in for a minute?"

"You're in, aren't you?"

"I'm serious. Do you have a sec?"

"Sure," she answered, nudging Gail toward the kitchen. "Can I buy you a beer? Something stronger?"

"No. Just an ear," she said slumping onto a stool at the counter. "You were right. He wants me to bury her blood-alcohol."

"What are you going to do?"

"I don't know," she groaned. She picked at a chip in the lively Mexican tile.

"He threatened to out me."

She looked up at Frank, clearly agonized.

"And you too."

"Amazing," Frank blurted. She sought refuge from this additional betrayal in the cop's time-honored use of crude humor. "You're not even getting any and they're twisting you. You'd think they'd at least have the decency to wait until you were getting properly laid before they blackmailed you."

"It's not funny, Frank. They've seen us around. One thing leads to another."

Frank was leaning on the opposite side of the counter. Her hand found the back of her neck as she marveled, "We can't send a man to jail for killing eight people — and a dog — but we can ruin one woman's career because she has dinner with another woman. What a country, huh?"

"I don't want to drag you into this," Gail said and Frank gave a short, hard laugh.

"Drag away, doc. This is stupid. This is so fucked. All of it. If they kicked me out tomorrow I don't know that that would be such a bad thing."

"Maybe you're ready to go but I just got here and I've worked damn hard to get here too. I don't want to lose it all now."

"Gail, you're not going to lose it all just because the

fucking mayor tells KABC you're a lesbian. He's a dick, you're a dyke. Let public sentiment decide."

"I wish it were that simple, but he's a very powerful player. He said in so many words that he can make things very ugly. For both of us."

"Whatever," Frank said. She drained her beer and pulled another out of the fridge. Slapping the top off against a ceramic opener set into the wall, she asked, "Sure you don't want one?"

"I'm sure. She was blind drunk, Frank. She killed *three kids* before their lives barely even got started. Talk about your public sentiment. That would bury him in a heartbeat. If I lie, I keep my job. Until the next ugly incident. But if I lie, I don't know that I could get out of bed in the morning. I hate this."

"Don't tell me you've never been asked to do anything like this before."

"Not this bad."

Gail looked at Frank as if she had an answer and Frank nodded. Bending over the counter Frank confided, "You know, I was thinking about this the other day. I offered a deal to the kid we originally thought capped Placa. He and his home boys talk to me, give me their alibi, and except for smoking someone, I'd look the other way. It wasn't right, but neither was losing a case against Ike. Sometimes it's okay to look the other way and sometimes it's not. There's just a hairline between right and wrong and I only hope I don't cross too far onto the wrong side.

"I've done things I'll never tell anyone about. Some of them seemed like the best choices at the time. I figure by and large I'm a pretty good cop, and I can do more good on the street than off. I can't help anyone if I'm not out there. I've made choices that kept me in the game, choices that I justified for the long run. Remember what they always told you when you were a kid? It's not who wins or loses, but how you play the game? Might be true in games but it's bullshit in politics.

It's all about who wins and loses, and that's all it's about. Problem is, you and I, we're still in it for the game."

Frank swallowed some beer. She hated the anguish on Gail's face. Wished she could wipe it away. Sonny Stitt blew *Sweet and Lovely* from the speakers and Frank thought, yes she is.

"You'll do the right thing, Gay. Whatever that is for you."

Gail nodded glumly.

"God! I *hate* this!" She ran her fingers through her hair, insisting, "I can't do it. I'll hate myself forever if I do. Goddamn it. But what about you?"

Frank lifted a shoulder.

"I'm not going any farther in my career than I already am. Surprised I made it this far, actually. If they busted me down to a DIII that wouldn't be so bad either. I could live with that. If they busted me out of the department . . . long as I get my pension, I don't know that I really care. At least not tonight."

"I thought you were so gung-ho. *Semper fi* and all that malarkey."

"I love my job. I never said I loved who I work for."

"I thought you worked for the people."

"That's true," Frank allowed. She studied the slim head on her beer and Gail said, "So I tell him no. There. The decision's made."

Gail snapped her fingers.

"Two brilliant careers over just like that."

"Ain't over 'til it's over," Frank smiled tiredly.

"Well however it turns out, thanks for listening. You're a good sounding board, you know that?"

"It's my job, ma'am."

"Hey, did you get my message last night? About Don Giovanni?"

"Yeah. Sounds dope."

"*Dope*?" Gail said wagging her head. "You've been on the streets far too long."

"Yeah. I need me some cult-cha."

"I'll give you cult-cha. Can I have a sip of that?" she asked, jutting her chin at the Corona. Frank slid it to her.

"How was your day?"

"Don't ask."

"It couldn't have been worse than mine," Gail said smugly.

"Don't count on it," Frank said, and Gail gradually wheedled the past forty-hours out of Frank.

"You know," Frank decided. "It's not even Ike so much. Yeah, that hurts, that one of my own men did this. I hate it but on some level I can even understand it. He's lost a few nuts. Something's rattling around loose in his head when it should be bolted down tight. Maybe he didn't come back from 'Nam right, I don't know. A lot of guys didn't.

"But the thing that gets me, is the institution. You know, I wanted to be a cop because my uncle was. I heard all his stories and I believed in good guys triumphing over bad guys. I *believed* that shit. And then when — well, some other things happened and I really believed that I had to be a cop, that I had to go out there and make a difference like my Uncle Al did. So I joined the force, swallowed the pabulum they fed us in the academy, and for a while I believed that our mission truly was "To Protect and Serve". Yeah, some bad things happened, but by and large I thought the LAPD was founded on good, solid values, that when push came to shove we'd do the right thing.

"Even today, until Nelson told me to let this go, I still believed they'd come through. I still believed they'd do the right thing. And that they didn't is killing me. No one gives a flying fuck about the Estrellas. They're just dopers out of the barrio. And I know it's that way, I'm not stupid. You don't spend seventeen years on the force and not know that it's all about the department. But when it comes to something like this, something really big, you always hope that someone'll do the right thing. That just this *one time* they'll do the right thing.

"And of course they didn't. Ike probably gets nothing worse than a boot off the force. My squad's coming apart at the seams. My own men think I'm a cheese-eater, and eight people are dead. And the fucking dog. And you know what the worst thing about all this is? As bad as all this shit is, the worst was having to go to Claudia's today and tell her there was nothing I could do. I couldn't even say how sorry I was, because she'd known all along what I couldn't — or wouldn't — believe."

Frank waved her empty beer.

"I'm babbling, doc. Sorry."

"No, don't be," Gail consoled. She reached for Frank's hand. "It's good for you. You need to talk this out. Keep talking."

Frank studied the crow's feet around Gail's eyes, the high cheekbones, and the little ear peeking out behind the shiny, dark hair. There were some wisps of gray at her temples that Frank hadn't noticed and she wondered if the doc touched them up.

"No," Frank said. "I think what I need right now is for you to dance with me."

She stepped around the counter and held her hand out to Gail.

"Would you do that?"

Gail took the offered hand, smiling, "You bet."

Frank held her lightly, but close. She inhaled the familiar peach shampoo, and underneath it, a dim, sexy scent that was uniquely, arousingly Gail's.

"I'm a horrible dancer," Gail warned into Frank's shoulder.

"Me too."

The song ended, but Frank kept leading, until Dexter's trumpet moaned into *Round Midnight*. Checking her watch, she joked, "They're playing our song."

"I didn't know we had a song."

"We do now."

"Meaning what, copper?"

"Meaning this."

Frank bent her lips to Gail's, lingering over them. They kept dancing, their lips exploring the others, until Frank traced hers along Gail's jaw, under the hollow beneath, on down the smooth and creamy silk of her throat. They moved together closely, dancing until they weren't following the music anymore but rather the rhythm of their own longing. When their lips parted for a moment, Frank whispered, "Stay."

Gail seemed reluctant, explaining, "This isn't how I planned it."

"How'd you plan it?" Frank teased gently. "Was I even in it?"

"Most definitely," Gail shined.

"So tell me how this should go."

Pressed together, ostensibly dancing, Gail said, "Well, first of all it was at my place. There'd be music — which we have — and lots of candles, and wine, and I wouldn't have just been blackmailed by the mayor and coming home from work. I'd be clean and lovely and in some very sexy but unrevealing slinky thing from Victoria's Secret."

"Hm. Well, I have candles and I have wine. And I can't do anything about the mayor, but I do have a shower and a clean T-shirt."

Gail laughed and Frank murmured, "Could that possibly be close enough?"

The doc pressed into Frank and didn't answer. They danced amid saxophones and tinkling pianos while Frank ached for Gail.

"I'm scared," the doc finally admitted.

"Of what?" Frank asked, not loosening her arms. She felt Gail take in a full breath, heard her say, "Of what you'll think. When you see me."

"And what do you think that'll be?" Frank said into the sweet hair, drowning in the scent of it.

"Probably nothing. But maybe you'll be repulsed."

"No," Frank whispered. "That's not going to happen. I promise. And it's okay if you're afraid. I don't want to push you into something you're not ready for, but you also need to know how much I want you, Gay. I want you so very much."

"Are you sure?"

With a quick, soft laugh, Frank allowed, "That's the only thing I'm sure of."

She gathered Gail even more closely, telling her, "You've got to do what's right for you, and if that means leaving, I'll hate it, but I'll understand."

Gail stepped away from Frank. Bringing her arms up around her neck she said, "I don't want to leave."

"Then stay," Frank pleaded. "Stay."

Gail held the cobalt eyes for a long moment before asking, "So where's that T-shirt?"

Epilogue

Frank sat in her work clothes, her shirt open to the sun. She was methodically killing a bottle of Glenfiddich and decided through her growing buzz that it was pretty hot. She should probably change into shorts before she melted, although melting into a puddle and disappearing didn't seem like such a bad idea. It had a certain macabre appeal to it, Frank decided. Like something out of Alice in Wonderland.

Swirling the whiskey in her glass, she silently implored, *Come on. Do your stuff.* She couldn't get drunk fast enough. She tried pretending she didn't hear the doorbell, but she wasn't that drunk. Yet. She stood slowly and made her way through the house, glass in hand. She was hoping it would be a Jesus solicitor behind the door. She was up for a good theological sparring and was disconcerted to see Gail standing there instead.

"Hi. I tried calling but kept getting a busy signal. Noah said you'd gone home."

"Here I am."

Frank opened the door wider and Gail stepped into the coolness of the house. Frank watched the doc impassively appraise the drink in her hand and the shirt hanging out of her pants. She knew her eyes were slitting up too. They did that when she was well on her way to oblivion.

"You do the post?" she asked picking her syllables carefully.

"Yeah. I just came by to see how you were. Noah was worried about you."

"He worries too much."

"He cares about you."

Touchy-feely stuff. Frank didn't want to go anywhere near that. Might ruin the effect of all that good scotch.

"What did you find?"

Sober enough to see Gail's confusion, she clarified, "When you cut."

"Nothing. Somebody emptied a .25 into him. It was a clean hit."

A clean hit.

Frank almost smiled, wondering if Gail knew she had just used police parlance for a justified shooting.

And justified it was, Frank told herself convincingly. Somebody had taken out Ike Zabbo last night. The sweeper driver at Hollywood Park had found him under his car in the back lot. Frank had handled her crew, letting them go home if they wanted to, but with strict orders not to bug Southeast or the Coroner's Office for information. It wasn't their case. In fact it had probably been kicked up from Southeast to Robbery-Homicide by now. Frank thought to ask Gail who was at the post, then decided she didn't really want to know. She swallowed the last of the drink, relishing its pure, raw burn. Then she realized she was being an impolite hostess.

"Can I get you a Coke or something? Too early for a beer?"

Indicating her empty glass, Gail said, "I'll have whatever you're having. It's been a long day already."

"Amen," Frank agreed. "Follow me."

She swiped a glass out of the cupboard and led Gail to the patio. Pushing a chair into the shade for her, she dribbled a finger of scotch into Gail's glass and resumed her basking. Gail was at an angle behind her and Frank could feel the pretty green eyes crawling all over her. She'd like to dive into those mossy green pools and never be seen again. Just sink down into Wonderland. Bye-bye.

Gail startled Frank when she perched next to her on the lounge chair.

"You're going to get burnt," she said pulling Frank's collar together.

"Worst of the sun's down," Frank argued, her free hand finding the rounded weight of Gail's hip.

"Still, you don't get a lot there."

Frank wanted to look at Gail but didn't dare.

"Do they have any idea who did it?"

Rolling a swallow of scotch around, Frank considered the question.

She'd gone by the Estrella's as soon as she could, glad there were no cops there. It was the time of day when the sun was sharp and merciless, the time of day that revealed every last flaw and detail, the time of day fading glories hated. She'd walked up the driveway, pressing past the Estrella's old car. Frank had studied the heat shimmying off the hood, resigned to the fact that summer was here. It sure would have been nice to get one last storm, but it hadn't rained in weeks and there was nothing but sunshine in the forecast. For a long while Frank had studied what looked like mud on the passengers side.

When she finally continued up the drive, Claudia had answered her knock. From behind the screen door, she could have been carved from wood. Frank asked how Toñio was.

"Okay."

She'd searched the weathered face, fuller than it was seventeen years ago, more deeply etched. But the eyes still burned bright and fierce. They asked for nothing and gave it in return. Claudia looked far beyond Frank's shoulder, resigned to enduring this fool one more time.

As if she were telling Claudia the time, Frank had said, "You know Ike Zabbo's dead."

Claudia had slowly shifted her eyes back to Frank's. The old adversaries wrestled wordlessly through the screen. Frank had eventually looked away.

"It's a nice day. Might want to wash your car."

Frank glanced at the Buick dancing in its heat waves.

"You've got some mud or something on the passenger side. Should get that off before it bakes on."

She'd left the vague shade of the porch, went back to the office, and told Foubarelle she was taking the rest of the day off. He'd spluttered and objected but she hadn't used a sick day in two years.

Now Gail was staring at her and Frank thought she really should get out of these hot clothes. Melting didn't seem so appealing anymore.

"Frank? Did you hear my question?"

"I heard it," she said into her drink. "No. I don't think they do."

She'd answered the question but Gail was still studying her. She lifted Frank's chin.

"Do you?" she asked quietly.

Frank stared into her glass.

"I'm gonna tell you a story. Probably 'cause I've had too much to drink but it's a good story. I think you'll like it. So once upon a time, a girl — she's ten — she's walking home from the corner market with her father. It's winter. It's dark

289

even though it's not that late. And it's cold. Not that that's relevant."

Frank heard herself slur a bit on the last sentences, made a note to watch that. She hated sloppy drunks.

"The father's carrying a bag of groceries. Dinner. Frosted flakes. Milk. Orange juice. And Ring Dings, 'cause his daughter had asked for them. You'll see in a moment why I remember the contents so clearly. They're walking. He's holding the grocery bag with one arm. His other's held out to his daughter. She's got her hand in his. His hand's big and warm and she feels safe next to him. Out of nowhere, a junkie jumps in front of them. He's got an ugly little gun. Snub-nosed .38 I realize later, when I become an expert in such things."

Frank's mouth was dry and she wet it with the good scotch. She resumed her story.

"All I knew then was that it was the scariest thing I'd ever seen. And this junkie was shaking it in front of us. He could barely point it, he was shaking so bad. And he's screaming at my father to give him his wallet. My father tried to calm him down. He pulled me behind him and he reached for his wallet. I felt it leave his pocket. I was watching the junkie. I was terrified, but I was fascinated, too. The junkie looked like a dog I saw some kids set on fire once. Desperate. Scared. He was Jonesing so bad. My father handed him the wallet and he grabbed for it. When he did, Dad dropped the groceries and lunged at him. I don't know why. He wouldn't have hurt us. He just wanted the money, but maybe my dad didn't want to give up his paycheck. He was a proud guy, stubborn. He worked hard for his money. I guess he thought he could take him. I don't know. The junkie's gun went off. My dad went down on his knee. He made a real heavy sound, then kinda toppled over onto the milk and frosted flakes and orange juice. The junkie took off. They never did find him. My Uncle Al was a cop. Handsome guy, like my father. Heavier, but it didn't matter when he was in his uniform. I though they looked like movie stars. Both of 'em. He drank himself to death. Got kicked off the force, drank all day. Blew his liver out at fifty-six. See, he was a cop. And someone killed his only brother and he couldn't do a damn thing about it."

Frank paused for another sip.

"I was in the station all night. My mom too. But nothing I told them was good enough. They never caught the guy. My mom got worse after that. She was manic-depressive and there were a lot more lows than highs. When I was in sixth grade, I started reading every criminology and every true crime book I could get my hands on. Devoured 'em. I was gonna be a cop. A good one. One who caught bad guys. Got good grades. Got scholarships to three universities. Kissed my mother goodbye. I wasn't gonna go down with her, I couldn't, and out I came to sunny California. Land of milk and honey. Became a cop.

"That's all I ever wanted to do was be a cop. And I've been a good one. Yeah, I've bent the rules sometimes. In the long run you have to. I remember Joe saying, 'Law and justice ain't the same thing, kiddo.' And I didn't believe him. Didn't want to. I *had* to believe they were the same thing, see? The law was all I had. It was all I had to put my faith into. And I know he was right. I knew it a long time ago. But I still like to pretend. It justifies what I do every day. And sometimes they *are* the same thing. And then it's a good day. When they're not, when law and justice are light years apart, then it's a bad day. And today was a very bad day."

Finches chirped in the oak over-hanging the yard. The faraway rush of cars sounded like surf. A couple yards over, kids voices rose and fell in play. Gail asked quietly, "Do you know who shot him?"

Frank shifted her face toward the sun, closing her eyes against its burn. Trying to forget the spatter on Claudia

Estrella's Buick, Frank marveled at the negative images playing against her eyelids. She thought maybe she'd like to take a photography class someday.

"Frank?"

Gail's hand was a command on her shoulder.

"No," she said to the invisible sun. "I don't know."

About the Author

Baxter Clare lives on a ranch in Southern California with her longtime companion, numerous houseguests, wild animals, and domestic pets. *Street Rules* is her second mystery.

Publications from
BELLA BOOKS, INC.
the best in contemporary lesbian fiction

P.O. Box 201007   Ferndale, MI 48220
Phone: 800-729-4992
www.bellabooks.com

LEGACY OF LOVE by Marianne K. Martin. 224 pp. Read the whole Sage Bristo story.   ISBN 1-931513-15-5 $12.95

STREET RULES: A Detective Franco Mystery by Baxter Clare. 304 pp. Gritty, fast-paced mystery with compelling Detective L.A. Franco   ISBN 1-931513-14-7 $12.95

RECOGNITION FACTOR: 4th Denise Cleever Thriller by Claire McNab. 176 pp. Denise Cleever tracks a notorious terrorist to America.   ISBN 1-931513-24-4 $12.95

NORA AND LIZ by Nancy Garden. 296 pp. Lesbian romance by the author of *Annie On My Mind*.   ISBN 1931513-20-1 $12.95

MIDAS TOUCH by Frankie J. Jones. 208 pp. Sandra had everything but love.   ISBN 1-931513-21-X $12.95

BEYOND ALL REASON by Peggy J. Herring. 240 pp. A romance hotter than Texas.   ISBN 1-9513-25-2 $12.95

ACCIDENTAL MURDER: 14th Detective Inspector Carol Ashton Mystery by Claire McNab. 208 pp.Carol Ashton tracks an elusive killer.   ISBN 1-931513-16-3 $12.95

SEEDS OF FIRE:Tunnel of Light Trilogy, Book 2 by Karin Kallmaker writing as Laura Adams. 274 pp. Intriguing sequel to *Sleight of Hand*.   ISBN 1-931513-19-8 $12.95

DRIFTING AT THE BOTTOM OF THE WORLD by Auden Bailey. 288 pp. Beautifully written first novel set in Antarctica.   ISBN 1-931513-17-1 $12.95

CLOUDS OF WAR by Diana Rivers. 288 pp. Women unite to defend Zelindar!   ISBN 1-931513-12-0 $12.95

OUTSIDE THE FLOCK by Jackie Calhoun. 220 pp. Searching for love, Jo finds temptation.   ISBN 1-931513-13-9 $12.95

WHEN GOOD GIRLS GO BAD: A Motor City Thriller by Therese Szymanski. 230 pp. Brett, Randi, and Allie join forces to stop a serial killer.   ISBN 1-931513-11-2 $12.95

DEATHS OF JOCASTA: 2nd Micky Night Mystery by J.M. Redmann. 408 pp. Sexy and intriguing Lambda Literary Award nominated mystery.   ISBN 1-931513-10-4 $12.95

LOVE IN THE BALANCE by Marianne K. Martin. 256 pp.
The classic lesbian love story, back in print!
ISBN 1-931513-08-2 $12.95

THE COMFORT OF STRANGERS by Peggy J. Herring.
272 pp. Lela's work was her passion . . . until now.
ISBN 1-931513-09-0 $12.95

CHICKEN by Paula Martinac. 208 pp. Lynn finds that the
only thing harder than being in a lesbian relationship is
ending one.   ISBN 1-931513-07-4 $11.95

TAMARACK CREEK by Jackie Calhoun. 208 pp. An in-
triguing story of love and danger.   ISBN 1-931513-06-6 $11.95

DEATH BY THE RIVERSIDE: 1st Micky Knight Mystery by
J.M. Redmann. 320 pp. Finally back in print, the book that
launched the Lambda Literary Award winning Micky Knight
mystery series.   ISBN 1-931513-05-8 $11.95

EIGHTH DAY: A Cassidy James Mystery by Kate Calloway.
272 pp. In the eighth installment of the Cassidy James
mystery series, Cassidy goes undercover at a camp for
troubled teens.   ISBN 1-931513-04-X $11.95

MIRRORS by Marianne K. Martin. 208 pp. Jean Carson and
Shayna Bradley fight for a future together.
ISBN 1-931513-02-3 $11.95

THE ULTIMATE EXIT STRATEGY: A Virginia Kelly
Mystery by Nikki Baker. 240 pp. The long-awaited return of
the wickedly observant Virginia Kelly.   ISBN 1-931513-03-1 $11.95

FOREVER AND THE NIGHT by Laura DeHart Young.
224 pp. Desire and passion ignite the frozen Arctic in this
exciting sequel to the classic romantic adventure *Love on
the Line*.   ISBN 0-931513-00-7 $11.95

WINGED ISIS by Jean Stewart. 240 pp. The long-awaited
sequel to *Warriors of Isis* and the fourth in the exciting
Isis series.   ISBN 1-931513-01-5 $11.95

ROOM FOR LOVE by Frankie J. Jones. 192 pp. Jo and
Beth must overcome the past in order to have a future
together.   ISBN 0-9677753-9-6 $11.95

THE QUESTION OF SABOTAGE by Bonnie J. Morris.
144 pp. A charming, sexy tale of romance, intrigue, and
coming of age.   ISBN 0-9677753-8-8 $11.95

SLEIGHT OF HAND by Karin Kallmaker writing as
Laura Adams. 256 pp. A journey of passion, heartbreak
and triumph that reunites two women for a final chance
at their destiny.   ISBN 0-9677753-7-X $11.95

MOVING TARGETS: A Helen Black Mystery by Pat Welch.
240 pp. Helen must decide if getting to the bottom of a
mystery is worth hitting bottom.   ISBN 0-9677753-6-1 $11.95

CALM BEFORE THE STORM by Peggy J. Herring. 208 pp. Colonel Robicheaux retires from the military and comes out of the closet. ISBN 0-9677753-1-0 $12.95

OFF SEASON by Jackie Calhoun. 208 pp. Pam threatens Jenny and Rita's fledgling relationship. ISBN 0-9677753-0-2 $11.95

WHEN EVIL CHANGES FACE: A Motor City Thriller by Therese Szymanski. 240 pp. Brett Higgins is back in another heart-pounding thriller. ISBN 0-9677753-3-7 $11.95

BOLD COAST LOVE by Diana Tremain Braund. 208 pp. Jackie Claymont fights for her reputation and the right to love the woman she chooses. ISBN 0-9677753-2-9 $11.95

THE WILD ONE by Lyn Denison. 176 pp. Rachel never expected that Quinn's wild yearnings would change her life forever. ISBN 0-9677753-4-5 $12.95

SWEET FIRE by Saxon Bennett. 224 pp. Welcome to Heroy — the town with the most lesbians per capita than any other place on the planet! ISBN 0-9677753-5-3 $11.95

Visit
Bella Books
at
www.bellabooks.com